In Memory of

"Glee"

Presented by

Jean and Richard Sanders

Indian River County Library

Upon Some
Midnights
Clear

A MARIO BALZIC MYSTERY

UPON SOME MIDNIGHTS CLEAR

BY K.C. CONSTANTINE

DAVID R. GODINE • PUBLISHER • BOSTON

First published in 1985 by
DAVID R. GODINE, PUBLISHER, INC.
306 Dartmouth Street
Boston, Massachusetts 02116

B 36 7442

LIBRARY OF CONGRESS CATALOGING IN PUBLICATION DATA

Constantine, K. C.
  Upon some midnights clear.

  I. Title.
PS3553.O524U6 1985   813'.54   84-48748
ISBN 0-87923-570-5

First edition
Printed in the United States of America

Upon Some Midnights Clear

BALZIC had had a deck built on the back of his house. There had been a porch, but it was narrow, and the wood had started to rot. The deck extended fifteen feet beyond where the porch had been, and it was made of chemically treated lumber that required only a coat of linseed oil and mineral spirits every couple of years. The frame had been bolted to the basement wall with steel rods, and the carpenters had assured Balzic that before the deck fell the wall of his basement would have to fall. The deck gave Balzic room to pace when his family was asleep and to drink wine and to talk to himself and to look at the stars. It also gave him an emotion he had never suspected he had in him: it made him feel rich.

Balzic was out on it, prowling from rail to rail in a heavy sweater and wool cap, wineglass in hand, gaping on a cloudless night at constellations he knew he'd seen all his life but could not name and telling himself that he was going to buy a book on astronomy so he could learn them, when the phone rang in the kitchen. He cursed without pause until he answered it.

"Yes?"

"Mario? Ed Sitko. You gotta come up to the hospital. Some lady got her head busted and all her money got stolen."

"She alive?"

"Yeah she's alive. Does she have to be dead before you check her out all her money gets robbed? Huh?"

"Why're you callin' me? You know who to call."

"That's why I'm callin' you. 'Cause I know who to call. This is bad here, this lady, what they did to her. This is real shit. You gotta come up here, I'm tellin' you."

"Eddie, I'm drinkin' wine, I'm lookin' at the stars, I'm walkin' around on my deck. What you're talkin' about sounds like a mug, you know? Call the station. Call the—"

"It is a muggin'. The lady had her whole Christmas Club get stolen. Over five hundred bucks. Except it wasn't a Christmas Club. She just saved it. And she went and got it out of the bank today and she was on her way home and some nigger rolled her. Right on Pittsburgh Street. In broad fuckin' daylight. I think it stinks. Old lady can't walk around in broad daylight, I'm telling you these niggers are really askin' for it, no shit they are—"

Balzic drained his glass and cradled the phone in the crook of his shoulder and neck and opened the refrigerator and grabbed the carafe that he filled from four-liter jugs. He poured his glass two-thirds full.

"Hey, Mario, you still there?"

"I'm still here."

"Well whatta you gonna do? You comin' up or what?"

"Eddie, don't misunderstand me. Your men—all over the entire fire department—I have never heard even one word of disrespect for you—"

"What's your point?"

"The point is, Eddie, if I see a fire or if one of my people sees a fire, we don't call you personally. We call nine-one-one and we—"

"Are you comin' up here and see this old lady or you gonna give me some speechy shit—"

"Goodbye, Eddie."

Balzic put the phone in its cradle and took his wine out onto the deck and leaned back and looked again at the Big Dipper and the North Star, the only elements in the sky he knew. He turned to his right to the south and looked at that vast flickering and sighed and sipped his wine and started to whisper that he should go to the hospital just to kick Eddie Sitko in the shins. He looked up again and said aloud, "I been alive so long I don't want to think about it and I look up at night and I can't name two things up there. That's disgusting."

He drank the rest of his glass of wine and went back into the house, wrote a note to his wife saying where he was going and left it on the kitchen table, and got his raincoat, and went out to his cruiser.

Though it was the third week of December the weather had been mild, with frequent but light rain and temperatures only once low enough for a frost. This night it was forty-five degrees and there was almost no wind. There had been sporadic drizzles in the afternoon, and the streets glimmered as the headlights from Balzic's cruiser shone on them.

He parked near the emergency entrance of Conemaugh Hospital and left his keys in the ignition. He got out and saw a bowlegged security guard hustling toward him and shaking his head from side to side.

Balzic held up his ID case so the guard could see it and then pointed with it to his car. "If you got to move that, the keys are in it. I don't know how long I'm gonna be."

"Oh I was gonna run your tail out of there 'til I seen it was you," the guard said. "Oh there ain't no problem though. You stay all you want. I'll watch out for you."

Balzic nodded and waved and pushed through the swinging doors into the emergency waiting room.

The waiting room was empty. Not only was no one present, the only sound was coming from a TV set. Balzic looked around as he walked to the registration and information desk and wondered how it was possible that on a Friday night in the week before Christmas no one was sitting in this room.

He was almost to the first hole in the first window above the first desk of two at the registration counter before he heard voices. They were the voices of dull exhaustion, of people complaining of too much work in too little time. He rang the bell. The conversation stopped, and a short, lumpy woman with overly large glasses halfway down her nose and stiff hair piled high atop her head came around a door and asked absently if she could help him.

He held up his ID case and asked if the fire chief was around.

"I don't think so," she said. "I haven't seen—oh wait. I did see him. Early. About five after eleven. When I first came on. But I haven't seen him since."

"He just called me from up here. Maybe he's someplace else."

"You might try the front desk."

Balzic turned away and then turned back. "Uh, it's a little quiet in here. I mean, I can't ever remember coming up here on a Friday night at one o'clock in the morning and seeing this room empty, you know?"

"Oh God this is the first time I've stopped since eleven. I've only been here a month so I don't know what it's like—but, uh, so you're the chief of police. I heard a lot about you. My sister's husband works for the street department."

"Oh yeah? Who's that?"

"Nicky Perrone. You know him? He just started a little while ago. Three months, I think."

Balzic nodded. "Yeah I know him. I mean I don't know him, I know who he is. He got hired? Full time?"

"No no no no. He's just fillin' in. Somebody got hurt or something. And somebody else got sick. You know how it goes."

"Yeah. I was gonna say, the budget the city's workin' on, I didn't think anybody was gettin' hired. Say, listen, you want to do me a favor? You get an old lady in here this afternoon, got knocked in the head or something? You remember anything like that?"

"Oh sure. That was Mrs. Garbin. Her husband used to work for the city. Years ago. Then he got hurt real bad on his leg. He worked for the, uh—"

"Sanitation department," Balzic said, nodding. "I remember him. Very well. Some kid he was working with dropped a garbage can on his leg, screwed up his Achilles tendon. Yeah. He took a disability pension. Garbinerri. So that was his wife, huh?"

"Yes, isn't that awful? Honest to God, you get robbed right in broad daylight in the middle of Pittsburgh Street.

All her savings, I heard. Close to a thousand dollars. Imagine."

"Uh, I heard it was not that much. So, uh, maybe you should not, uh, you know—"

"But imagine! Right before Christmas. That's such a shame."

"Uh-huh. Yeah. Well, I don't know what the amount was, but I have an idea it was probably less, if you know what I mean."

"Well, no matter how much it was it's still a darn shame. These niggers—honest to God—everything they get and they don't want to work and who pays for it? Us, that's who. Fools, that's what we are. They want welfare they oughta work, do something, my God."

Balzic had heard the speech so many times since the 1960s that he believed he had developed an immunity to it, had developed a way of appearing to listen when he had tuned out after the first time he heard the word "welfare." But this time he was dealing with something else and was compelled to interrupt the woman.

"Who said it was a nigger number one, and number two, who said this particular nigger—whoever he's supposed to be—was on welfare?"

"Well—why that's—I just heard it, that's all. It's all over the hospital."

"Look here, Missus, uh?"

"Mrs. Sandusky. Virginia."

"Mrs. Sandusky, these rumors—and that's what they are—please don't repeat them. I have enough trouble over the holidays, especially Christmas. I don't need something else to worry about, you understand?"

"I—I guess."

"Well, you think about it. Please. Okay? Goodnight."

Balzic turned in time to see Eddie Sitko coming around the bend of the corridor some ten yards away.

"Christ it's about time," Sitko said. "What took you so long?"

Balzic scratched his throat and walked away from the reception desk, out of Mrs. Sandusky's hearing. "Eddie, exactly what do you expect me to do here now? Huh? Am I supposed to talk to this woman? Now? It's almost one-thirty?"

"No—nah, Christ, you don't have to talk to her. I did all that."

"Oh really? And the next time some goddamn tank car springs a leak on the Conrail line I'll just go down and take care of it myself, is that okay with you?"

"Huh? I don't follow you."

"I said the next time some tank car springs a leak I'll go down and take care of it myself. You follow that?"

"Yeah, I got you now. But, oh, you're kiddin' me, right? I mean, that's different."

"Oh? How's it different? Tell me, I want to hear how it's different."

"Well with chemicals you got to know what to do. And you don't—what the fuck're you talkin' about?"

"Uh-huh. What I'm talkin' about is *you* know how to ask this old lady what happened to her, right?"

"Hey, Mario, quit bustin' my balls, huh? I mean I was here when she got brought in and nobody was around, so I talked to her, that's all. I tried to call your guys two or three times, I couldn't get no answer. So I just kept talking to her. And she told me everything. Honest."

"Okay, so now you got me up here, and this lady can't

say anything until tomorrow anyway, so exactly what am I doin' here?"

"What you're doin' here is listenin' to me. I already checked this out with all my officers and what we decided—"

"Oh now wait a minute."

"Just listen! Listen, I'm tellin' you. What we decided was we're gonna do some things and—"

"Eddie, Eddie, Jesus Christ you couldn't tell me this over the phone?"

"Tell you what? You don't even know what I'm gonna say."

"Oh I know what you're gonna say and the answer is the same one I would've given you over the phone. Honest to Christ, Eddie, sometimes you're really out of line, you know it?"

"Listen, on the phone you'd've hung up on me—which is what you did anyway, prick. And you can't hang up on me while I got you here, huh? Can you? Huh? Huh?"

"The answer is no," Balzic said, turning abruptly and walking toward the door.

"What answer is no? Whatta you mean no? You didn't even hear the question yet," said Sitko, hustling along beside Balzic and ducking in front of him when they reached the exit.

Balzic stopped. "Get outta my way. I'm not gettin' mixed up with another one of your goddamn campaigns. I told you that after the last one. Seven hundred and some bucks *still* not accounted for in that one and people are lookin' at me funny ever since. Get outta my road, I'm tellin' you."

"Mario, we *got* to have you. And nobody's lookin' funny at you about nothin'. That's a load. Nobody ever accused you of—"

"Nobody accused me! You got a couple assistant chiefs still don't talk to me. Those fuckers think it went in my pockets. You gonna argue with that? Or you gonna get out of my way?"

"Okay," Sitko said. "Okay. Be that way. Go ahead. Let a couple of stupid fuckers keep you from doin' what's right. From what *you* know is right."

"Aw give it a break for crissake. G'night." Balzic stepped out of the waiting room and then leaned back in. "Just so there's no misunderstanding here. I'm not signing anything, I'm not opening any accounts, I'm not countin' anything, I'm not carryin' anything, and I don't want to hear from anybody that you said I was gonna do any of those things."

"Man oh man, talk about a fuckin' Scroogey."

"Good night, Eddie."

Sitko followed him out. "We put the arm on everybody, we can raise two grand nothin' flat. And that ain't even bringing the newspaper into it. Or the radio station. Throw them in, we get four thousand easy—"

"Good night, Eddie," Balzic said, walking toward his cruiser.

"We'll get three thousand without you—"

"So do it."

"Four, maybe five with you."

"Sounds like you got to find a substitute."

"What're you so fuckin' hard-assed about? Jesus Christ."

Balzic stopped and wheeled about. "Hey, you listen, I don't care what it is. World War Two vets with no legs that're gonna fall outta their wheelchairs or little kids that need a kidney, or whatever the fuck you got in mind. I don't sign nothin', count nothin', carry no money, not one goddamn thing so some prick can say I looked like I ripped off two dimes! You hear? I been down this road twenty times with you. And now you want me to do it for some woman I haven't even talked to yet. Where's your brains?

"You know what this smells like to me? It smells like an insurance job, only this lady doesn't have any insurance, so she's gonna get ripped off right before Christmas—"

"Oh Mario, Jesus Christ, you're really gettin' warped, you know that?"

"Just listen a minute. You know how many insurance burglaries I got to contend with now? You have any idea how many stolen cars we find burned? Pros just strip 'em, they don't waste time burnin' 'em. So who burns 'em? Kids burn 'em. Kids and guys who can't make the payments on 'em is who burns 'em, that's who. And now you got a lady who lost her life savings one week before Christmas. Eddie, I'll make you a bet. I'll bet you a hundred bucks against a dime she doesn't have any insurance—"

"Aw, Mario, for crissake—"

"You want to bet or not?"

"I don't even want to think about what you just said. If you saw this woman—you know who it is? Her husband used to work for the city for—"

"Jack Garbin's wife is who it is."

"Holy shit. You know who it is and you keep on thinkin' what you're thinkin'—Christ Almighty, I don't believe it."

"You gonna take the bet or not? Yes or no."

Sitko looked at the macadam of the parking lot and shook his head and whistled. "I'll be a sonofabitch. Mario, you have been a cop too long, no shit you have."

"You want to make the bet, you know where to find me," Balzic said. "But no matter what, don't you use my name in no goddamn fund-raiser, I'm tellin' you. You want to raise money for this lady you do it without me. I'm not raisin' a nickel for anybody I haven't talked to.

"But you know what pisses me off? You really want to know? You could show me pictures of arson, you could tell me all about it, tell me what books to read and who to talk to, but if I didn't see some bastard strike a match I wouldn't fuckin' dare tell *you* how a fire got started. But you happen to be in the hospital when somebody gets brought in with a busted head and all of a sudden you not only know what happened, you also know how much was robbed and that a nigger did it. And when I tell you it sounds like somebody's trying to work a number, you tell me I been a cop too long. And all I was doin' was mindin' my own business on my deck and drinkin' some wine. Man, no shit, good night."

Balzic turned to go to the cruiser and found the bow-legged security guard shrugging and working his lips as though he believed there was something he ought to be saying or a duty he ought to be performing. "It's okay," Balzic said. "We been hollering at each other for thirty years. We always holler. Forget about it."

Out of habit, Balzic drove by the station on his way home. He regretted his habit the moment he turned off the street into the parking lot because directly in front of him was the large, oblong, gleaming face of Billy Lum, bright with the excitement that came from someone else's wrong luck of having been in front of him at a wrong moment. Lum was in his early thirties, chocolate brown with a pocked complexion, with a huge growth of hair surrounding a circle of skin in the top rear of his elongated head. He had a ropey neck, heavy shoulders, muscular arms, and large scarred hands, all of which he'd gotten from years of emptying garbage cans into the backs of garbage packers owned by his father.

Lum was the oldest son of a man whose packers carried half of Rocksburg's residential garbage and most of its commercial, and whose bills were paid on time in full. Lum should have stood first in line to inherit a garbageman's empire. There was one problem: though Lum and his father worked with each other six days a week and had for years, they did not speak to each other except in the briefest way about the most necessary things. Lum dumped garbage into a packer driven by a man who had announced publicly and often that he had no intention of allowing his oldest son to become anything but a well-paid laborer. Lum, still stinging from that knowledge in a way even he only dimly understood, took his revenge on the rest of the world; he was too afraid of his father to take it any other way.

Lum, in handcuffs, was being led up the steps into the duty room by Patrolman Larry Fischetti. Lum was laughing scornfully at Fischetti and talking loudly, defiantly, obnoxiously. He stopped abruptly at the door and squinted in Balzic's direction.

"Hey, Ballzy. Hey, mah man, hey. C'mon in. Get with the program!"

Oh shit, Balzic thought, and groaned aloud. He parked and turned off the ignition and was getting out of his cruiser when Patrolman Harry Lynch drove in. Lynch got out of his cruiser carrying two plastic evidence bags. He had almost reached the steps before his noticed Balzic and then came and bent down by Balzic's window.

"You want to know what that stupid bastard did this time?"

"To be honest with you, Harry, I don't really want to, but I know neither one of us has a choice so go 'head."

"You're gonna love this," Lynch said, shaking his head. "This redneck—I don't know where the hell he's from, West Virginia I heard somebody say, but maybe he was saying Waynesburg. Anyway, this redneck gets all boiled up and winds up in the Black Legion where he gets into an argument with guess who. And guess who just happens to be able to get his hands on a .357 magnum. And it ain't his, understand—he was just 'able to get his hands on it.' Don't you just love this fucker's lies? I mean, they're such goddamn beauties and he knows you know they are, but he tells 'em anyway. Shit."

"So what happened?"

"I don't know what happened. I don't know in what order. All I know is I got a white guy in the hospital— must've had all the luck in the world, honest to Christ, it went right between his ribs right here"—Lynch pointed to his own ribs on the left side—"and didn't touch nothin'. Not one goddamn thing. Blew a gutter in him but that's all. I mean it knocked him right off his feet, and he cut his head on a table or something when he went down, but that .357 just tore away a bunch of flesh, that's all.

"You got witnesses?"

"Oh shit we got more than we can count. That joint was packed—"

"Who will testify? That's the key phrase—will they testify?"

"Well Christ we got the shootee. And we got the shooter. With a piece. And right here in these two bags"—Lynch held them up—"we got two slugs. They're all busted out of shape, but what d'you want from a .357? They went all the whole way through that bar and stopped in the wall. And I took good measurements—and pictures too! Got my Polaroid and took a whole pile of pictures."

"That's good, Harry. I'm glad you did all that other stuff. Because you know there are no black witnesses."

"Not this time. I got plenty. I'm tellin' you."

"Harry, you know better than I do that nobody black is gonna testify against him."

"Well . . . fuck 'em. We got the shootee. And that's all the witness we need."

"Just as long as he talks."

"Why wouldn't he talk?"

Balzic took his glasses off and rubbed the bridge of his nose where the frame dug into it. "What kind of question is that, Harry? Huh? Ah, never mind. Let's get in here and see what we got."

⁓※⁓

Balzic had reached just the first step leading up to the duty room of the station when he heard the commotion inside. There were sharp voices and shouting and scuffling.

Balzic, followed by Lynch, bounded up the steps and into the duty room and found it packed with bodies. The smell of beer and perspiration stung Balzic's nose. The sight of the large group of men, ripped and tattered, bloody and bleeding, halted him at once. The uproar of voices instantly offended him.

He elbowed his way through the men—there were at least twenty—and got through the lifting door in the counter to see Desk Sergeant Vic Stramsky having an impossible time trying over the roar of voices to hear what patrolmen

Joe Grgorich and Andy Mitosky were saying. Rookie Patrolman Ed Zigmun was having no success keeping the noise down.

The disorder brought a rise of sourish juice to the back of Balzic's throat. He reached for his ring of keys, found the key he wanted, went to the shotgun cabinet, and unlocked it. Then he found another key and opened the lock securing one of the 12-gauge riot guns to its rack. He took the gun, stepped up on a desk, pumped a shell into the chamber, and bellowed, "Shut up! Shut up goddammit!"

The voices stopped. No one moved.

"The next sonofabitch who opens his mouth without being asked is gonna explain to me why he's talkin'. And he's gonna do that with the barrel of this up his nose—is that clear?"

There was some scuffling of shoes and some breaths drawn in and let out; otherwise, there was no sound.

Balzic looked around the room. "I don't like noise. I don't like people runnin' their mouths just to see if they work. Now every one of you. You drop your pants down around your ankles and turn and face that wall away from me. Do it now! Drop 'em! Do it! And when you've done that, you put your hands behind your heads and keep 'em there!"

There was neither hesitation nor murmur of protest. As soon as Balzic stopped talking, every civilian in the room began to undo his belt and fly front and to shove his trousers down to his ankles.

Zigmun's mouth slowly opened and he stood looking bug-eyed at the civilians and then up at Balzic on the desk and back at the civilians.

"Zigmun," Balzic said when he was satisfied the room

was quiet. "Get up and watch these people. First one talks without being asked a question, you shoot him. Don't kill him. Just take one of his hands off. You people—before you start to talk—you try to remember where your hands are."

Balzic stepped down off the desk and then handed the riot gun up to Zigmun after he'd scrambled up on it.

"All right, Vic," Balzic said to Desk Sergeant Stramsky, "what's all this about?"

"Oh this is just gonna thrill you," Stramsky said softly, shaking his head. "Right here, right in front of us, we have a group—no, two groups of American veterans. Veterans of Foreign Wars in fact."

Balzic closed his eyes and shook his head.

"One of these groups of men, these veterans, is from old Big Two and Korea, and the other group is from—"

"Vietnam," Balzic said under his breath.

"You got it. The fellas with the long hair and the red hankies around their heads, well, they're all paid-up dues members, by Christ, and the ones with the short hair, they're also all paid up, but there's a lot more of them than the other ones—which you can see."

"I don't believe this," Balzic said darkly. "So what was the beef?"

"The beef is—and this is just as near as I can figure it— the beef is who lost the Vietnam war, followed naturally by, uh, what would naturally follow."

"Okay okay, I get the picture. Uh, if you get no problems, no wise guys, etcetera, book 'em and get 'em the hell out. They break up the VFW?"

"Not totaled from what I hear, but they put a job on it."

"Well fuck it, that's between them and the club. Call the duty magistrate and work something out on a fine and costs. Do whatever you have to to move 'em out. I don't want any of these guys locked in, understand? If they can't go minimal bond, we'll lock 'em in, but otherwise, out, okay?"

Stramsky nodded.

Balzic turned and tried to locate Harry Lynch.

Lynch was fidgeting by the third and last of the interrogation rooms. He was looking through the stack of Polaroid photos he had in hand when Balzic approached.

"We got the bastard this time," Lynch said as Balzic neared. "We finally got him on something that'll stick."

Balzic grunted something unpleasantly skeptical and brushed past Lynch into the tiny room in which sat Billy Lum, grinning his best catch-me-if-you-can-but-don't-forget-you-have-to-prove-it-motherfucker grin.

Balzic shut the door and straddled the chair opposite Lum across the small, square, cigarette-burned and coffee-stained table.

"Bal-zeek! Mah man! Wha's happenin', mah man?"

"What's happenin' with you, Billy?"

"Hey, you first, mah man. Hy y'all doin'?"

Balzic rubbed the tip of his nose. "I think I'm doin' all right, Billy. I was doin' a lot better a couple hours ago, but, hell, that's the way it goes."

"Hey, me too! No shit. I was doin' fine couple hours ago. Then that mothafucker Lynch put these on me"— Lum held up the wrist-restraints—"and threw my ass in the back of his car, man, and I ain't done nothin' yet. She-it."

"Really?"

"Yeah really. I mean, real-ly, man. I'm up the Legion, man, mindin' my own damn business, talkin' trash, gettin' some taste, boom, boom, man, two shots or firecrackers or somethin', I don't know what, people fallin' down, hollerin', carryin' on, screamin'—shit, pus, and corruption everywhere—and the next thing I know, here come Lynch bustin' through the door, don't ask no mothafuckin' question, come right straight at me, be tellin' me put my hands behint my back and don't say nothin' or he goin' open my mothafuckin' head, man. And the next thing is I'm outside and my poor black ass is gettin' throwed in the back seat."

"Your 'poor black ass'? Is that what you said?"

"Oh Bal-zeek, don't be jivin', man. Call my lawyer, man, and let me get on home. You know this is jive. Lynch don't even know what's happenin', man. That dude been cappin' on me for years, ack like I done somethin' to his daddy, man, I don't know what he got against me. Cat's prejudice or somethin' I swear to God."

"Billy, let's skip this part, okay? Let's go to—"

"This part? Huh? Skip what? Say what?"

"Let's skip the bullshit you give the tourists, huh? The shit you give all the dumb little white girls at the community college, huh?"

"Bal-zeek, you been listenin' to lies about me, man. There ain't no truth to that shit, man. I don't be fuckin' with no paddy broads. I'm a soul brother. I love my soul sisters—"

Balzic bent his forehead into his hand and closed his eyes. He sighed and pushed his glasses back up his nose.

"Listen," Balzic said after a moment, "you want to tell

me about this? I'm giving you an opportunity to tell me what happened first. Now you can take this opportunity or you can let me find out everything from other people. And then when a magistrate asks me whether you were cooperative, I can answer with one of two words. Yes. No. Yes he cooperated. No he didn't cooperate."

"Aw man, call my lawyer up, man, and don't be puttin' all this jive out. My man get here and I be gone in fifteen minutes and you know it, so what's all this shit?"

"A guy's in the hospital with a gunshot wound, Billy. What do I know? Tell me something."

"No shit." Lum made his eyes go as wide open as he could. "Gosh oh golly oh gee. Is God going to take him away, Mister Po-liceman?"

"Harry!" Balzic bellowed at the closed door behind him. Then he stood quickly and went to the door and opened it in time to see Lynch hustling toward him.

"What're you doing, Harry?"

"I was checking the state police lab. We got a problem."

"Nobody there, right?"

"Yeah, how'd you know?"

" 'Cause it's Friday night and there's never anybody there. Fuckers think they work in a bank. That's what you're saying, right, we can't get a metals test?"

"Yeah. That's the problem," Lynch said, nodding somberly.

"Well, we just got to work around it, that's all."

"Oh that'd be good evidence, Mario. We'd really have the bastard."

"Harry, we ain't gonna get it, so forget it. Besides, it ain't worth diddly anyway. Tell me again what you have. From the beginning."

"Well, I got the call from Stramsky—shots fired, Black Legion, da-da, da-da. I get there, people are still comin' out, runnin', hollerin', you know. I get inside, the place is real quiet except for the noise the people are makin' tryin' to get out. There's some quiet talkin'. That's all. This white guy's on the floor by the bar, and about a foot away from Lum's hand, his right hand, is the piece.

"Hey, there's nobody else at the bar. He's just standin' there drinkin' like nothing's happening, this guy's on the floor, he's bawlin', and he's bleeding all over the place from his head and the side of his chest, and Lum is just standin' there drinking beer. So I walked over to him and I got my piece out and I ask him if that piece on the bar is his, and he says no it ain't his and what made me think it was, did it have his name on it, something smart-ass like that, and I said put your hands behind your back and he said something else smart, and so I put my piece right behind his ear and I told him do what I told him or I was gonna light the inside of his head up."

"Then what?"

"Then he puts his hands behind him, I put my cuffs on him, I tell him to kneel down and put his forehead against the bar and keep it there. I tell Jimmy Payne call Mutual Aid, which he does, and I look at the white guy see whether there's anything I can do for him and there wasn't, so I went back out the car and got my Polaroid and loaded it up and started talking—oh, wait a second, I took the guy's belt off and I was gonna put a tourniquet on him and I said Christ, that's dumb, so—I mean, where was I gonna put it, so I mean, you couldn't put no, uh, there was no way you could put pressure on any place to stop it, you know?"

Balzic nodded and rubbed his face. "Then what?"

"Then I went back and took the pictures. I took about ten or twelve, I guess, before the Mutual Aid guys got there, and then I stopped to help them out, and when they left, I put Lum in the cruiser and then I went back in and took the rest of the pictures and got the slugs outta the wall. And then I took measurements and while I was doing that I was talking to Jimmy Payne. Turns out he called it in."

"So what'd he say?"

Lynch shook his head. "Nothin'. He had his head down. He heard the shots, said they hurt his ears, he dove for the floor, didn't hear any more shots, so he got up real slow and peeked over the bar and everyone was runnin' for the door, and then he stood up and looked over the bar and saw this dude with blood all over him. And that's all he'd say. Except that he saw the gun. But he never saw anybody holding it, understand?"

Balzic nodded. "Then?"

Lynch shrugged. "Then he called here and then Stramsky called me and that's the start."

"D'you stop at the hospital? Or did you tell somebody to stop there?"

"Oh yeah. I sent Frank Lomicka up there. And I ain't heard from him. He's probably still there. That asshole's probably still in the operating room."

"Uh, what about these witnesses? You really, uh, you really actually got some black people said they'd testify and they gave you their names and addresses?"

Lynch closed his eyes and his ruddy face reddened considerably. He opened his eyes and looked at the floor. He looked up and started to speak twice, but neither time did he say a word, and his eyes closed again.

Balzic looked over his glasses. "You lost it, right?"

"Hey, listen, Mario, honest to God I'll find it. It's gotta be here. Either here or in the cruiser. I didn't look there yet, but that's where I was goin' when you called me."

"Look, Harry, forget it. I mean I hope you find your notebook, but it's not gonna make any difference about the witnesses. You understand me, right?"

No answer.

"Harry? Am I right? Huh?"

"Yeah I guess. But I really did get four witnesses, Mario."

"I'm sure you did. No doubt. But let's concentrate on other stuff, okay? First thing, get Lomicka on the phone and see what's going on up the hospital. Maybe you can give him a hand up there. But check that out first, and then we'll see where we are, okay?"

Lynch nodded. "I'll find it, Mario, I will. I always do."

"Take care of the other stuff, worry about your notebook later." Balzic put his hand on Lynch's shoulder and gently prodded him toward the counter door.

"How we coming, Vic?" Balzic called out to Sergeant Stramsky.

"We're gonna run 'em over to Aldonelli's office four at a time. He agreed on nominal bond." Stramsky approached Balzic and lowered his voice. "What happens if they don't have a dollar—we gonna lock 'em in?"

"Christ, take it outta petty cash."

"Uh, Mario, we don't have any petty cash. Don't you—"

"Oh shit I forgot. Uh, well, listen, tell Aldonelli I'm good for it. Just get 'em the hell outta here, all right?"

"Aldonelli ain't gonna go for it."

"For crissake, it's only a goddamn dollar apiece. You

mean our credit's so bad we ain't good for twenty dollars? Or thirty? Jesus. Well try it anyway. Let's just see where we are, okay?"

Balzic turned and went back to the interrogation room and found Billy Lum on his feet and walking from wall to wall.

"Who told you to stand up?" Balzic snapped, shutting the door with his foot. "Sit down!"

"Don't be hasslin' me, Balzeek. And get my lawyer on the phone, man. I'm gettin' tired ridin' this shit."

Balzic took off his wool cap and rubbed his scalp hard. He sat in the chair nearest the door and rubbed his scalp some more and then put his cap back on. "I'm gonna say this once, Lum, so pay attention—"

"Oh man, don't be campaignin', man, got-damn."

"—so pay attention," Balzic said, lowering his voice. "You put your black ass in that chair. Now. Or you ain't gonna see your lawyer for at least twenty-three hours. You payin' attention?"

"I be a mothafucka."

"You'll be what?"

"Nothin'. Man, she-it," Lum said under his breath, sliding over to the chair and dropping slowly into it.

"Okay, Billy. Let's try it again. What happened in the Legion?"

"I already told you."

"Tell me again."

Billy Lum sighed heavily, noisily. "Aw man, gimme a cigarette."

"No."

"Whatta you mean no? Where the fuck we at? Russia?"

"I said no."

"Hey, man, look here. Take the money outta my pocket and go get us a pack, man."

"I don't smoke."

"You smoke all your damn life, Balzic, whatchu talkin' 'bout?"

Balzic put his elbows on the table and rubbed his forehead. "I haven't smoked in almost five years, Billy."

"Balzic, you jive, man. Every time I be comin' in here, first thing you done was give me a cig-a-rette, man."

"Not the last two times I brought you in—"

"Two! Two! I ain't been in here twice in the last five years, man! And last time I was in here, goddammit, Balzic, you was smokin' 'cause I remember, man, y'all tried to say I cut that stupid bitch Eloise Burnside."

"We didn't *try* to say it, we said it. Because it was true."

"True, shit. You didn't prove it. And you don't prove it, it's a lie! Every mothafucker know that's right."

"Why don't you skip the dumb-nigger routine and talk to me like a man for once."

"Mothafucker, call my lawyer and let me get outta this pigpen. Talk to you like a man, shit. You ain't funny, Balzic."

Balzic leaned back in his chair and folded his arms. "You 'mother' me again, Lum, and I'm gonna put leg-shackles on you and I'm gonna tell Harry Lynch to go get a big towel and wet it and I'm gonna tell him to go to work on the backs of your legs. And before you open your mouth, just remember that you haven't been booked yet. There's no record that you're in this building. And there won't be until Lynch writes it up and Stramsky gets finished with that mess out there, and he won't be finished for a while, and Lynch can't find his notebook. And one more thing. No matter how many suits your lawyer files against us, after it's over not one of them will change the way you feel after Lynch gets done. Just one more 'mother.' Just one."

Billy Lum's eyes narrowed ever so briefly. For a split second, his fury got out of his control and it showed brilliantly in his eyes. He knew he was at Balzic's mercy and hated it and hated Balzic and let himself slip until that hatred gleamed through. Just as quickly, he was smiling and rolling his eyes in mock horror.

"Hey, Balzic, hey, mah man. You know I just be jivin', man. I don't mean nothin'. Just talkin' shit."

"I'm not."

"Well, shit, whatchu want to know, man?"

"I told you what I want to know. What happened in the Legion?"

"Man, it was what I said already. I'm standin' at the bar talkin' shit and I hear these—"

"Before you heard the noise, what happened?"

"Nothin' happen."

"You said you were talkin' shit. Who were you talkin' shit to?"

"Oh man, I don't know. Some soft leg."

"Which soft leg?"

"Man, I don't remember. I was talkin' to couple bitches—"

"Which ones? Give me some names."

"Labell somethin'. Labell Taylor. But she went on home. She ain't from Rocksburg anyway. I don't know where she from."

"Labell Taylor, huh? What's she look like?"

"I wasn't payin' no attention to that. I was jus' talkin' trash."

"Tall? Short? Fat? Skinny? Old? What?"

"Balzic, I never talked to the bitch before, man. I don't remember what she look like."

"You can't remember anything about her—not one little thing, like whether she was short or tall? Huh?"

"That's right. I can't remember not one little thing."

"Okay, you can't remember anything about her. Who else? You said you were talking to a couple bitches. What about the other one—or two?"

"Same thing, man. Never saw 'em before. Didn't even know their names, man. Jus' juicin' and talkin' shit, man. I wasn't tryin' to get no leg."

"And just like that, bang bang, and a white guy is on the floor bleedin' all over the place."

"That's it."

"Where was this white guy before you heard the noise?"

"Never saw him. Didn't even know he was in there."

"It's Friday night in the Legion and a white guy's on the floor bleedin' and you never saw him—until after you heard the noise and you turned and saw him on the floor. Right?"

"Right on, Balzic."

"Which way did you turn?"

"Which way did I turn? She-it, I don't know. What difference do it make?"

"You can only turn two ways, Billy. You can turn to your left or to your right. Which way did you turn?"

"I told you I don't know. Who cares anyway?"

"I do. Which way?"

"I don't remember, man. Can you dig it? I don't know."

Balzic rubbed his cheeks and then his chin. "Let's run this one down one more time, Billy. You're standing in the Legion, on a Friday night, talking trash to two women, when you hear some noises. Firecrackers, gunfire, you don't know which. Next thing you know, a white guy—who you never saw before—is on the floor bleeding. Then Officer Lynch appears, finds a .357 Colt Python revolver on the bar very near your right hand, he takes you into custody, puts you in the back seat of his cruiser, and you don't know anything about anything, is that about it?"

"Right on, Balzic. You got it."

Balzic nodded slowly. "You're telling big ones, Billy, and you're forgettin' that there's no record of you bein' in the building yet. Before you say anything else, I want you to think carefully about that fact. There is no record of you bein' in this building."

"Balzic, man, why you gotta be threatenin' me, man? What I ever do to you, man? You ack like I done somethin' personal to you, man. What is all this stuff about me not bein' in the building, man? Why you wanna talk on me like that?"

"I'm talking to you like that because I want you to have all the facts before you decide not to cooperate—"

"Cooperate! Co-op-er-ate! Man, I'm tellin' you everything I know the answer to. What else I got to do?"

"Answer everything. It's simple. Just answer everything."

Lum dropped his chin and looked up at Balzic. "Man, I can not tell you what I do not know. My brain only hold so much, and if what you wants to know ain't up there, then, shit, it's shame on me, but I still can't help it."

Balzic stuck his thumbnail into the center crack in his lower teeth and pried up a particle of food. "Let's try it from a different direction. What time d'you get in the Legion?"

"I was there twice. Which time you want me to talk about?"

"Any white guys get shot the first time?"

"I don't think. Uh-uh."

"Then talk about the second time."

"Okay."

"Well?"

"Well what?"

"Well what time did you get there?"

"I don't know. Ten o'clock. 'Leven. I don't have a watch."

"Five years ago you were stopped by the state police for, uh, driving erratically, I believe. You were stoned. Blown right out of your skull. Remember?"

"Don't remember nothin' like that."

"And you had three of those Japanese quartz watches, those ones that retail for about three hundred apiece. Remember?"

"Balzic, you know ain't nobody prove I was blowin' no weed and didn't nobody prove I didn't buy them watches, man, and if you can't prove it, it's a lie."

"What'd you do with the watches?"

"What watches?"

"The ones we were just talkin' about."

"Ain't nobody proved I even had no watches, man, so I don't know anything 'bout no goddamn watches."

"Big Jimmy Payne says he saw you fire two shots tonight. And we have at least four other—"

"Big Jimmy don't be talkin' 'bout me like that. Big Jimmy talk all kinda shit, but ain't no way Big Jimmy goin' stand up in no trial and swear on no Bible what you say. Big Jimmy too cooled out for that."

Balzic squeezed his temples with his left thumb and middle finger. "How long you gonna persist in this dumb-nigger routine?"

Billy Lum leaned back in his chair and smiled. "I only answer the way I'm aks."

"It's gettin' late, Billy," Balzic said, standing and sighing. "I'm gonna ask you once more to cooperate—"

"I answered everything you aks." Lum drew out the last word.

"—and when the DA's people want to know why I recommend no bond—"

"No bond!"

"That's right, no bond, and when they ask me why—"

"C'mon, Balzic, it's only a goddamn assault with a prohibited weapon and we both know you don't have a case on that little legal turd, so what the hell're you talkin' about no bond—"

"Oh, indeed. Little legal turd, huh? Tired of Dumb Lum, huh? Maybe you're even gonna get enough intelligence to know how long you're gonna sit before I tell anybody you're here. Or is that too much to ask?"

"You got no case, Balzic. You got a piece on a bar two feet away from my hands when Lynch came in. I just heard you tell Lynch you got nobody to give me a test see whether I fired a gun. And we both know nobody in the Black Legion is gonna talk on me."

"You're forgettin' somebody."

"I ain't forgettin' nobody."

"The shootee, Lum. The shootee."

Lum's lips turned down negatively and he shook his head slowly, forcefully. "Ain't nobody in the Black Legion gonna talk on me," he said again. "You ain't got no case. So why don't you call my lawyer so I can get on home."

Balzic crooked his finger several times at Lum. "Let's go. You're gonna sit in the dark for a while."

Lum rolled his chin over to his right shoulder. "Maaan, sheeee-it. . . ."

"Up. On your feet and movin', I'm tired, I want to go home."

There came a sharp rap on the door. Stramsky opened it and poked his head in. "See you for a second?"

Balzic followed him out and closed the door. "Yeah?"

"Lomicka just called. The shootee just took a walk."

"What? How the hell is that possible?"

"Well, apparently they just had to stitch him up. Or staple him, or whatever the hell they're doin' now."

"They didn't knock him out and Lomicka didn't ask, right?"

"Sounds that way. Lomicka's pretty embarrassed."

"So where's Lynch?"

"He just got there when Lomicka was callin'."

"So did either one of 'em—did anybody in the hospital make the guy? Nobody went through his clothes? Checked his wallet?"

Stramsky shook his head no.

"Oh Jesus. Lum just sat in there, grinnin' at me, jerkin' me off, tellin' me we don't have a case, and here we are, two cops and everybody in that hospital working on the shootee—while he's awake—and nobody has the presence of mind to ask him what his name is and where he lives. And that bastard Lum is gonna walk again."

Balzic chewed his teeth and fumed. "I'm takin' Lum downstairs. That sonofabitch is gonna give up some time for this. Nobody calls his lawyer until the watch changes, got that? And then I'm gonna stick it to him on the bond."

"Stramsky nodded. "Oh. Hey. We got four guys can't put together a dollar between 'em."

"So?"

"They want to be locked in."

"What?"

"I'm tellin' you. Go ask 'em yourself. Some kind of fuckin' protest or somethin'."

"What?" Balzic's voice was squeaking upward.

Stramsky sighed and shrugged several times. "Go ask 'em, what can I tell you?"

"Those guys over there?" Balzic jerked his thumb at four bedraggled, bloodied men in their middle to late twenties. He walked quickly toward them, shaking his head as he went.

"All right, what is this? This protest crap? What protest? What's goin' on?"

"That's right," said the shortest of the four. He had a mass of dried blood that spread from his left nostril to his left ear.

"What's right?"

"This is a protest. Lock us up. We're not movin'."

"What're you talkin' about?"

"Everybody got to make their statement somehow, man, and this is where we make ours," said a blond fellow with a badly swollen lip and blood caked over his jaw and down his neck.

Balzic looked at his shoes. "Fellas, it's late, my patience is gone, I'm tired, I'm gettin' crankier by the minute. I don't think you belong here, I don't want you here, but I'm not gonna put up with any shit either. So somebody better explain."

The four looked at each other and then seemed to agree

by a series of shrugs and lifted thumbs and pointed shoulders that the short one should make the explanation.

"Okay. This is fine with me," he said, pulling at his nose. "Ain't no veteran in America, in the whole goddamn America, the whole goddamn history of this country been screwed like the guys that served in 'Nam. And guys are writin' their congressmen and that shit and writing letters to the papers and for what? For nothin', that's what. We can't even go in—like us, here. We go in the VFW, every damn one of us is a member, dues paid right up to the month—and we go in there—every time we go in there some motherfucker starts some shit, man."

"Right, yeah, goddamn right," the others chimed in.

"And you know what it's about, man? Huh?"

"I'm listenin'," Balzic said.

"It can start out about a hundred different things, man, but when all the bullshit's over, when they get down to it, man, these fuckin' people look at us like we're some kind of shit 'cause the fuckin' U.S. lost, man. Like it was our fault. Like we weren't tryin' or some fuckin' thing."

More nods and groans of agreement.

Balzic licked his lips and held up his right index finger. "I don't want to interrupt you, but I can see where you're goin'. I mean, I sorta understood all that before. But my question is this: if you're gonna have a protest—and I ain't sayin' whether you should or you shouldn't or whether you have a beef or don't have a beef—but exactly whatta you think's gonna be accomplished, uh, I mean, just what're you tryin' to, uh, no. Just who do you think is gonna be impressed by this protest if you're gonna be locked in here? I mean who's gonna see you? Who's gonna listen?"

"We're gonna have a fast, man," said a heavyset fellow with his right eye puffed shut.

"No, no, no. Wait a second. You're not gonna have any fast here 'cause you're goin' tomorrow morning. Out. In fact. Now that I think about it, out now. Go'wan. Out. Go home. I don't want to hear nothin'. Beat it."

"Hey, man, you can't do that," said one who had previously been quiet. "We caused a disturbance. We were in a fight. We broke up a club. That's assault and battery or something. Disturbing the peace. We broke the law. You guys arrested us, we admit it, we plead guilty. That's fair. That's right. You got to lock us up. That's the law."

Balzic canted his head in the direction of the last speaker, a fair-skinned, smooth-faced fellow who looked barely nineteen. Even the several large abrasions on his cheek and jaw did nothing to age him.

"Don't tell me the law," Balzic said. "If I don't arrest you or book you or sign the information against you, you ain't even here. So do me a favor. You want to have a protest, a fast, you don't wanna eat, then fine. You have one to your hearts' content. Only not here. Now take a walk."

The shortest one promptly sat on the floor. He had a little trouble doing this as his trousers were still down around his ankles. The three others immediately followed his example.

Balzic closed his eyes and sighed. "All right, all right, then if you don't want anybody makin' sense with you, then listen to this. I got two guys hustling people over to the magistrate, uh, two in the hospital, Zigmun there, Stramsky, and me. That's seven. I can have all seven here in about three minutes. Four tops. I guarantee you that within a minute you will be in the parking lot, and there's a very good chance somebody will be hurt. Maybe bad.

"Now you guys are veterans, and so am I and so is Stramsky. We feel certain, uh, what do I wanna say here? Uh—a kinship with you. We feel for you. We don't wanna fuck with you, not for a second. Least of all not for something as dumb as that thing you're complainin' about, losin' the war in Vietnam, Jesus. I don't have a bitch with you guys. Except this—and pay attention, 'cause I'm not kiddin'.

"This is my headquarters. This is my office. This is where I work, this is where my people work. And my rule is, nobody fucks with it. Not you, not anybody. So the choice is yours, either you go or we make you go. Take your pick. Out on your own or we put you out. You got ten seconds to decide, startin' now."

"Aw fuck it, man. Let's do it outside."

"Hey. I got it. Let's do it with our clothes off. Bare ass. Huh? Whatta you say?"

"Hey, right. Right!"

"That'll attract some fuckin' news media, huh? Attract them eyewitness news motherfuckers, them channel-eleven-we're-the-ones-to-watch motherfuckers—"

"Right! Those action-news-puts-you-there motherfuckers."

Balzic put up his hands and glared at the four of them until their exuberance subsided. "I wouldn't do that. I mean, you do what you want. But two things. Hear? Two things. Number one, that's indecent exposure and then we're right back where we started. Two, it's supposed to get very cold tomorrow, like, I heard, maybe five or six degrees. And I'm just prick enough to not arrest you until morning. So you guys give it some thought. In the meantime, out!"

Balzic started toward the door, but had taken only the first step when the spokesman lunged off the floor and swung at Balzic. The blow caught him flush on the side of the neck and sent him reeling sideways against the desk. By the time he righted himself and turned around, Stramsky and Zigmun had pinned the spokesman against the wall. Stramsky had his right forearm across the spokesman's throat, had the spokesman's right arm stretched against the wall, and had the heel of his right shoe dug into the spokesman's right instep. Zigmun had the other arm and was standing on the other instep.

"More you twitch," Stramsky said, "worse it's gonna feel. It's up to you."

Balzic picked up the calendar and stapler that had gone flying when he banged onto the desk. Holding his neck, he said to the three other vets, "Get your pants up and get out and I don't mean five minutes from now. Don't even think about arguin'. Don't even think. Just do it."

The vets scrambled to their feet, hitching and tugging up their pants, their eyes darting from Balzic to the vet pinned against the wall to Stramsky and Zigmun and back to Balzic. Without a word, they shuffled and slouched toward the door and then out.

Balzic watched them go. When they were outside, he turned to the vet Stramsky and Zigmun were holding.

"Let him go." Balzic waited until they released him and until he coughed and hacked and gasped for air and achieved a semblance of normal breathing.

"So," Balzic said. "So you can't stand freedom, huh? So you wanna punch your way into prison, right?"

"What're you talkin' about?"

"Oh you know what I'm talkin' about. You know positively, perfectly well what I'm talkin' about," Balzic said, moving toward the vet until he was less than a hand's width away from him. "You got a name, tough guy?"

"Murlovsky."

"Well, Mis-ter Murlovsky. So you wanna go to jail, huh? You wanna get inside, huh? You wanna get in there and tell the other tough guys how you don't take shit from nobody, huh, least of all from cops, is that it?"

"I don't know what you're talkin' about."

"Course you don't. You think you wanna be a real man among real men, don't ya? You think you wanna tell outlaws about what a real rebel outlaw you are, don't ya, huh? Well, you'll do that no matter what I say now, or what anybody says now or ever, but I'm gonna tell you about guys who punch cops in police stations. You listenin', huh?"

"I'm listenin'."

"Good. Then try this on for size. You think you're a man? Huh? Shit, you're not even a baby. You think you wanna go to prison, huh? Bullshit. You wanna go where you don't have to make a decision about what you do next. You know what a cell is for guys like you? It's a womb. It's a place where you get fed and you get clothed and housed and you don't have to do a fuckin' thing except breathe. Some guys break out of prisons. Guys like you break *in*. For guys like you, a cell's your biggest escape. So you go inside, and you brag to all the other assholes about how bad you are, how tough you are, but I just told you what a candy-ass you really are. And now you can't even use the excuse that you don't know what you did."

Balzic turned to Stramsky. "Put him in with Lum. Give him something to remember."

As usual when Balzic had been excited late at night, he had trouble getting to sleep. And as usual when he had trouble getting to sleep, he was awakened before he got much sleep at all. In this case, he was awakened by the telephone at 7:05—less than three hours after he'd come home from the station.

He was up and moving, with his eyes barely open, groping toward the phone his wife held out to him. She helped him find it, closed his hand around it after it dropped once, and then fell backward on her side of the bed, sighing.

"Yeah?" Balzic grunted.

"Mario, it's Royer. Sorry to bother you. I mean, what time you went out of here last night—"

"Uh-huh. So?"

"We got problems. I don't—look, if I could've done it, if I could've thought of some way to handle this without bothering you, I would've. I mean, one of the things I can handle, but the—"

"Uh, what is it?"

"Lum's screaming his head off—"

"What about?"

"Not about anything. He's just screaming. You know, making noise as loud as he can. He's not sayin' anything particular."

"You don't know that he does that? Really? You don't know that?"

"No."

"Well he does. Every time we lock him in for more than a couple hours, he starts hollerin'."

"Yeah, but what happens when people start showin' up for work in the other offices? He's making a lot of noise."

"Yeah, I can hear him. Well, usually he doesn't last too long. His voice goes. Wait him out, that's all I can tell you. He'll quit pretty soon. Besides which, it's Saturday. Remember? Remember who works on Saturdays?"

"Oh. Uh, the other thing is, those vets last night?"

"Which ones?"

"The ones that were gonna protest or something? Remember?"

"Yeah."

"They're outside now. They said they're gonna wait till eight o'clock, then they're gonna take their clothes off."

"What's the weather like?"

"Cold."

"Then forget about 'em. They're not gonna do it for long even if they do it at all. Anything else?"

"Yeah. We already got a call from one TV station and from two newspapers about 'em. They all say they're all coming."

"Listen, you can't worry about stuff till it happens. I'm goin', I'm goin' back to sleep, 'kay? Okay?"

"Yeah. Sorry."

Balzic grunted and hung up the phone, turned, and on his second step jammed his little toe on the leg of the bed. "Oh Jesus! Oh Christ! Son of a—"

"What happened? What's the matter?" Ruth was up and

crawling toward him. "Oh you stubbed your toe. Oh, oh, poor baby, poor baby."

Balzic eased himself into the bed and bent down to massage his toe.

"You want some ice for it?"

"No no no I don't want any ice."

"Hey! I didn't step on your toe—"

"I didn't say you did."

"I didn't call you up either."

"I didn't say you did that either."

"Well don't snap at me. All I did was answer the phone and ask you if you wanted some ice."

"Hey, cut me some slack, okay?"

"No. You cut *me* some. I went to sleep late too."

"What? What? What the hell's goin' on here? I bang my toe, you ask me if I want some ice, I tell you no and you're all out—"

"I'm not all out of anything. It was your tone. It was snippy. Snotty."

"Snippy?"

"I said snotty."

"You said 'em both," Balzic said under his breath. "Listen, I'm out of line, okay? I'm—"

"It's not okay. But you're out of line, that's for sure."

"—I was gonna say, I was tryin' to say I'm sorry. You gonna let me? Or ain't I allowed?"

"No." Ruth scrambled back up the bed, jammed herself under the blankets, and snatched them up to her chin.

Balzic started to say he was sorry, thought about it, put his tongue on an upper molar, and said, "I'm gonna take a shower. Get dressed. Go look at the world. Uh, I'm sorry I was snotty. And I am whether you let me or not."

No answer.

"I'm sorry I was snippy too."

"Oh go get your shower."

"I'm goin'. I'm on my way. Keep an eye on me. This is me goin' right here."

<hr />

Balzic turned off South Main into the City Hall parking lot at ten after eight. He jammed on the brakes and closed his eyes and dropped his chin and put his hand on top of his head. "Oh Jesus fucking Christ," he said aloud. "Why?" He closed his eyes and squeezed them shut, then he picked up his head, shoved his glasses back up his nose, and looked again at what awaited him.

Two of the three Vietnam vets he'd thrown out of the duty room last night were naked except for their shoes and socks. They were standing by the foot of the steps leading into the duty room. The third, fully clothed, was feeding rolled-up newspapers into a fire in a barrel.

Just beyond the vets, Fire Chief Eddie Sitko was standing with his hands on his hips gawking at their nakedness.

Off to the side was a tall, hulking figure with unruly hair and ill-fitting clothes. Balzic had never seen him before, but he guessed from the way the fellow was hovering about that he was probably a reporter.

Desk Sergeant Joe Royer was looking uncomfortable at the top of the steps.

Balzic shook his head, eased off the brakes, and drove around the vets until he got to his parking slot. He turned into it and shut off the ignition. His eyes were still burning from lack of sleep, and he had to force himself to get out of the cruiser.

Eddie Sitko was walking toward him, saying, "What the fuck's this?"

Balzic shrugged.

"You gonna bust these guys or what?"

"They're vets, Eddie."

"I'm a vet too. So what? I don't take my fuckin' clothes off just on account of that."

Balzic shrugged again and started toward the steps.

"Well you gonna let 'em stand around like that? What kind of vets?"

"Vets vets, how many kinds are there? Vietnam vets, I don't know. They got some kind of bitch. Ask them. I'm sure they'll be happy to tell you."

"Well you just gonna let 'em stand around naked like that?"

"Eddie, I already discussed it with them. Last night. I told 'em what their choices were. One of the choices was I was gonna let 'em freeze."

"They ain't gonna freeze with that fire there. You could bust 'em for that. There's an ordinance against open burning."

"It's in a barrel. I don't think that qualifies as open burning."

"That's a technicality. Arrest 'em, then let some magistrate figure it out. Meanwhile, they ain't standin' around makin' a joke out of you."

"They're not makin' a joke out of me."

Sitko shrugged. "They're right in front of your place. They was up in front of one of my places I'd turn a three-inch hose on 'em."

Balzic dug some dried soap out of his ear. "Eddie, I'm glad you're a fireman."

"Huh? What's that mean?"

"Just what it sounds like. I'll see ya, I got to go."

"Hey wait a minute. I wanna talk to you about Mrs. Garbin."

Balzic was already walking quickly toward the steps. "I don't want to talk about it."

"Well wait up a goddamn minute."

"I don't want to hear it, Eddie, honest to God I don't."

Sitko was calling after him, and the large hulking figure, splay-footed, was lumbering toward him, and all Balzic wanted to do was get inside and get some coffee and maybe a doughnut or some orange juice.

"Excuse me," the hulking figure with the unruly hair said. "You are the chief of police here, is that correct?"

The tone of that voice put Balzic off immediately. It was so well modulated that Balzic couldn't decide whether this stooped hulk with wiry, wild hair was going to show him to a table or try to sell him a cemetery plot.

"I'm the chief. Who're you?"

"Rob Lesser. I'm with the *Gazette*."

"If you're sellin' ads, you got to talk to the FOP people. I ain't allowed to buy ads."

"Selling ads? Of course not. Why would a newspaper sell ads to the police?"

Balzic cleared his throat. "For the policeman's ball. Look, maybe one of my people can help you. I'm busy right now."

"You don't understand. "I'm not an ad salesman. I'm a reporter—"

"Like I said, maybe one of my people can help you." Balzic started up the steps.

"Why does he think I'm selling ads?" Lesser asked no one.

"Beats the hell outta me, kid," Eddie Sitko answered, following Balzic up the steps. "He knows salesmen dress better than you do."

"What? What—what does that mean?"

"Hey, take it easy, kid, I was just pullin' your chain. Mario! Hey, Balzic, what the fuck! I'm not gonna chase you all over your goddamn—slow down a second, will ya!"

"I'm not listening to any fund-raising crap. I don't have time."

"Jesus," Sitko said, stopping once he'd got inside and wincing at the sound of Billy Lum's voice screeching from the downstairs lockup. "What's all that about?"

"Christ, he started up again," Royer said. "He quit about two minutes ago."

Rob Lesser came into the duty room then and said, "I'm not an ad salesman. What do my clothes have to do with it?"

"You gotta put up with that screamin'? If he ain't hurt, why d'you put up with it?"

"I'm supposed to turn a hose on him too, I guess."

"Christ, Mario, this place is like a zoo here this morning."

"Hey, if it bothers you, leave."

"Oh no, you're not getting rid of me that easy—"

"Is the coffee made?" Balzic asked Royer.

"I really am a reporter," Rob Lesser said in his modulated voice, "and you can verify that fact by calling my employer. I don't have credentials yet because I just this week began."

Balzic made his way to the automatic coffeepot and motioned for Royer to take care of Rob Lesser. Balzic mouthed the word "Out" as he poured a cup of coffee with his back to Lesser.

"Pardon me, sir," Royer said to Lesser, "but you'll have to leave."

"Leave? Why do I have to leave? I can't leave. I've been sent here to question the chief about—"

"Chief's busy. He can't answer questions now."

"But he's pouring coffee. He's getting ready to drink coffee—it appears to me."

Balzic turned and peered over his glasses at Lesser. "It appears to you, huh? Well watch this. I'm gonna *dis*appear to you." Balzic set off grumpily toward his office.

"Hey, Mario!" Sitko cried out. For crissake I gotta go to work, will you listen a minute."

"Hey, go to work. Who's stoppin' you? I *am* at work."

"Why is he hostile? Did I say something wrong?"

"You'll have to leave, sir," Royer said.

"But I'm on assignment here. I can't return without a story."

Balzic reached his office, ducked in, and banged the door shut.

"Mario!" Sitko shouted.

"Go. Leave. Goodbye. I am not talking to you about that woman until I talk *to* her, *about* her," came Balzic's muffled shout.

Sitko turned away from Balzic's office door and said, "Hey, Royer, whatta you givin' that kid the rush for? He's here to get a story. Hey, kid, uh—what's your name again?"

"Lesser. Rob Lesser."

"Hey, Mr. Lesser, have I got a story for you. You're

gonna love this. Your boss is gonna love it. He's a good friend of mine. Tom Murray and I go way back. And your readers, hey, they're gonna become your fans, that's how much they're gonna love it."

Balzic's door flew open. "Eddie, I'm warnin' you, don't do that until I check that lady out."

"Oh," Sitko said, smiling hugely. "Does it, uh, does it appear to you that I might be gonna say something about a certain lady we both might know, huh? Is that the way it appears to you, Mario, old buddy? Ha?"

"I'm telling you, don't."

"And how do you know what I might be gonna say to this young gentleman here?"

"I'm tellin' you, don't sic that kid on it until I check it out."

Sitko put his arm around Lesser's shoulders. "Listen, don't pay attention to him. You come on with me. We'll go have some coffee, we'll talk, I'll tell you all about it."

"But I was supposed to question the chief about those Vietnam veterans outside. That was my assignment. I can't return without—"

"Forget those clowns. Look at 'em, out there fuckin' naked. I'm gonna tell you a real story. It's gonna break your heart. You'll be cryin' when you're writin' it, honest to God. . . ."

Sitko led Lesser out the door.

The last thing Balzic heard was Lesser saying, "Why is he hostile? Is he always hostile? Or did I say something wrong?"

Balzic chewed his teeth, hustled back into his office, and turned his wheel-file until he found the home phone number for the managing editor of the *Rocksburg Gazette*. He dialed the number and knocked on his desk with his knuckles until Tom Murray answered.

"Balzic? What do you want? Make it fast. I'm busy."

"Okay. Pay attention. I'm busy too and I'm not gonna explain. Eddie Sitko just walked outta here with his arm round one of your reporters, Lasher, Lasser, something—"

"Lesser."

"—yeah. And he's gonna give him a sob story about a lady who says she got rolled and lost her life savings or her Christmas Club or some crap. Eddie's got his nose open for a charity thing. You know how he is. I told him to knock it off until I checked the lady out which I have not had a chance to do yet."

"So?"

"So put some brakes on the kid until I check it out."

"No."

"No? Just no? Whatta you mean no?"

"No. Just what I said."

"Why the fuck not? Whatta you mean no? Why not yes?"

"I don't tell reporters they can't write stories."

"Oh what the fuck, what're you gonna tell me, some crap about you don't want to mess with their enthusiasm or some crap?"

"That's it. You got it."

"Oh bullshit. Bullshit! You can't give me—"

"You can't give me anything either. Bye. Oh, Mario?"

"Huh? What?"

"You know what they say now. Have a nice day."

"Murray, you stonehead Irish prick—"

The click followed the laughter.

Balzic wanted to throw the phone against the wall. He closed his eyes and tried to blot out the events of the day so far. He had a vision of retirement, of himself on his back on a beach with a wet terrycloth hat over his face, his feet in the surf and his ears filled with the sounds of seabirds and wind.

"Aaaaaaaaaghhhhhhhhh. . . ."

Balzic winced. If it's possible, he thought, for someone to die from making ugly noise, then Billy Lum should have been dead years ago.

Balzic jumped up and lurched back into the duty room, intending to do something both legal and sensible about Lum. Royer stopped him before he'd gone three steps. Royer was pointing toward the windows, on the other side of which was a brightly painted panel truck with a television transmission dish on its roof. Even before the truck stopped, as Balzic and Royer watched, the side doors were opening and technicians were jumping out.

"What're you gonna do about that?" Royer said.

"Me? I'm not gonna do anything about it. They can take all the pictures they want, ask all the questions, I don't care. I hope the vets are happy. But it's all gonna add up to zero, 'cause they're not gonna show those bare asses on television. So where's that gonna leave those guys then?"

"Aaaaaghhhhhh. . . ."

"Oh Jesus Christ I'm takin' that asshole outta here before my head splits open. Who's the duty magistrate? Huh?"

"Aldonelli."

"Call him and tell him I'm comin' and who I'm bringin'. Then call Lum's lawyer and tell him what's goin' on. Then, after I bring him back here, you find somebody to haul him down to the county lockup."

"What about the vet down there, the one that smacked you?"

"I'm comin' to that. As soon as I get Lum out of here, turn that clown loose."

"What?"

"I know, I know what you're thinkin'. But that clown wants to have the state make up his mind for him, and I'm not gonna do it. He wants to get locked up, he's gonna have to do something a lot worse than punch me in the neck."

"Mario, I think you're makin' a big mistake. Everybody in the department is gonna know what happened tomorrow. The whole goddamn town'll know by the end of the week. I think that't the wrong message to be sendin'."

"Maybe it is," grumbled Balzic, "but it's the one I'm gonna send, and that's that. And when I get finished with Lum, I'm goin' up to the hospital to see some lady. Meantime, make those calls."

Balzic ducked around the corner and bounded down the stairs. He was almost to the bottom before he remembered the keys, went back up and got them, and then went bounding down again. He flipped the switch for the one overhead light in the four-cell lockup, then pulled open the steel door leading to the cells. In the first cell, Lum was stretched out on the metal bed, pretending to be asleep. On the floor, his arms wrapped around his knees, sat Murlovsky, trying not to be blinded by the light. He looked like a schoolboy who couldn't resist the temptation to look at a solar eclipse.

Balzic opened the door to their cell. "Let's go, Lum."

"What about me?" Murlovsky said.

"What about you? C'mon, Lum, on your feet. Move it!"

"Oh got-damn." Lum sat up, holding his hand over his

eyes. He had been here many times before and knew how to protect his vision.

"Whatta you mean, what about me? This nigger's crazy. I don't have to be treated like this. He screamed all night. When he wasn't doin' that, he was braggin' about how many white girls he fucked. You can't do this to me, you can't—"

"Why not? You wanna get locked in bad enough to punch me in the neck, then I'm gonna lock you in where I feel like lockin' you in."

"Say what? He did what? He punch you in your neck? Ain't that a bitch. Where was I at?"

"Get up, get out, and get up the steps. You, Murlovsky, close your mouth. Somebody'll be down for you in a little while."

"Punch you in your neck, ha. Hoo! Got-damn," Lum said, cackling and sputtering as be boogied out of the cell and up the steps.

"Keep talking," Balzic said. "Keep talking."

<hr>

"The charges, Mario, uh, what are the . . . ?" asked District Magistrate Anthony Aldonelli.

Balzic swallowed and thought for a moment. "Uh, how about these okay? You ready?"

"I'm ready," Aldonelli said, poised at his electric portable typewriter.

"Okay. Assault. Reckless endangering. Firearms violation—"

"Oh, man," Billy Lum said. "This ain't right. My lawyer s'posed to be here, man. And 'firearms violation'! She-it, you got to be more specific than that, man."

"Unlicensed handgun, how's that?"

"What handgun, man? Huh? What handgun you tryin' to connect me with, man? Huh? What one? Not that one Lynch say he found on the bar, man. Ain't no way you connect me with that handgun, man."

"—put that down, okay?"

"I got that. It's down."

"She-it. This a got-damn bunch of bullshit."

"And let's not forget attempted homicide."

"No mothafuckin' dope charges? May as well make me the mothafuckin' dope king of the black world, man. Mothafuckin' dope emperor, man, you goin' charge me with all that other bullshit, she-it, how come you leavin' out dope charges? Huh? Might as well put down there a thousand pounds of weed, and two tons of coke, too, she-it, why not? Man, where the fuck my lawyer? You call him? Huh? Did you call him or not, man, I want to know."

"Quit hollerin'. I called him. I don't know where he is, but he's been called."

"Ohhhhhh man . . ."

"Uh, Mario, what's, uh, whatta you want the bond?"

"Hey! Hey! What're you askin' him for? 'Whatta you want the bond?' Bullshit! You don't ask him. He's the cop. You're the goddamn magistrate, you don't—"

"Hey. You. Shut up. That's enough. You want contempt charges to deal with here? I'll decide who says what here. You keep quiet."

"I think fifty ought to do it."

"Fifty! What! Where the fuck—what the hell you mean fifty? Where the hell'm I s'posed to get five thousand dollars, Jesus Christ, Balzic, you crazy or what?"

"Fifty thousand it is," said Aldonelli. "You know the procedure, right?"

"Fifty! Where the hell am I gonna get five thousand dollars? Are you two crazy? This is a goddamn assault and weapons charge and that ain't no—that ain't worth ten thousand for crissake—"

"Attempted homicide makes it a little bit different. I have certain latitudes here. Discretion's mine. Besides, I'll accept property. I know your father."

"Aw motherfuck this, man. My father ain't talked— don't be talkin' to my father, man, that's bullshit. You say you know my father, then, goddamn, you know he don't speak to me, and you know that, you know he ain't postin' none of his property for me."

"All he has to do is present a title to one of his trucks," said Aldonelli. "I'll accept that."

"Oh, yeah, right. And all I gotta do to fly is grow some fuckin' feathers, man, and a beak." Billy Lum shook his head. "Why you lettin' this happen, Balzic? Man, I am seriously fuckin' disappointed in you, man. I have never done you like this, man. And you know my old man don't have no time for me, man. You know he ain't gonna sign one of his trucks over, man. So why you workin' me like this, man? Shit. . . ."

Balzic closed his eyes and sighed heavily. "Maybe I'm just gettin' tired of cleanin' up after you. Christ knows I been doin' it long enough. First time I busted you, you were fourteen years old—and I have no idea how many times we busted you since."

"Twenty-six," Lum said.

Balzic shook his head and laughed ruefully in Aldonelli's direction. "Notches on the rapsheet. Billy Lum's six-gun against society. You can't believe the crap he's put out about himself. One day I was in Muscotti's and he was talking to this white girl—God only knows where she was from, the moon maybe, and he was actually comparing himself to Robin Hood. And instead of bows and arrows, he was talkin' about his spreader, his shotgun, remember that one, Lum? Huh? You didn't know I was listenin' to that one."

"Aw later for you, man."

"Later for me, huh? Uh-uh. Later for you. I hope no-body comes up with five grand and I hope you know how to count to a hundred and seventy-nine, 'cause that's how many days you're gonna spend waiting for your trial. Let's go. On your feet. And don't say another word. Or I'm gonna ask a hundred thousand, how d'you like that? If nobody's gonna go five bills for you, who d'you think is gonna go ten? Huh? And then maybe I'll talk somebody into a couple continuances, huh? How'd you like that? It might be ten months before you come to trial, you'd just be sittin' on your brains down there in Southern Regional. I like it myself. Whatta you think of it? Huh? You ready to go, or you wanna say something else?"

Balzic was staring out of the duty room at the four Vietnam veterans, two naked and two clothed (the one named Murlovsky who had spent the night in the same cell as Lum had rejoined them), when he got the call from Magistrate Aldonelli telling him that attorney Leonard Bayer had produced the $50,000 bond certificate for Billy Lum's release not a half-hour after Balzic had escorted Lum out of the office.

"Swell," Balzic said as he hung up. "He'll be out before he's in. What a world. . . . Hey, Joe, don't bother taking Lum down to the county lockup. His lawyer'll be here in a couple minutes. I'm goin' up the hospital. Hey, did anybody turn anything on that guy Lum shot?"

"I haven't heard anything."

Balzic headed for the door, grumbling as he went.

Outside, at the bottom of the steps, a microphone was thrust into Balzic's cheek. He recoiled. "Watch it, huh?"

"Chief, about these Vietnam veterans. Don't you believe—"

Balzic pushed the microphone away and glared at the tall, young, handsome, carefully groomed man with the resonant baritone voice who was attached to the microphone.

"You wanna move, please?"

"Chief, these veterans have alleged that you—"

"Hey, you smack me in the face with the mike, you don't even know you did it, and even though I asked you to please move, you're gonna stand here and ask me more questions?"

"Chief, these veterans have alleged that you and—"

"Will you get outta here!" Balzic shouldered his way around the television reporter, and hurried to his cruiser. The reporter and his technicians trailed after Balzic, trying to keep up.

"Chief, if I could just have a moment—"

"So you can hit me in the face again?"

"These veterans have alleged that you—"

Balzic turned to confront the reporter when they reached his cruiser.

" 'Sorry's' not in your vocabulary, is it?"

"Chief, these veterans have alleged that you refused to listen to their—"

"Refused to listen! Is that what I did? Hey, apparently we got a lot in common. Maybe we oughta get together sometime, have a couple beers, and not listen to each other. Whatta you think?"

"—they have alleged that you refused to listen to their complaints of harassment—"

"Aw go have a stroke for crissake. Jesus." Balzic turned and flopped into his cruiser and drove off toward Conemaugh General Hospital.

Before he had driven a block, Balzic called Royer on the radio. "Hey, Joe, do something, okay?"

"Yeah. What?"

"Get somebody to check out those vets. I want to know who they are, when they were over there, what they did, when they got back, what they been doing, the whole number. Find Rugsy. Tell him to do it. Tell him forget about whatever he's doing, okay?"

"Okay, Mario. I'll get Rugsy on it. Out."

After a few minutes he turned into the entrance ramp of the brand new municipal parking lot on the southeast side of the hospital. A bronze plaque on a five-foot-high obelisk proclaimed: "Edward J. Sitko Parking Garage." Below the words there was an amateurish likeness in bas relief of the city fire chief.

Above the entrance ramp, white stenciled letters on a red background announced that there were SEVEN LEVELS. 25¢ FOR FIRST HOUR. 15¢ EVERY HOUR AFTER. SECURITY FOR CAR, DRIVER.

Balzic took the ticket from the machine and drove in as

the bar lifted. He shook his head and chewed his lip and thought, Jesus Christ, fire chief for all those years, bust his ass for nothing, not a dime. And then one day, whether you want it or not, they name a garage after you. They don't even ask your permission, and they think it's a great honor. They could've named the training tower after him . . . the Edward J. Sitko Fire Training Tower . . . at least there would have been a fire every once in a while. Sitko's semi-eternal flame. He would've got a boot out of that. But a goddamn garage? The Edward J. Sitko Parking Garage? Jesus fucking Christ . . . and they didn't even have the decency to let him die first. Wonder what they're gonna stick my name on. Goddamn sanitary landfill probably. . . .

Balzic found an empty stall on the fourth level. He walked quickly to the elevator, took it to the second level, and then walked through the covered archway to the hospital, marveling at its more recent additions. In less than a year, the hospital board had annointed the construction of the parking garage, a new pharmacy and professional annex, and a cancer chemotherapy unit to the south of the main building. Then they took their collective breath and consumed a half-block of houses and a parking lot to the west and were now turning that vacant ground into a new emergency unit.

Somehow, during a worldwide depression, the board of directors of Conemaugh General had managed to find the money to finance seemingly their every construction whim. Balzic suspected that, no matter how bad the economic times, there were two institutions in America that would never want for money: churches and hospitals. Christians would always give money to the churches to secure life everlasting, and Jews would always give money to hospitals to secure life as long as it could be made to last.In between were the Christian-Jews, or the Jewish-Christians, who prayed for life without end while writing checks to forestall the end of life. Nothing wrong with that, Balzic thought, as he tried to imagine how many people would be out of work without such prayers and check-writing. Out of such prayers were hospitals built, and new wards and cancer units and parking garages to serve the staff and the visitors. Out of such prayers came memorials to fire chiefs. . . .

Balzic made inquiries and was directed to the fourth floor. He found the nurses' station and asked for the supervisor. A minute later, a fiftyish woman with a dark complexion approached him at a stern pace. She had a taut, angular body and the brittle expression of one determined never to gain weight.

"Who wants to see me please?" The words were spoken with neither pause nor inflection.

"I do," Balzic said, holding up his ID case.

The supervisor took the case from Balzic's hand, scrutinized the photo, and glowered up at Balzic. Without a word, she handed the case back. "Well?"

"I'd like to talk about your patient, uh, Mrs. Garbin?"

"She's not my patient. She's a staff patient."

Balzic licked his lips and thought whether he wanted to continue. "Is somebody from the staff around?"

"It's Saturday morning. The staff is extremely thin."

"Then maybe you could help me—if you would."

"It's doubtful that I can. And I am busy."

"Of course you are. You have a lot of work here, I

know that. People think, hey, you're the boss, you sit around, tell everybody what to do—"

"Do you want information? Is that it? Then ask. Trying to butter me up isn't going to get it any faster. I am up to my eyes in work. Do you mind?"

"Uh, sorry," Balzic said, shrugging feebly. "Okay. Tell me what you think about Mrs. Garbin."

"What do you mean what do I think about her?"

"You haven't had a thought about her? Not one?"

"Well, of course. But how do you mean? I don't know what you're looking for."

"Listen, this is not a test. Your answers aren't gonna please me or not please me. I want to know what you think about this woman."

"But I haven't that much contact with her."

"In the contact you had with her, what did you think?"

"I know you're searching for something, Officer, but I don't know what—"

"Look, lady, I'm searching for anything. See, what we got here, never mind. What I got is a bunch of rumors about Mrs. Garbin, what happened to her, how much she lost, and so on, and it's close to Christmas, see, which is a very emotional time. People get all out of joint around the holidays, especially this one. Now there's a story gets going about an old lady gets rolled, loses a bunch of money, and certain kinds of people start in to thinking a certain kind of way, and the next thing you know I got five or six problems where before I only had one. So, you're the first person I talk to about this lady—not the first, but the first who might be a little objective, you know? So I want to hear your impressions, I want to know what you think. And if you haven't been around her enough to get an impression, then tell me somebody who has. That's all, okay?"

The nurse had listened with crossed arms and pursed lips. "I think I'm the wrong person for you to talk to."

"Uh, who might the right person be? Do you know?"

"Sorry. Can't help you." The supervisor shrugged emphatically and turned and strode into her office.

Balzic looked around, not sure even why he was still standing there, never mind what he was looking for. He felt a gentle tug on his sleeve and turned to see a chubby, pink-faced nurse motioning for him to follow her out into the corridor.

Out of sight of the nurses' station, the pink-faced nurse stopped and said, "Our supervisor is, uh, well, don't hold it against her. This isn't her year for men. Her husband left her about six months ago, and last week she found out her son's gonna marry a divorcee with three kids. So right now, men are a big pain in the behind, if you know what I mean."

"Okay," Balzic said, nodding. "So whatta you know about Mrs. Garbin?"

"Not much. Mrs. Garbin's not talking to anybody— 'cept the fire chief."

"She's not saying anything?"

"About what got her in here, no, not to any of the nurses. All it is, is, how are you, I'm fine, did you move your bowels, yes I did, here's tomorrow's menu—but I don't think you'd be interested in that."

"How many times has she talked to the fire chief?"

"Twice that I know of. He was here when she was brought in and then again today."

"When today?"

"Right after I came on duty."

Balzic nodded. "Uh, she get her own doctor yet?"

"No, residents and interns, that's all, they're checking on her, but there's nothing serious. Just some bruises on her forehead, a cut on her nose. She'll be out tomorrow, or the day after for sure."

Balzic frowned and shrugged. "Well, thanks. Appreciate your help. What room's she in?"

"Four-seventeen, right over there."

Balzic patted the pink-faced nurse on the arm and turned toward room 417. When he walked in he found Mrs. Garbin propped up watching a television set that hung on metal brackets from the ceiling. She was a frail woman, bones jutting everywhere, with a dark complexion and great dark circles under her eyes. Her nose was long and hooky, and she had no teeth—or if she had them, they weren't in her mouth. Her white hair was yellowing and hung straight off an irregular part in the middle of her narrow head. She struck Balzic as being someone who had never taken her pleasures in food.

"Mrs. Garbin?"

She glanced at him irritably and her eyes returned at once to the TV screen. "I was wondering when you was gonna show up."

"You remember me?"

Mrs. Garbin chewed her gums, but said nothing. She continued to watch a religious show on the set. Balzic glanced up at it. A man obviously delighted with himself was singing. In a small circle in the left corner of the screen, a woman was signing the words for the deaf. She looked almost as exuberant as the male singer.

"I'd like to ask you some questions, Mrs. Garbin. Do you mind?"

"You'd ask 'em no matter what I did, so what?"

"I can come back some other time."

"You're here now, may as well get it over with."

"Mind if I turn the sound down?"

"I can talk to you and watch that at the same time. I can do two things at once."

"Okay," Balzic said, sighing and taking off his raincoat. "Would you tell me what happened, please?"

Mrs. Garbin did not take her eyes off the screen. "This nigger jumped out of a car and hit me in the head and face twice and took my money."

"What time did this happen?"

" 'Bout six o'clock."

"Yesterday evening?"

"That's right."

"Where'd it happen?"

"On Pittsburgh Street. Right where Third Avenue crosses it."

"Which corner were you on?"

"By that Boron station."

"So you were opposite, uh, the real estate place, uh, G and G Realty, I think."

"Yes."

"Which way were you walking?"

"Up the hill. I was going home. I just come from Frank's Market. Paid my bill."

"Frank stay open that late? I thought he'd be closed by five."

"I stopped in the Sons of Italy. I had couple beers, talked to Jack's brother. He was tendin' bar."

"Jack? Your husband Jack?"

"Surprised any of you city guys can remember his name."

"Uh-huh. So then you were walkin' home, facing traffic, right?"

"Traffic's only gone one way there for 'bout twenty years. At least."

"So, uh, what kind of car was it? D'you happen to notice?"

"Nope. Never even seen it."

"A black guy got out—"

"A nigger got out."

"Uh-huh. So he got out, hit you twice, right? With what?"

"Whatta you mean with what?"

"What'd he hit you with? His hand, a stick, a brick, what?"

"I don't know, I never seen it."

"Well what was moving, his right hand or his left hand?"

"Just told you I never seen it coming so how the hell would I know which hand he done it with?"

Balzic took a deep breath and exhaled slowly. "What did he look like?"

"A nigger."

"Was he black? Or the color of a Hershey bar? Or a—"

"Why don't you just ask me who it was 'stead of asking me all these description questions?"

"Do you know who it was?"

"Sure I know who it was. It was that garbage collector's bastard Lum."

Balzic's mouth dropped open in spite of himself. He stuck his tongue against the inside of his lower lip and pushed out. After a moment he said, "D'you tell this to anybody else?"

"Told it to anybody who asked me."

"Well, for instance, did you tell it to Eddie Sitko?"

"Sure I did."

"Uh-ha. Okay. You sure you told him?"

"I just said so, didn't I?"

Balzic ran his tongue over his teeth and chewed his upper lip. "Mrs. Garbin, uh, could you, uh, would you describe Billy Lum?"

"What the hell for? We both know what he looks like. I mean you ought to, for cryin' out loud. You arrested him enough times. Sonofabitch been gettin' away with murder for long as anybody can remember. You don't know what he looks like, that's your problem. It sure ain't mine."

"Mrs. Garbin, these are serious charges here. Assault, battery, aggravated assault, robbery—"

"Goddamn right. Robbery. Don't forget that one. Five hundred and two dollars. I've been savin' it up for three years. Three bucks a week. An extra dime or nickel here or there. Sometimes a quarter. But at least three bucks every week. Pinching pennies, squeezin' 'em till Lincoln hollered, and that nigger got it all and all I get is a trip in here on my Medicare card and that's with a hundred-dollar deductible, and you? Look at you. You're in here questionin' me like I'm the one who robbed him. I can see it in your eyes, Balzic."

"You're not lookin' at me."

"I don't have to look at you. I know. Just like all the rest of them bastards work for the city. Begrudge me and Jack every goddamn penny of his disability. I don't have to look at you. I quit lookin' at all youns bastards years ago. I know what you're thinkin'."

"Mrs. Garbin, let's get something straight—"

"I don't have to get nothin' straight from you."

"Well, you're gonna hear it whether you want to or not—"

"Go blow it out your ass."

"Uh-huh. Well, I don't care where you think it's coming from, but this is the truth. I don't have anything whatsoever to do with city pensions. I don't have anything to do with disability. I have never been asked to pass judgment on whether anybody gets a pension or doesn't, and I've never volunteered any advice about anybody's right to a pension or to a disability check, is that clear?"

"Like I said: go blow it out your ass."

"Mrs. Garbin, your opinion of the truth doesn't change it. I have never once begrudged you or your husband whatever you or your husband gets from the city—"

"Big deal. You're so generous, cheese oh man."

"Let's get back to the other thing."

"Yeah. Let's."

"Uh, if I brought an information in here with Billy Lum's name on it, accusing him of assaulting you and robbing you, would you sign it?"

"You just go bring it and see if I don't."

Balzic rocked back and forth on his heels and toes. He picked up his raincoat and put it on. "Mrs. Garbin, I'm gonna check some things out. I'll be back."

"Take your time. I ain't goin' nowhere."

"Goodbye."

"Till you arrest that nigger bastard and get my money back there ain't nothin' good, and don't you forget it."

Balzic shrugged, grunted a goodbye, and left Mrs. Garbin to the religious show on the TV set. He hurried to the nurses' station and asked if he might use the phone. A nurse told him to help himself and pointed out a phone not in use, but just as Balzic picked it up, the supervisor appeared and told him curtly that a pay-phone was located in the visitors' lounge near the elevators.

Balzic replaced the phone in its cradle and, humming a nonsensical tune to keep from cursing, set off toward the visitors' lounge. When he got there, the pay-phone was being used by an emaciated, tattooed, toothless man in a wheelchair. Balzic studied the man's tattoos for a moment and tried not to eavesdrop. The man had an anchor and a winged serpent on his upper left arm, a cluster of roses with the word LOVE in the middle on his left forearm, a dagger dripping two drops of blood on the inside of his right forearm, and a tiny bird in flight on the left side of his neck. The bird's beak was open and created the illusion that it was about to bite the man's left earlobe.

"Yeah?" the man snarled suddenly, after listening for what seemed to Balzic almost a minute. "Yeah? Izzat a fact? Well go to hell yourself. You hear me? Huh? Go to hell yourself!" The man slammed the phone onto the cradle, missed it, and caught it as it bounced off the arm of his wheelchair. An IV bottle hung from a stainless steel pole on the left arm of his wheelchair, and a urine-collection bag was taped to his right ankle.

After he hung up the phone, he proceeded with great deliberateness to remove the IV tubing from the needle taped to the back of his left hand. Once he had done that—and without moving away from the phone, so that no one else could get near it—he then removed the catheter from his penis. This was not done without great grimacing and several pronounced and pained expirations. Then, as Balzic watched in bemused horror, the man coolly inserted the end of the catheter tube into the IV syringe still embedded in a vein in his left hand. He then appeared to be trying to insert the IV tubing into his penis.

Balzic cleared his throat loudly and said, "I think that's a mistake."

"Who astcha?" the tattooed man said, concentrating furiously on trying to insert the IV tubing into his penis.

"Nobody. But I think that's a bad move."

"If nobody astcha, how's come you're still givin' answers?"

Balzic watched for another second, then wheeled around and bolted back to the nurses' station and told them what he'd just observed.

"Oh cripes," one of the younger nurses said, dropping a metal clipboard she'd been writing on and breaking into a trot around Balzic.

Balzic closed his eyes and shook his head. After a moment's thought he looked around, spotted a phone, and went to it. Just as he reached for it, the supervisor reappeared with pursed lips, folded arms, and contemptuous eyes.

"I know you told me where the pay-phone is, lady," Balzic said. "But I don't wanna go down there again. So I'm gonna use this one, okay?"

"It is not okay. That is a nurse's phone. You are not a nurse. Put it down and leave."

Balzic did not put the phone down. Instead, he dialed the station.

"Did you hear me? I said put that phone down!"

Balzic looked at the supervisor and listened to the ringing. "I'm not goin' to the pay-phone, lady. I was just down there and I didn't like what I saw and I'm not goin' back. So if you don't want me to use this phone—and I don't see what the big deal is anyway, you got two other phones here—if you don't want me to use this phone, you're gonna have to take it away from me. You wanna try that? Huh? Remember, you can't call the cops, 'cause I'm the chief of the cops here. So? Whatta you gonna do? Where's this little power-struggle gonna wind up? Huh?"

"Rocksburg Police. Sergeant Royer speaking."

"Balzic. Two things. First, find Eddie Sitko and ask him if a certain woman in the hospital ever mentioned any names regarding her so-called assault and robbery. Okay?"

"Okay."

"Second thing, get me the number for the Black Legion."

"Hold it."

Balzic heard a wheel-file being flipped. He glanced at the nursing supervisor, who was chewing her molars and breathing noisily. Balzic pushed his glasses back up his nose and listened carefully as Royer told him the phone number for the Black Legion.

Balzic depressed the receiver buttons, lifted his finger, got a dial tone, and dialed the number, looking openly at the supervisor all the while.

"Legion."

"Is Jimmy Payne around?"

"Who wants to know?"

"Chief of Police Balzic."

"Uh . . . jus' a second."

After a moment, filled with muffled words, the same voice came back on to announce: "He don't start work till six o'clock. You want him, you goin' have to call him at home, understand?"

"Does he start at six every night?"

"Every night but Monday. Ain't nobody work on Monday."

"You know his phone number?"

"Uh, he don't be likin' nobody get that number, understand? Hold it, hold it, he just walk in now. Ho, Jimmy! Ho! Phone call. . . ."

Another moment passed. The nursing supervisor continued to glare at Balzic.

"Yeah?"

"Jimmy Payne?"

"Talkin'."

"This is Balzic, chief of—"

"I know who you are."

"Tell me, you work every night for the last week?"

"Uh-huh. 'Cept Monday."

"Start at six every night?"

"Little before. Sometimes a lot. Like today."

"Were you there last night at six?"

"Uh-huh."

"Was Billy Lum there?"

"When?"

"At six o'clock when you started. Was he there?"

"Yeah. He was playin' cards."

"You absolutely sure of this?"

"Yeah, I'm sure."

"Were there a lot of people there then?"

"I'm not sure. Dudes playin' tonk, bullskatin'. Ten maybe."

"But there were other people there besides you and Lum?"

"Oh yeah. Sure."

"Okay, Jimmy. You might have to testify about this, you hear? And it doesn't have a damn thing to do with what happened later on. Okay? Thank you very much for your cooperation. Goodbye."

Balzic hung up and then, glancing around to see that the other nurses were not overtly observing him, he locked gazes with the supervisor and bowed from the waist, throwing his arms out briefly, grandly.

"One day," she said flatly, "you'll need me and I'll remember what you just did."

"You do that, Sweets," Balzic said, " 'cause it'll be a long time before I forget you. 'Bye."

He hurried back to Mrs. Garbin's room and found her preoccupied still with the religious show on the TV set. He knocked on the jamb and took one step into the room.

"Now what?" she said, glancing hotly at him.

"Mrs. Garbin, uh, you're gonna have to reconsider your accusation. I'm not saying you have to change it, but you are gonna have to think about it some more."

"Oh yeah? How's come?"

"Because Billy Lum most probably was not where you say he was at the time you say he was. Other people say he was someplace else at that time."

"Other niggers probably."

"Doesn't matter who they are, Mrs. Garbin. If a half-dozen or so people walk into the magistrate's office during the preliminary hearing and say Billy Lum was someplace else, all we're gonna do is waste a lot of time and money if you keep saying he assaulted and robbed you at the time you say he did. Now you don't have to tell me anything right now—"

"It was him. I seen him clear as I see you."

"—you don't have to change anything now. But I want you to think about it some more."

"I don't need to."

"Well, you just think about it some more anyway. Uh, your husband at home?"

"Where else would he be? And who wants to know? You?"

"Yes, ma'am."

"What for?" She had pulled herself up stiffly to a sitting position, and she began to scratch her forearms.

"Just want to stop in and see him, say hello, that's all. You mind?"

"Leave him alone. He don't need any baloney with you. Just leave him alone."

"No, I'm gonna go see him. I'm gonna ask him about this money you been savin' up—"

"He don't know nothin' about it. So just leave him alone."

"I can't leave him alone, you know that. He doesn't know anything about it—nothing at all? You tryin' to surprise him?"

"I never told him nothin' about it. So he don't know nothin' about it. You wanna find out about it, go find that Lum bastard. Ask him where it is, you wanna ask somebody so goddamn much. Go 'head."

Balzic shook his head and ran his tongue over his lower teeth. "Uh-uh, I'm not gonna ask him about it. He's already got enough trouble. No, I'm gonna talk to Jack, to your husband."

"You leave my old man alone."

"Ma'am, you know better than I do that I can't leave him alone."

⚬◦❈◦⚬

Balzic got the Garbins' address from the admissions office after he found that they had no phone listed in the directory. It was a street on Norwood Hill, the highest elevation in Rocksburg, where nearly all the people had come from

— 71 —

the Abruzzi Mountains of Italy and the rest from Calabria and Sicily or were descended from those who had. Balzic loved Norwood in the summer. Summer meant terraced gardens abloom with vegetables, especially tomatoes and peppers and garlic and basil and dill and mustard seed, and men with hard round bellies arguing over how best to increase their produce or how to cure it or preserve it or pickle it and women in sleeveless cotton dresses with their arms brown from hanging out clothes and telling each other that the men didn't know what the hell they were talking about. Balzic tried to drive around the hill at least once a week all summer long just to smell it.

And every Fourth of July, Mother of Sorrows Church held a street bazaar to raise money and to celebrate the anniversary of the burning of its mortgage and the founding of the country; and Balzic took his wife and mother so his mother could see her friends and so Balzic could eat pork sausage made with hot, red peppers and garlic and fennel seeds and drink the wine that came out of the cellars in the hands of proud, suspicious men. It was a standing joke that if you liked their wine, they'd be proud, and if you didn't, they'd want to know how you found out about the bazaar and who invited you anyway.

But Norwood in winter had no such charm. Its streets were steep and narrow and frequently glazed with ice. The city salt and ash trucks never bothered with Norwood, and the inhabitants of the hill became, it seemed to Balzic, as difficult as their streets. He did not look forward to talking to Giacomo Garbinerri, because, among other reasons—if Balzic remembered it right—Jack Garbin had quit planting a garden at about the same time he had stopped going to the Mother of Sorrows bazaar, which was the same year he had been forced to give up his city job and start collecting a disability pension.

Balzic had to park half a block from the house because that was the only space he could find. Cars were parked bumper to bumper on both sides of the street, which, like all the others on the hill, was made of large, yellow bricks and had been laid out before anybody there had owned a car.

The Garbins' house was typical of the houses on Norwood Hill. The lots were narrow and deep and the houses were built to fit the lots. They were generally four stories high—cellar, first floor, second floor, and attic—usually sixteen feet wide and thirty-two to forty feet deep. All had been built of wood, but most were covered either in aluminum siding or in asphalt tile that was supposed to imitate red bricks. And the Garbins' house, like almost all the others, had a front porch built over a coal bin—though most of the houses were now heated by natural gas—and a metal awning extending out from the porch roof to keep off the weather. There were concrete circular flowerpots on each end of the four steps leading up to the Garbins' front porch from the sidewalk. To the right of the steps was the wintry remnant of a rock garden. There were four juniper bushes close to the house, and all gave evidence of a devoted clipper.

Up on the porch, as Balzic knocked, he saw two aluminum chairs that had been turned upside down and were leaning against the house. He could see that they'd been painted several times; chips in the paint revealed at least three layers, each a different color.

Jack Garbin opened the door with a surprised grunt. He had several days' growth of white beard. He was much thinner than Balzic remembered him, and the fact that he wasn't wearing his false teeth gave him a flaccid gauntness. He was wearing a green cotton work shirt and trousers to match, and he was barefoot.

"Hello, Jack."

"Is that you, Mario?"

"It's me. Uh, may I come in?"

"What's this about?"

"It's about your wife."

Garbin grunted and looked down at his bare feet. "Come on in. Just lemme go put some slippers on."

Garbin backed away from the door, made a vague gesture with his right hand, and hobbled off out of Balzic's sight. Garbin's right heel was fully three inches off the floor at each step and that forced him to walk in a wobbling, bouncing gait that must have given his back fits.

He leaned his head around the corner and said, "I ain't got nothin' to drink. If you're gonna want somethin' you're gonna have to go get it yourself, you know? Huh?"

"I don't want anything. I'm fine."

"Oh. Well, sit down. I forgot where I put my slippers."

"They're out here, Jack. In front of the TV."

"Huh? Oh. Forget my . . . ," Garbin said, wobbling and bouncing back into the living room. He spied the slippers, black leather with the left heel mashed down and the right heel cut away. He put them on with his back to Balzic and then he eased himself onto the couch next to the TV set. The couch cushions were all sprung out of shape and made a loud metallic sound when Garbin settled down.

He reached for a package of cigarette papers and a pack of tobacco on the table by the couch and quickly rolled a cigarette. He lit it with a wooden match. After he shook the match out, he licked his thumb and forefinger and pressed the burnt match for a second and then laid it carefully in a large ceramic ashtray. There were no other butts or matches in the tray, though the room was heavy with the smell of smoke. Garbin coughed each time he exhaled smoke. "Oh crap," he said, and heaved himself off the couch and left the room.

Balzic could hear the clinking and a faucet being turned on and then off. In a moment, Garbin was back, his face looking only slightly less flaccid. He had put his teeth in.

He plopped on the couch again and it twanged again. "Okay, okay, so now—so now what? Huh?"

"Well, first off, how you doin'?"

"Oh cut the baloney. You didn't come up here to find out how I'm doin', huh? I mean we can see how I'm doin'. Huh? Look around. How's it look like I'm doin'? Furniture's forty years old—and it was ten years old when Mag's mother gave it to us. Gave it to her. Can't sit down nowhere in this room without that old bag stabbin' me in the rear end every time."

"So you ain't doin' too good."

"Aw just skip it, huh? We both know what you want, what you're here for, so let's get to it, huh? And before you get started, I don't know nothin' except what she told me. So what am I gonna tell you, huh?"

"I don't know. Why don't you start by telling me what she told you?"

"You already know what she told me, huh? She told me the same thing she told you, so now why you wanna make me say it all over again, huh? I'll tell you why. 'Cause you think something funny's goin' on here, that's how come you're here. And we both know that. So now whatta you want me to tell you, huh?"

"I don't know. What d'you want to tell me?"

"Aw will you cut it out answerin' me questions. Don't answer me no questions. Answer me answers when I ask you something. This is my house. Don't go messin' around with me in my house, huh?"

"Jack, I'm not messin' with you—"

"Aw baloney. You was a snoopy kid when we was kids and you growed up a snoopy guy. You was a cop before you was a cop, don't tell me, huh? I knew you was always gonna be a cop."

Balzic shrugged and tried his best to smile.

"What'd you think I was gonna be, huh? D'you think I was gonna wind up like this, huh? Cheese. Rollin' cigarettes in the Depression. 1935. Still rollin' cigarettes. Sometimes I think the Depression ain't never been over— ah, what's the use. Well what'd you think I was gonna be, huh? Just another number down the DPW, huh? Tell the truth. Is that what you thought, huh?"

"I don't know, Jack. I don't know what I thought."

"Heh. That's probably 'cause you didn't think nothin'. Hey, you get outa school, you go to the Marines. Yeah. I remember that. Me, I don't even get drafted. I'm 4-F. They turn me down. I ain't—I got a, what you call, a heart murmur. All my life I got this here murmur, nothin' happens to me, no heart attacks, no coronaries, no nothin'. But it keeps me out of the draft. So I make a pile of money the whole war making them artillery shells and then the war's over and who needs shells, huh? And—and then, there I am. I bought this house, I got married, and youse guys are all comin' back, all big heroes youse guys, and I ain't even got a job. How do you like that, huh? I went from bum to king to bum in five years. Whatta you care, huh?"

Garbin rolled another cigarette.

"Boy oh boy," he said, "what a screwin' that was. All of a sudden, nobody needs artillery shells anymore. And everywhere I go, apply for a job, some S-O-B, he wants to know, am I a vet? No I tell him. I was 4-F I tell him. So then what? So now I'm 4-F all over again. I was 4-F because I was 4-F, ain't that a kick in the ass, huh? You was 4-F, you was good enough to make shells, but when they don't need shells no more, then you're 4-F all over again. You go to the back of the line. You gotta get in line behind all youse guys. Youse vets. Hey, the big heroes. Some heroes. Yeah. Some heroes. Some of those big heroes they didn't fire a shot. They didn't fire a shot the whole time they was in. You think I don't know about that, huh? I heard all about it. . . . And what did I wind up doin', huh? I'll tell you what. Pickin' up garbage, that's what. Pickin' up other people's crap, that's what. Me and a bunch of niggers. Me and a bunch of *tuzones*. . . ."

Garbin sagged from the effort of his speech. He tried to smile but looked too tired even for that. Suddenly he brightened and said, "Hey Balzic, you wanna have some wine, huh? I was fibbin' before when I said I didn't have nothin' to drink. It's good stuff. Old Castellucci makes it, you know him?"

"Which one is that? I know a bunch of Castelluccis."

"Egidio. The old guy. Must be ninety. The one they cut off his legs a couple of years ago with the diabetes, you know him?"

"Oh I know who he is. But I don't know him."

"Son of a brick makes the best wine in Norwood, honest to God. He got a cousin or somethin' works in the produce business up in the Strip, you know, in Pittsburgh? And he always gets him these real good grapes, man oh man. Hey, sit still, I'm gonna get you some, honest, you're gonna love it."

Garbin hefted himself off the couch and wobbled out of sight. Soon he returned with two large jelly glasses half full of a liquid almost black. Balzic smelled it and it gave off a chianti-like aroma. He held it up to the light and its deep, deep burgundy-black color struck him with its clarity. He tasted it, rolled it around his mouth. It was dry as kindling and its peppery, flinty taste was as good as some commercial wines Balzic had drunk and better than a whole lot of them.

"This guy makes this in his cellar?"

"Yeah. Ain't that a kick, huh? Think of that. Making this in your cellar. Pope oughta make him a saint. You know how much he charges me for this? Huh? A buck and a half for a gallon. Hey don't quote me on that, huh? He ain't s'posed to sell it—"

"I know all about that. A buck and a half?"

"Yeah. Hey. Sometimes when I can't sleep, you know, when it's three, four in the morning and I'm so all woke up I could holler, boy, I come down and pour myself a big glass of this and, oh, I take about fifteen minutes just to drink one glass. Oh, I savor it. And its puts me right back to sleep."

"This is damn good stuff here," Balzic said.

"Oh, I tell ya, I feel very fortunate that he sells it to me. You know, most people try to buy it from him, he says nothin' doin'. 'Cause he only sells it to a couple guys up here on the hill and I'm lucky."

"How come he sells it to you?"

"I don't know. I never done nothin' for him. All I do is tell him when's he gonna show somebody how to make it, you know, 'cause he's gonna die someday—I mean, we're all gonna die some day, so I ask him who he's gonna teach how to make it and he just laughs. He got I don't know how many kids and grandchildren and great-grandchildren. Must be seventy of 'em show up every year on his birthday, and that's when they drink most of what he makes. Then he sells me some and then he gives some to that old lady lives down the street, uh, what the hell's her name, I can never remember her name. He gives her some. I don't know why he sells it to me. I think he feels sorry for me."

"D'you ever ask him?"

"Nah. What would I wanna do that for? What if I ask him and he finds out he ain't got no answer? Then what? Then maybe he decides he got other people he oughta sell it to. Then I'm outta luck. I ain't gonna fool around with it."

Balzic nodded and grunted agreement. "Well, I wouldn't want to fool around with losin' this, that's for sure." Balzic took another mouthful and held it and then eased it down his throat slowly. "My, my," he said. "My, oh my . . ."

Garbin emptied his glass in two quick swallows.

"Hey, uh, listen, Balzic, uh, I don't know what my wife's doin', huh? You listenin' to me?"

"I'm listenin'. I didn't say she was doin' something though, did I?"

"Nah, nah, I didn't say that, you know what I mean? Huh? Nah, I didn't say you said she was doin' something. All I meant was I don't know what she's doin', you get me now?"

"Yeah. I get you. So, uh, where'd she, uh, I mean, where'd she get this money? This is a lot of money here. You know, she's talkin' like five hundred dollars here. That's a lot, you know?"

"Well five hundred ain't so much. I mean, these days, hell. What's five hundred? What can you do with that, huh? Hey, you used to be able to buy a brand new Chevy for that. Ha. No more. No more. Uh-uh."

"Still, I mean, five hundred's not something you sneeze at. You gotta get it somewhere. Don't you think?"

"Yeah, well . . . I guess you do."

"See, that's my point. I don't understand where she got it. I mean, what're you living on here—if you don't mind my asking."

"No, hell no, I don't mind. Hey, you could check, you don't have to ask me. I mean you could check yourself if you want. But no, I don't mind. I just—all we get is the two checks, you know. One's the city, I get the disability from the city, and then the other one, that's the Social Security. And the rest, uh, that's, uh, we get the food stamps, you know, huh?"

Balzic nodded slowly and then he finished his wine.

"Hey lemme get you some more."

"Oh no no no. Listen, I don't want to take that from you. You keep that for yourself. This it too good to share with some nosy bastard pokin' around in your life."

Garbin was raised half upright, poised on the edge of the couch. "You sure now? I got plenty."

"No, no. I'm fine." Balzic faked a grimace. "Well, I'm not fine, you know. My back's botherin' me."

"Aw no kiddin', you got a bad back? Huh? Cheese, look at you, you look in good shape there, and here you got a bad back. Man, who'd've thought that, huh? Listen, another glass of this won't hurt you at all. Another glass of this you'll forget all about your back."

Balzic shrugged feebly and smiled a sheepish little smile. "Well, maybe one more wouldn't hurt, huh?"

Garbin heaved himself up with a grunt, snatched Balzic's glass, and hobbled away. In a moment he was back. He handed Balzic the glass, filled almost to the brim, and eased himself back onto the couch, the springs thwanging under his bony weight.

"Listen," he said, barely above a whisper. "I don't know how I should say this or not, you listenin'?"

Balzic nodded and leaner forward.

"See, I don't know nothin' about this money. I mean, I don't know—see, lemme think how to say this—I don't know nothin' about it, I mean I don't know how else to say it."

"You mean you don't know that she had it? Or you mean you don't know whether she ever had it? Like that?"

Garbin heaved a great sigh from deep in his diaphragm. He licked his thin lips and scratched his nose. "See, I don't know nothin' about it, that's what I'm tryin' to tell ya." He paused to suppress a belch. "See, it's like she never told me nothin' about this."

"That she was saving it? Or that she had it? Or that she didn't have it? Or that she was thinking maybe about doing something like this?"

"Huh? Whatta you mean, doin' something like this? Did she do something, is that what you're askin' me? D'you think I think she done somethin'?"

"I don't know. You tell me."

"Well, I don't know, see. That's what I'm tryin' to tell you."

Balzic scratched his nose and leaned farther forward.

"Jack, listen, I think you're livin' pretty close to the bone here. I think you know every cent that comes in, and I think you know every one that goes out. I think you're the man here. And I think you would know that. So I'm not really sure what you mean when you say you don't know."

Garbin hung his head and shook it slowly from side to side. He dug in his ear with his index finger and then examined the tip of his finger.

"Uh, Balzic, I been tryin' to tell you a couple different ways. I don't know how—I can't say it no different way. I really don't know nothin' about what's goin' on here."

Balzic glanced about the room and finally brought his gaze to focus on Garbin's grayish pale eyes. "I think, uh, I think I better be going on home, Jack. I think I better do that before you get me another glass of this wine."

Balzic stood up and emptied his glass with a lot of appreciative noises. "Boy oh boy, that old man really knows what he's doin', doesn't he?"

Garbin nodded tentatively. "Oh yeah. Sure. Doggone right he does."

Balzic walked quickly to the door. "Listen, don't get up. I can get out by myself. But, hey, Jack, if you should happen to remember anything about this money, any little thing no matter how small you think it is, you wanna give me a call? Huh?"

"Huh? Oh yeah. Sure, sure. If I can think of some—oh yeah, I'll give you a call right away."

Balzic started to open the front door and then looked down at Garbin, who had twisted around on the couch and was frowning up at him.

"Listen, uh, I think you ought to, you know, talk this

over with your missus. I mean, you don't mind me giving you this little advice, do you?"

"Huh? Oh heck no. No. That's okay. Well maybe, maybe I might."

"You know, the man of the house should know about these things. Us guys, you know, we can't be lettin' women take over the money thing, huh?" Balzic winked. "Christ, they take the money, then pretty soon, where are we, huh? Pretty soon all we are is goddamn dollars and cents. What kind of respect is that, right?"

"Oh. Yeah. Right. Absolutely. Hey, one thing leads to another. Pretty soon all they think we are is a goddarn bunch of George Washingtons, huh?" Garbin tried very hard to laugh, but what he wound up doing was coughing heavily.

"That's what I mean," Balzic said, letting himself out quickly. He hurried down the steps, putting on his coat as he went. He had one arm in and the other half in and was walking too fast and hit a patch of ice on the bricks in the middle of the street and went down with a thump on his buttocks that jarred him enough to bounce the stem of his glasses off his left ear. Fortunately, he landed on the fleshy part of his rump and much of his raincoat and liner was under him when he went down.

"I know what this is for," he said under his breath, looking up at the heavens. "This is for that lie about the bad back, one, and, two, it's for all that shit about the man of the house and the money. Listen, I've told worse ones than those two—"

"Hey, you. Go home, boozey!" came a raspy deep voice from the sidewalk.

"What?"

"You heard! Go home! Get ta hell outta here!" The voice approached above fast shuffling steps.

Balzic felt a sharp rap on his thigh. "Hey! What the hell you doin'?"

Another rap on the thigh followed. He was being kicked. Balzic rolled away and scrambled awkwardly to his feet. He hit another icy brick and went down on one knee. His left arm was caught in the sleeve of his coat and the coat was knotted behind his left shoulder.

"Shame you, you boozey! Get ta hell outta here! Go home!"

Balzic could feel himself gaping idiotically at the stooped figure confronting him: covered in black from head to foot, black babushka, black cloth coat, black stockings, black low-heeled shoes, a woman with rubbery lips pierced him to his stomach with her furious gaze.

"Sonsobitch! Drunk! Bum! Go home! Get ta hell outta!" She was barely five feet high even with her two-inch heels. Her face was a crosshatch of wrinkles. The tip of her nose seemed to rest on her lower lip. Her blackish eyes were bright with indignation. She came at Balzic with her hands made into fists, the right one drawn back to deliver her most righteous blow.

Balzic tried to hold up his right hand, which made him lose his balance because his left hand was still bound up in mid-sleeve, and he went down on his right knee and shoulder on the street. He struggled mightily to regain his balance and then lurched to his feet and began to shuffle away from the woman.

"Hold it, lady! I'm not drunk. I fell on the ice—"

"Ya. Sure. Lyin' bum. Get out before I smack you one."

"Oh Christ!" Balzic said. "Listen, you. My car's right

over there." He tried to point with his right thumb behind him and almost lost his balance again. He steadied himself. "I'm gonna go to my car now, missus, and you better stop messin' around with me, you hear!"

The woman tried to spit at him. Saliva dribbled over her lower lip. She wiped her mouth and tried to spit again. This time no saliva issued; all that came forth was a strenuous *ptew*ing.

"Aw knock it off, lady, Jesus Christ."

"Hey! No swear you, drunka bum! I gonna calla cops."

"Aw cut it out, lady. I am the cops. Go home. Get outta here. You're startin' to make me mad."

"You mad? Huh? You wanna fight? Come ona you. Let's go. I fight. Come on!" She sidled toward Balzic, slowly, menacingly, her fists in front of her.

"Lady, I'm trying to tell you. I am not drunk. I am the cops. I am the chief of police. I'm tryin' to get to my car. Now get outta here and let me alone." He jerked his left arm to try to free it, but it remained snarled in his coat.

The woman darted forward and stung him with a roundhouse slap on his ear and cheek. His glasses went flying. He danced backward several steps out of her range.

"Lady, I'm not jokin'. Knock it off and go home! I'm tellin' ya—knock it off and go home!"

"Come ona, you sonsobitch. Put uppa you hands and fight! Don'ta run. Come on. I likea fight. Come on. Come on . . ."

"Hey, Ma! Ma! Whatta you doin'?" came a male voice from up the street to Balzic's right. Someone bounded down some steps and then came toward them gingerly on the sidewalk. "Ma! What're you doin'?"

"I'ma beat ta hell outta drunkie."

"Oh, Ma, honest to God, what're you doin'?" A portly young man wearing only a flannel shirt and thin cotton pants hurried to get between his mother and Balzic. "Momma, what're you doin' out here? You can't do this. Momma, come on! Jeezou . . . hey, man, you okay?—oh holy cow. Momma, what's wrong with you, honest to God."

"I'm okay," Balzic said.

"Like hell you are," the woman snarled. "I knocka you down two times already, sonsobitch."

"Oouuuuuuuu Momma, honest to God, you can't do this no more. You can't do this! Someday you're gonna do this and somebody's gonna call the cops and you're gonna go to jail and then what're you gonna do? Huh? What're you gonna do in jail? Momma!"

Balzic struggled mightily and finally got his coat off. Then he found his glasses, making sure to keep behind the son talking worriedly to his mother. She kept crowing about how many times she had knocked Balzic down and about how he was a drunken bum.

"Sonsobitch gotta no guts. He won'ta fighta me. Scaredy cat."

"Momma, please, Momma, please come home, okay? Please promise me you won't do this no more, okay? Momma? You listenin' to me?"

"How many times she done this?"

"Oh this is the second time," the son wailed. "Look at her face. She wants to fight! This is goofy. Momma, you gotta stop! Please stop." He had hold of her hands now and was trying to bring them down from shoulder level.

"She get hurt the first time?"

"No. She smacked some old guy in the mouth. Busted

— *86* —

his false teeth. He wants the money to get 'em fixed. Jeez oh man. Momma, quit squirmin' around. Stand still! Please, Momma, stand still, pleeeeeeeease! Oh, man, I'm freezin'. . . ."

"What's your mother's name?"

"Hey, why don't you just take off, man, okay? I got enough trouble here. I don't need to fill out no goddamn questionnaire."

"Sonsobitch! Scaredy cat! Boozie!"

"Listen here. I'm trying to help you out. But just remember, your mother already kicked me twice and, for your information, I am the chief of police—"

"What? Oh no. Mommaaaaaaaaa! Honest to God, what're you doin'? Oh no. You the chief, no kiddin'? Please don't joke about this. My God, you are the chief. I recognize you. Holeeeee crap, Momma . . ."

Balzic worked on his coat, buttoning the liner sleeve to the outer coat. "Uh, what've you been doin' about this? Her?"

"There ain't too much I can do, man, uh, sir. I mean I can't watch her twenty-four hours a day. I gotta go to work, you know?"

"Uh-huh. Got any relatives?"

"Oh man, she got 'em all pee-ohed at her. None of 'em's talkin' to her. Her sisters don't talk to her, her brothers—Momma, stand still!—her brothers don't talk to her, I don't know what I'm gonna do. 'Cept I ain't puttin' her in no home for the mentally vegetables, that's for sure."

"Okay, okay. I get your meaning. She, uh, she trust anybody? She talk to anybody?"

"Just me. The neighbors won't talk to her. Nobody talks to her but me and I'm goin' nuts she keeps this up. This is really, oh, Jeez, I don't know what this is, this fightin' with people. . . ."

"She doesn't trust anybody—not even a priest maybe?"

"Oh crap. Two weeks ago she started hollering in Mass. Oh God you can't believe it. Started hollerin' out loud 'bout the priest was a drunk. Momma, stand still! Hey, man, I gotta get her home. I'm freezin' out here."

"Go ahead," Balzic said. "But listen, you know Father Marrazo?"

"From St. Malachy's? Yeah I know who he is."

"I think you better go talk to him. You got a real problem here and you need to talk to somebody. Marrazo's a good man. He knows a lot of stuff and a lot of people. There might be some things you could do that you haven't thought of yet."

"I bet I have—never mind. Jeez it's cold, I gotta go. C'mon, Momma, c'mon, let's go, okay?"

"Sonsobitch. Scaredy cat. I hit him good one. You see? Huh?"

"I seen it, Momma, okay? I seen it."

"Good. I'ma glad you seen it."

"Oh holy cow, Momma, come on!"

Balzic watched them totter off, the son taking his mother's elbow and leading her delicately up the sidewalk. When they were almost out of sight Balzic noticed that the son was in his bare feet.

Balzic stared at those bare feet and shrugged wearily and said to himself, for crissake, it's Saturday. I don't need to be out here. I need to go home, lock the doors, unplug the phones, I need to collapse. I need to get the hell off this street and think about what's for dinner and what to drink. I need to take a hot shower and ask Ruthie if she still remembers my name and what she wants for Christmas. I don't even know what day Christmas is. I haven't bought one gift. That old lady really smacked me one in the face, Jesus that stung . . . I need to go home, I need to go home and throw myself on somebody's mercy. . . .

When Balzic got home, he walked into an empty house. On the counter next to the stove he found a note from his wife, which read:

Dear Mister,

We've gone to the malls, both of them. We're going shopping. We is your mother and me. I am your wife. You saw me recently. I think it was November. It's December now. It's holiday time. Christmas, New Year, fa la la la la, deck the halls, presents and decorations and things like that. You remember presents. We give them to each other at this time of year. Your mother and I are going to buy some to give to each other. We'd probably buy some for you but we can't remember your size. Are you the same size you were last year at this time?

After we finish shopping, your mother and I are going to take ourselves to dinner. We don't know where we're going yet, but I told her it ought to be someplace expensive 'cause we owed it to ourselves 'cause we couldn't get anybody we know to take us. She agreed. She said we ought to have champagne. I agreed. We'll be home unless a couple guys pick us up.

I almost forgot. There's a big green tree on your new deck. It goes in the red stand which is down in the cellar. If you have an hour or two, maybe you could put the green tree in the red stand and put them both in the living room next to the fireplace. The tree goes on top.

I have just read over what I wrote so far and it's pretty smart-assy. I don't care. I've been into the wine. So has your mother. We're going shopping. I have the checkbook and all the charge cards. Both of them. Ho ho ho.

Merry Saturday night.
—The Missus.

P.S. If we don't get picked up after dinner, we're going to the bingo at St. Malachy's, so we won't be home till around 11 or so.

"Well," Balzic grumbled, "so much for throwing myself on somebody's mercy."

He shed his coats and tie and tossed them across the arm of the couch in the living room. Then he went back through the kitchen and out onto the deck and stared at the big green tree. He stared carefully at it for a long time. Then he went back into the kitchen, opened the refrigerator, and surveyed its contents. There wasn't a casserole in sight, or a pasta salad, or tuna salad, or anything in any of the plastic containers or glass bowls that looked like it might have been left as a way of satisfying anybody's urge to dispense mercy. He closed the refrigerator and reached in the same motion for a jelly glass in one of the cabinets above the sink. Then he bent down and opened the cabinet under the sink and took out a magnum of red table wine, which he uncorked and poured into the jelly glass almost to the brim.

Well, he thought to himself after taking a tentative mouthful, there is still mercy to be found in the hearts and hands of California winemakers.

He went back out onto the deck and studied the big green tree again. It looked as big and unmanageable as it had before. The longer he looked at it the bigger it got, and the less manageable. He went back into the kitchen and tried to remember the last time he had put up a Christmas tree. He couldn't.

He emptied the jelly glass and held it up and squinted at it. He took it to the sink, rinsed it out and set it on the rubber drain-mat, and got a bigger glass out of the cabinet. He filled that almost to the brim and held it up.

"Now that's the right size," he said, resting his rump against the sink. He took a mouthful of wine, held it, sloshed it from cheek to cheek, and let it go down slowly. He canted his head and glared at the door to the deck.

I'm not going out there, he thought. That tree's gonna be bigger than the last time I looked. It's gonna be bigger, the needles are gonna be sharper, the trunk's gonna be crooked, and I don't even wanna know where the stand is . . . last time I tried to put up a tree I broke a lamp and got a needle stuck up under my thumbnail . . . Jesus Christ, Marie was ten years old—or was that Emily? God, Ma was pissed off, Ruth was pissed off, Marie was cryin'—or was that Emily cryin'? Jesus Christ, I can't remember which one was cryin'. Ruth said I was scaring the kids, Ma said I was scaring Ruth, and I wind up in the damn emergency room gettin' the needle out . . . goddamn pine needle, lost my thumbnail . . . now who would think a goddamn pine needle could be that sharp and wouldn't break . . . that damn needle went in there almost a half-inch . . . nah, three-eighths of an inch . . . God, was that ten years ago? No, couldn't be. Hell, Marie's twenty—or is that Emily? Jeezus, I can't remember which one's older . . . ho-leeee shit, Sitko's right. I been a cop too long. I been mindin' everybody else's business so goddamn much I can't remember which one of my daughters was born first . . . no wonder Ruthie's pissed off . . . no wonder . . . she has never gone out of the house and not left me something to eat . . . well she ended that record tonight, bozo. . . .

Balzic raised the glass to his lips and drank, but the glass was empty. He refilled it. He took another large mouthful.

Truth be known, Balzic, if you dare admit it, you have never done anything but hate Christmas since you been a cop . . . worst holiday of the whole goddamn year . . . Memorial Day, Fourth of July, Labor Day, none of 'em, New Year's Eve, none of 'em's as bad as Christmas . . . all the professional drunks are drunker and all the amateurs think that's the time they're supposed to turn pro, and all of them feeling so goddamn lonely and so sorry for themselves they just gotta do something stupid . . . I'm not puttin' up that tree, I don't care how much Ruthie's pissed off . . . I mean I care she's pissed off, but I'm not gonna hurt myself just to make her not be pissed off at me. . . .

Balzic pursed his lips and scowled at the door to the deck. Then he went to the phone and called the station.

"Rocksburg Police. May I help you?"

"Who is this?"

"Sergeant Stramsky. Who's this? Is that you, Mario?"

"Yeah. Hey, listen. Anybody around down there wants to make five bucks?"

"Huh? Five bucks? What for?"

"Puttin' up a Christmas tree."

"Puttin' up a tree? Yours?"

"Yeah. Of course it's mine."

"Your wife did it, huh?"

"My wife did what? What're you talkin' about?"

"Last year she swore she was never gonna put the tree up again. Don't you remember?"

"When'd she say that?"

"Last year. Yeah, down at the Eagles. Christmas party, remember?"

"Uh-uh. I don't. But I guess I should've. Well? Anybody around?"

"Yeah, one of the city electricians was just here a minute ago. I think he's in the can now. I'll send him up. Is that all?"

"Yeah, yeah. Thanks, Vic. G'night."

Balzic hung up and filled his glass again and took it into the living room. He dropped onto the recliner and leaned back so that the footrest came up. He turned on the floor lamp and held the wine up to the light, moving it nearer and farther and watching with pleasure as the light played on the glass and the wine and changed its color. He sipped some and held it up to the light again, sipped some more, and then watched the light play on it. . . .

He awoke with a jump. There was pounding on the front door, the doorbell was ringing, somebody was shouting, "Chief! Chief! You okay? Hey! Ho, Chief! You okay?"

Balzic struggled to get up, just catching the glass before it rolled off his lap, and got on his feet with a lurch and walked stiffly to the door. He succeeded in getting the locks open only after he freed both hands by putting the glass in his teeth.

"Who is it? Whatta you want?"

"Yo, Mario, you okay? Jeez, I been knockin' and ringin' the bell and hollerin' for I don't know how long here. I

— *93* —

looked in the window and you looked like you was dead or something, I don't know what. I got worried, you know? So I just kept ringin' and hollerin' and, like, if you didn't open up when you did I was gonna call Stramsky to get his ass up here, you know?"

"Yeah, yeah. Whatta you want?"

"Stramsky, uh, Stramsky said you got a tree—hey, it's me, Finoli. Electrician—you sure you're okay?"

"Oh oh oh, yeah, c'mon in. I don't have my glasses on and I fell asleep, drank too much too fast and really zonked out. No, c'mon in, I'm okay."

"So whatsa matter? Lights don't work or what?"

"No, see, let me explain. It's not the lights. It don't have anything to do with electricity. The tree, see, you got to put the tree up."

"Stramsky said you wanted an electrician."

"Yeah, well forget about what he said. I don't need—I need somebody to put my tree up."

"Your tree? You can't do that?" Finoli looked very confused. "Oh. Okay. So where's it at?"

Balzic told him where the tree was and where the stand was.

As Finoli brought the stand up from the cellar he said, "So how'd you hurt your back?"

"Who said anything about my back?"

Finoli grinned and shrugged. "Well, you know. Can't put up your tree, I figure there gotta be something wrong with you. I mean, you look okay. So it must be your back. Lotta guys look okay and they can't do nothin' it's their back.'

"My back's fine. My back's okay. There's nothin' wrong with my back."

— 94 —

"Oh."

Finoli took the stand out on the deck. About six minutes later, he came to the door and said, "You wanna hold the door, huh? I'll bring it in. You want it in the living room, right?"

"Yeah, right."

Balzic held the door, and Finoli carried the tree in off the deck, through the kitchen, and into the living room where he set it in the corner Balzic had cleared for him. The tree stood perfectly straight.

Finoli stood and admired his work, "So, uh, how long you had the heart thing?"

Balzic squinted at Finoli. "What heart thing? What're you talkin' about?"

"The heart, the heart, ya know." Finoli poked himself in the chest.

"You think there's something the matter with my heart?"

Finoli shrugged again. "Hey, you know, if it ain't the back, it's the heart. I mean, what else is there?"

"What else is there what? What the hell are you talkin' about?"

Finoli threw out his hands and slapped his stomach with both hands several times. "Hey, you know. If it ain't your back and you look okay, I mean, it's got to be your heart. I mean, Jeez, you can't put up your own Christmas tree, there gotta be something serious wrong with you, you know?"

Balzic put his hand on Finoli's shoulder and steered him toward the front door. "Five bucks enough? Huh?"

"Jeez, I only been here fifteen minutes. Three bucks is plenty?"

"Take five. Here." Balzic handed him the bill.

"Hey, you give it, I'll take it. Hey, don't get me wrong. I didn't mean nothin' personal about your heart attack. I—"

"Finoli, there's nothin' wrong with my heart. I didn't have a heart attack."

Finoli peered up at him. "Look, I know guys don't like to talk about it, somebody's always making jokes how you're afraid to, uh, you know, you're, uh, afraid to be a man in bed and stuff like that and then you, you're a cop—"

"Finoli, there's nothing wrong with my heart. There's nothing wrong with my back—"

"Well there gotta be something wrong with you! Holy crap, a guy don't put up his own Christmas tree, I mean, what the hell, huh?"

Balzic chewed his teeth and nodded many times. "Hey, okay. I'll tell you. I had a heart attack. Little one. Nobody knows. But don't worry about it, 'cause I'm getting over it. Thank you very much for puttin' up my tree. Merry Christmas. I'll see you around, okay?"

"Hey, it was my pleasure. Same to you. And listen, they can do all kinds of things now. The important thing is, don't strain. My uncle told me. Don't even strain yourself when you go to the bathroom. You gotta be real careful about that."

"Okay, Finoli, good night. I'll be careful. Merry Christmas." Balzic did everything but shove him out the door.

Balzic hadn't taken more than a step away from the door when somebody knocked on it. Balzic turned back and opened it. It was Finoli again.

"Listen, I just wanted to tell you one more thing."

"What's that?"

"About the bed thing, you know. With the wife?"

Balzic waited.

"My uncle says you can't get in a hurry. You just gotta be patient. When the time's right, you'll know it. And it'll be better than ever 'cause you appreciate it more."

Finoli's sincerity was genuine, but Balzic laughed anyway.

"I'll remember that, I will. I'll think of you, too. And your uncle. Tell him I said Merry Christmas."

"Aw he's dead. Yeah. Last year."

Balzic pursed his lips, waved, and eased the door shut. He headed for the kitchen and the red wine under the sink, grumbling every step of the way that even bargains have their price.

⁐⚬⁓

Balzic woke on Sunday morning with a start, nearly upsetting the recliner. His wife was peering down at him.

"Why don't you go get in bed?" she asked him. She was dressed for church.

"Uh, Jeez, what time is it? You comin' or goin'?"

"Going. It's quarter to ten. C'mon, get up and drink some water, brush your teeth, and go get in bed for a little while. You'll feel lousy you stay there."

"I feel lousy already. I don't have to stay here. Uh, d'you have a good time yesterday? Last night?"

"It would've been a lot better time if you were there. But, yeah, we had a good time."

Balzic rubbed his eyes, scratched his scalp, and sat up. "Where'd you go? To eat I mean."

"I'm not telling you. I will tell you what I had though. I had swordfish. So did your mother. And we had a bottle of asti spumante—which I don't like, but which she loved. So I liked it a little bit myself."

"I thought you liked that."

"It's too sweet. But last night it didn't matter."

Balzic got on his feet. He could still taste the red wine. "You mean all those times you drank asti, you really didn't like it and you said you did?"

"That's right." She started toward the front door. "Ma's in the car. I'm goin'. Go upstairs and get in bed."

"Why'd you say you liked it if you didn't?"

"Because your mother likes it. I'll see you. Do you want me to wake you up when we get home or not?"

"Uh, yes—no. I need to sleep. Uh, you shouldn't say you like something if you don't. It confuses me."

"It confuses you, but it makes your mother happy. 'Bye."

She was out the door before he could say anything else. He stared at the door for a long moment, pondering what had just been said. What he thought they'd been talking about was what kind of sparkling wine she liked, and it wasn't the kind he thought she liked. But that last thing she said, Balzic thought, that didn't have anything to do with wine. That had to do with who she spent most of her time with and who she felt obliged to make happy and who she didn't.

"Shit," he said aloud, trudging toward the bedroom and undressing as he went. "She's leaving messages for me all over the place, and I'm not gettin' them too good. . . ."

He sat on the edge of the bed and scratched his sides and took off everything but his underwear. He picked dead skin off the sides of his feet and thought about something Iron City Steve was always ranting about: What's Christmas without Easter? Yeah, that was it. Only it ought to be: What's Christmas if your wife's pissed off at you? Who gives a shit about Easter if you can't stand Christmas, and find me a cop—married or single—who can stand Christmas, and if your wife's pissed on Christmas, who thinks about Easter? That ain't for months. . . .

He hung up the clothes that didn't smell and put the ones that did in a basket in another closet. Then he pulled down the bedcovers and crawled in. Every time he closed his eyes the movies started: Jack Garbin and his wife . . . Jack Garbin hobbling around and rolling cigarettes, embarrassed by his furniture and befuddled by what his wife was up to . . . his wife scratching her bony arms and snapping and snarling like a wounded dog . . . Billy Lum gleaming and sweating and spitting out one mouthful of lies after another . . . an old lady coming at him with her hands ready for war . . . vets coming at him with their hands ready for war . . . falling down in Norwood, his glasses flying, his face stinging . . . falling across a desk in the station, his ears ringing from a blow on the neck he never saw coming . . . old ladies and young punks and it's not like this in the movies Hollywood makes . . . Ruth and Christmas trees . . . Ruth making promises other people remembered but he didn't . . . Finoli and Christmas trees and heart attacks and bad backs and social lies to scrounge some wine from Garbin and social lies to grease the way for Finoli and Ruth and asti spumate . . . confusing me and making Ma happy, what the hell is that all about . . . Kee-rist my neck hurts and my ass and my elbow, how come my elbow hurts? Is that from Norwood or is that from that shit Murlovsky? I'm gonna be sore tomorrow . . . I'm too old for this shit . . . all these people . . . all these people. . . .

"All these people," Balzic whispered. Then he whispered it again and again. He didn't know why he was whispering it, except that it had a soothing sound to it, a rhythm. It was relaxing to say it and he kept saying it. It was a way of turning off the movies when he closed his eyes. It made them all run together, made them all blurry, made them lose their distinctions, made them all less imposing, less individually frightening. It turned them into a harmless glob of thought that became a friendly sound and a friendlier rhythm. It put him to sleep.

◦⟞✖⟝◦

He spent the rest of Sunday in bed, waking fitfully every couple of hours, then falling asleep again. Sleep was his great escape. There were times when he got in his cruiser and drove around aimlessly with the radio off and that was fine when it worked, but it was not his first-string escape. There were times when he drank and he drank something every day and some days he drank himself into a deep escape, but even that was not his top-shelf escape. His top-shelf, first-string, state-of-the-art escape was sleep. When he didn't want to think about the wreckage of a hangover, he got into bed and stayed there. When his mind saw only problems and when his body felt only aches, he shut it all down in bed. Ruth had said to him many times in their marriage that she didn't know anyone who could fall asleep as fast as he could or who could sleep as long as he could. He'd told her every time that it was something he learned during the war. He was only partly sure how he'd learned it. It was something he'd done because his body told him very quickly that finding a way to rest would give him a better chance of staying alive. He was telling her the truth.

He had learned it the first day on the beach at Iwo Jima. He had told himself that only three things would allow him to get out of there. One was the ability to dig. The lower you were the less chance you had of catching shrapnel, and Balzic refused to be defeated by the ash that kept sliding back into the holes he dug. It was almost like shoveling water, but compared to the consequences of not digging, it was easy. Another was the ability to move quickly, and for that you had to be rested. All around him were people who couldn't rest, couldn't sleep, and in a matter of days—if they lasted that long—they were too fatigued to move quickly when they had to. He wasn't sure how or why he'd thought of it. He just had. He imagined himself a dog. Dogs could appear to be sound asleep, could curl up and sleep all day, but when something alarmed them, they could be awake and alert and aggressive in an instant and then, when their alarm passed, they could curl up and sleep again as though nothing had happened. The third thing was luck because without that it didn't matter how well you could dig or how fast you could move. But luck he couldn't control; digging and sleep he could, and you had to do something to try to survive or your mind would have exploded and then it wouldn't have mattered what happened to your body. . . .

So Balzic slept until Monday morning. Between the time he finished his vegetable juice and before the water for the instant coffee came to a boil, he spied the article on the front page of *The Rocksburg Gazette* his mother was reading. It sent an acidic rumble up his throat.

"Hey, Ma, let me see that, okay?"

"See what?" She folded down the corner of the paper and peered up at him. She was sitting at the table in her chenille robe, and she had not touched her own coffee. She had been clearly absorbed by something in the paper.

"The paper."

"You can't wait?"

"Oh. You're not done."

"Whatsa matter you—I look done?"

"Hey, Ma, you don't have to get hot, you know. I just asked you—"

"I know." The corner of the paper went back up.

Balzic slid his tongue up against a molar. He eased down on one knee in front of his mother and started to read the article at the bottom of the front page.

The headline was: "Fund For Victim Gathers Strength." It had the byline of Mary Hart. Balzic cringed. He felt his stomach growling and the juice starting to rise again.

"Funds for the victim of a brutal assault and robbery on Friday continue to accumulate in the trust account set up in her behalf by the Rocksburg fire chief while the victim remains confined to her bed in Conemaugh General Hospital.

"Gifts of all sizes keep rolling into the fund, set up by Fire Chief Edward F. Sitko within hours after he learned that Mrs. Jack Garbin, 61, of 700 Dorsey Street in the Norwood section, was brutally beaten and robbed of more than $700 in broad daylight on Pittsburgh Street.

" 'We're getting it from all over,' Sitko said. 'Every one of the hose companies has kicked in at least $100 and that was just what was collected among the men.' The chief said that total alone meant over $900 would be earmarked for the victim.

"Chief Sitko said further that many firemen are canvassing their neighborhoods and that money was already coming in. 'Tony Prittica collected over $75 in two hours himself in the Hilltop section of Norwood,' the chief added.

" 'The guys in the morra league up at the Hilltop Club

gave almost $60,' the chief said, praising the civic spirit and generosity of the morra players.

"Alan Cecconi, attorney for the fund, named The Garbin Christmas Club because the victim's loss was her Christmas Club which she had just cashed in, said he thought that it was not inconceivable that the fund might reach five figures. 'The way it looks now,' Cecconi said, 'three or four more days like the first two and we'll reach $10,000 easily.'

"Mrs. Garbin, confined since the robbery to a hospital bed with deep bruises and lacerations of the face, expressed her complete surprise at the generosity of the members of the community. 'I don't know what to say,' she said, when this reporter relayed the news of how The Garbin Christmas Club was growing. 'I'm just so grateful,' she added with tears in her eyes.

"When informed that police have failed to turn up a suspect in the assault, Mrs. Garbin said she wasn't surprised by that. She said the police weren't very cooperative. 'They didn't seem to care too much one way or the other,' she said.

"Strangely silent has been the reaction of the Rocksburg Police Department to all inquiries by this reporter to learn of any progress being made to bring this vicious robber to justice. Repeated calls to Chief Mario Balzic's office and home have gone unanswered."

Balzic quit reading and lurched upward off his knee, startling his mother.

"Sorry, Ma. Hey, listen. You answer the phone a lot in the last two days? People askin' for me?"

"People always askin' for you."

"No. I mean has some old lady been callin' here a lot?"

His mother pursed her lips and said, "I don't know. I answer no phone for you yesterday, I'm sure. Day before, I don't think. Can't remember. Ask Ruthie anyway. I don't answer phones when she's here. Whatsamatter you, huh?"

"Nothin', nothin', never mind. Where is she? She up?"

"I don't think. She was sick last night. Her stomach is upset."

"Huh? She throwin' up? Huh? What time? I didn't hear anything."

His mother laughed. "You never hear nothing when you sleep since you born. Who you kiddin'?"

"C'mon, Ma. Why didn't you wake me up?"

"What was you gonna do? Huh? You don't do nothin' anyway. When was you ever do somethin' when Ruthie or you kids get sick, huh? Ruthie takes care of the kids when they sick, Ruthie takes care of Ruthie when she's asick. Whatta you do? Calla doctor, that's what. Calla doctor, sit around for a while, then run, run, downa Muscotti's. You, yousa no good when somebody's sick, Kiddo. I'm tellin' you."

"Hey, Ma, you know how many times I heard this lecture—and it don't apply to me anyway and I'm not gonna answer to it, you know? You should've woke me up."

His mother scoffed out a burst of breath. "Hey, you so concern about your wife, huh? Go see now. Go. Go 'head. She's in bed, probably still feel like hell. Go see, g'wan."

"Okay," Balzic said. "I will. Uh, you sure you didn't answer the phone yesterday?"

"I told you—no. What'sa matter you? What're you standin' here for? Go see Ruthie." She folded the newspaper and whacked him across the arm with it.

"Hey! What'd you do that for?"

" 'Cause sometimes you make me so mad."

"What'd I do to you? What for? What're you talkin' about? What'd you hit me for?"

"Go see you wife, okay? Go see you wife. I don't say nothing." His mother carefully unfolded the paper and pretended to immerse herself in reading it.

Balzic, shaking his head and sighing, turned away and went to the bedroom, where he found his wife covered up to her chin and looking drowsy but awake. He sat on the edge of the bed and ran the back of his fingers across her forehead.

"Hey, how you doin'? Ma said you were sick last night. Why didn't you wake me up?"

"Mario," Ruth said, rolling her eyes broadly, "why would I want to wake you up? Huh? So you can get sick? Every time somebody throws up, you throw up."

"Ah come on. I do not."

"Mario, why do you always deny it? You know you do it. Every time one of the kids got sick and threw up and you were around—you didn't even have to be around. All you had to do was hear it and the next thing you'd be pushing her out of the way so you could throw up."

"That's bull. That's baloney. You're exaggeratin'!"

Ruth shrugged herself up on her elbows and laughed.

"Mario, honest to God, it's like you got amnesia when we talk about this. You don't remember how many times whenever one of the girls got sick like that I used to hope you'd have to leave, go arrest somebody or something, honest. Taking care of the kid, that was okay. But, boy, taking care of you *and* the kid, that was too much for me, boy. And then you come around and want to know why I don't wake you up? Aaah. Sheese."

"Okay, okay. So how you doin'? You okay now?"

"Sure I'm okay. I'm here aren't I?"

"Well, good. I'm glad. You want something? Some juice, toast, what?"

Ruth shook her head no. "Not now."

Balzic shrugged. "Okay. So, uh, listen, not to change the subject real fast, but, uh, you get a lot of calls yesterday from that old shit-bitch Hart?"

"From who?"

"From that old bag Mary Hart. She call here a lot?"

"Not once."

"You sure? Never mind. Forget I said it." Balzic chewed his lower lip.

"What did she do now?"

"Aw it's on the front page of the paper. You'll see it—I mean if you feel like readin' it."

"Can't you tell me now?"

"Well, among other lies she told is one that she says she called here repeatedly and got no answer."

"She didn't call even once. Not yesterday. Except for church, I didn't go out of the house yesterday—which is something I need to do. Real soon, you hear what I'm sayin', big boy? Real soon."

"Okay, okay, I get your meaning. But look, tell me again 'cause I need to know: No calls for me from that bag of bullshit? Right?"

"Mario, I can see you're very angry about this, but don't start on me. I've been taking calls for you for a long time, and I never missed a call yet, so just climb down off your mad horse and—"

"Okay okay okay, I just need to make sure. I got to go. I'll see you." Balzic bent down and kissed her on the forehead. Then he stood and headed for the door.

"Mario?"

"What?"

"I know you're getting ready to do something bad to somebody, and—just be careful how you talk to her. That woman has caused you a lot of problems—"

"Look," Balzic interrupted her. "She's already caused me problems today. And—never mind. I'll see you later."

Balzic went back to the kitchen, went to the wall phone, and punched the buttons for this station.

"Rocksburg Police. Royer speaking. May I help you?"

"It's Balzic. Is Rugsy around?"

"He just went in the can. Whatta you want?"

"Tell him stop whatever he's doin' and check every bank and savings-and-loan in this town. I want to know where Jack Garbin or his wife has an account or had an account and what kind it is or was. And if he, she, or they didn't have any accounts, I want to know that too. Got it?"

"Got it. Anything else?"

"Yeah. Ask him to get what he's got on those four vets I asked him about and get it ready for me. I want to read that too."

"When you want this? When you get here?"

"Yeah, but I won't be there for awhile. I'm goin' down the paper, the *Gazette*. I want to talk to some people down there."

"Okay—hold it, here's Rugsy now."

The phone changed hands.

"Sergeant Carlucci."

"It's Balzic. I want you to check something."

"Yeah? I'm listening."

"Check all the banks and all the S and L's to see if Jack

Garbin or his wife had a savings account or a Christmas Club."

"I was gonna do that. I was just waiting for them to open up."

"Well, don't miss any, you hear?"

"I won't. But I'll bet a week's pay she doesn't have any. That old lady's running a game. I know her all my life, Mario. She's a pain in the ass, that woman. I mean, she got reasons, you know, but everybody got reasons. She's still a pain in the ass."

"Rugsy, uh, you get anything on those vets?"

"Yeah, I got that too. Called the VA. Three of 'em's okay. They were all in Vietnam. But none of 'em were in combat. One guy was a helicopter mechanic, another one was a truck driver, another was in a supply outfit—clerk, I think. The fourth one never made it through basic. He got a General Discharge. That's Murlovsky, Joseph G. Unfit for military service, that kind of number. All petty stuff. But he also got a prior."

"Oh yeah? For what?'

"A and B, kicked down to simple assault and malicious mischief. But he got fifteen days, six months' probation."

"What was it about?"

"He got in a beef in a Legion hall on the Northside, Pittsburgh. Sound familiar?"

"Good work, Rugs. You're my man. Keep checkin' those guys. Find out how that thing in the Vets got started. See if that Murlovsky was in the middle."

"I'm working on that. It's gonna take awhile."

I know. Stay on it. I gotta go." Balzic hung up and headed for the front door, giving his mother a pat on the head as he went by her.

The *Rocksburg Gazette* building looked like what it produced. It was all rectangles: the building, the windows, no matter which way Balzic looked at it, it reminded him of the shape of a newspaper. It was made of cinder blocks, and the windows were covered with some material to cut the glare on the inside, so they appeared from the outside to be opaque. It was the grayest, dullest, least inviting building Balzic had ever seen. He'd said that the first time he saw it; he thought it now as he bounded up the three steps leading to the front door.

Inside the foyer, a receptionist–switchboard operator sat behind glass with just her face and shoulders showing. She slid aside a window to inquire if she could help him. Her voice had an awful nasal sound that made words like "four" have two syllables.

"I want to see the managing editor and I don't have an appointment. I'm the chief of police."

"Mr. Murray's not at his desk at this moment. Would you care to wait?"

"I know where his desk is, I can find him."

"No one is permitted in the newsroom without an escort. It's for security purposes. I'll ring again. Just have a seat, please." She slid the window shut and punched a button.

Balzic could see her lips moving but couldn't make out what she was saying.

She slid the window open again. "Mr. Murray's at his desk now. He says it's all right for you to go back."

Balzic reached for the door on his right, but when he turned the knob nothing happened. He looked back at the operator. She was reaching downward. There came a buzz and the door popped open. Balzic snorted to himself.

He walked along a narrow corridor toward a door marked NEWSROOM. Once through that, he found himself walking toward Tom Murray as he was slumped forward over an ancient typewriter and jabbing at it with his index fingers. Cigarette smoke swirled upward around his head.

Murray glanced up briefly at Balzic and nodded toward the metal chair beside his desk. He continued to stab at the keys, inhaling deeply on the cigarette in his mouth. Ashes dribbled on the keys and on his lap.

"You look like hell," Balzic said. "You ever put anything in your body besides smoke and beer?"

Murray paused in his typing and squinted through the smoke at Balzic. "You come here to make smart cracks about my personal habit? Or you got something else in mind?"

"Something else. But just lookin' at you, I gotta tell you, you look like hell."

"You're repeating yourself. What else?"

"Okay, okay. It's about the, uh, queen of the rednecks. She's—"

Murray held up his left hand and gingerly pulled off the cigarette that had stuck to his upper lip with his right. Once he'd freed it and sputtered a few times, he said, "I have no control over her."

"You have no control—what kind of crap is this? She works here, doesn't she? You run the joint, don't you?"

Murray butted out the cigarette and reached for another from the pack next to the typewriter. That pack was empty. He fumbled in his sportcoat draped over the chair behind him and found another pack. All the while he was doing that and opening the pack and lighting another cigarette he kept shaking his head and saying, "No no no no no. . . ."

"What is this 'no no no' shit? You the boss here or not?"

"When it comes to her I'm not the boss. I'm not anything. I don't give her assignments. I don't edit her copy, I don't do anything. As in nothing. That should be clear enough, even for someone with the limited intelligence of a cop."

"Oh that's cute. Whatta you mean when it comes to her you don't do anything?"

"Hey, Balzic. I know being a cop can turn anybody's brain into a bag of mucus, but how many ways do I have to say it? I am not responsible for what that woman writes— or types or whatever she does. I did not hire her, I do not have the power to fire her, I function here only on the condition I am not included in any suit brought against this paper because of her. How's that? Little clearer now?"

Balzic screwed up his face and looked over the tops of his glasses at Murray.

"So in other words, when she writes bullshit you can't do anything about it, is that what you're tellin' me?"

"Very good, Mario, ver-ry good. There's hope for you yet."

"She works, uh, for your boss then?"

"You're getting even better. You're starting to show real promise."

"And he doesn't care what she writes."

"Rrrrright. Oh, you're catching on so quickly. I'm so proud of you."

"Yeah, well, I'm glad I'm making you proud. But this time she's gone over the edge. This time—"

"This time," Murray interrupted him, "you're talking

to the wrong person. You have a beef with Miss Hart, then you should be talking to Miss Hart. And if you look real close you can tell that she is not me.'"

Balzic sighed and closed his eyes and scratched his scalp. "Okay, so—so, I'm talking to the wrong person. So okay. So when I start talking to the right person, I just want you to know what it's about, okay? Huh?"

"You want sympathy?"

"C'mon, man, what is it with you? Do I want sympathy. Jesus Christ. If I—"

"So what's your bitch? She wrote something about 'repeated phone calls went unanswered,' right? And nobody at your house got any phone calls, right? And somebody was home all the time, right? So if you don't want sympathy, what do you want? You want me to tell you something else is new? She's been doing this kind of thing for fifty years. You want to hear about all the interviews she invented? What's your boredom threshold? You know how tough libel is to prove in this country? You want to hear how many times we've been sued? You want to know how many times those suits never came to trial? You want to know how much this paper's paid out in settlements? You want to hear how many times this paper has never printed one fucking word about any of those suits?" Murray leaned back in his chair and snorted.

"I have only one nightmare," Murray went on. "I'm standing in front of Saint Peter and he's got a whole stack of *Gazette*s on the floor beside him, and he looks at me and he says, 'There was a gap in the news.' And I say, 'What gap?' And he says, 'You never reported the suits against you. Why is that?' And I say, 'Because the publisher had a lot of money.' And he says, 'But your publisher's not trying to get in here. *You* are.'

"So, what do you have to tell me that's new or different?"

Balzic shrugged. "Hey, maybe it's not gonna be a big deal, but I think your paper may be part of a fraud."

Murray clasped his hands behind his head. "I'm listening. But it's not my paper, let's not overlook that little fact. I just work here."

Balzic let out an exasperated sigh. "It's the paper you run."

"I am the managing editor. I don't *run* anything. And you ain't Saint Peter."

"Look, I can see where you're trying to split yourself off from this thing, but, uh, when the shit hits the fan, it's gonna be your fan, and I thought you might like to know about it."

"I do want to know about it, but I also want to disabuse you of any notions you might have of whose newspaper this is and where I function in it. This newspaper was here before I was born and it'll be here after I'm dead." Murray's tone was different suddenly. His voice almost broke. He coughed several times, small ones at first, but then they became deeper and his narrow shoulders shook with the effort. When he stopped, his face was crimson and his eyes were glistening with tears.

"Jesus Christ, Murray, you okay?" Balzic squinted as he watched Murray take out a soiled handkerchief and spit into it.

"No."

"What's that mean?"

"What the hell do you think 'No' means? It means I'm not okay. It means I don't really give much of a crap about Mary Hart or the Garbin Christmas Club—and least of all about this goddamned newspaper. And for crissake, don't try to make me be more specific. I have taken pride in not being sentimental—though Christ knows why anybody would take pride in that—uh, you got something else you want to talk about?"

Balzic felt his eyes darting from Murray's face to the walls to the floor and back to Murray's face and he couldn't stop them from darting and he began to feel extremely, self-consciously, uncomfortable. He dropped his gaze to his hands resting on his knees and shook his head no.

"Hey, Tom, I'm sorry I bothered you about this. If there's—"

"Oh shut up for crissake. Everything's taken care of. There's nothing I want or need or that has to be—everything's taken care of."

Balzic stood up abruptly and started to go, but Murray reached out and caught his forearm.

"There's one thing," Murray whispered, shifting uneasily in his chair.

"Hey, name it. Whatever—name it." He leaned close to Murray so he wouldn't have to talk above a whisper.

Murray swallowed hard twice. "Uh, a funeral's not my idea. You know, I don't give a rat's behind about religion, but my family's, uh, my family's Catholic. And, uh, we talked it over, and they, uh, they insist that they're gonna have one, uh, I mean, I won't be in any position to argue about it. Uh, so, uh, what I'm trying to say is, uh, I'd be honored if you'd be driving, uh, if you'd lead the parade. . . ."

Balzic started to speak, but stopped and just nodded and reached down and patted Murray twice on the shoulder. He bolted away from Murray then, knowing that if he'd tried to speak he wouldn't have been able to.

Outside, in the air, walking toward his cruiser, Balzic felt himself breathing through his mouth, almost gasping. He was cold, a lot colder than the temperature should have made him feel. He jammed his hands deep into his pockets and stopped walking and looked up at the sky. The clouds were thick and low and grayish on their undersides and in some places a dull metallic blue, and they were oozing along. The sky was no different from countless other wintry skies he'd looked at in his life, but this one seemed full to bursting with the news he'd just heard.

He and Murray went back a long way. He'd been walking a beat and Murray had been a sportswriter and both of them were just back from World War II. They'd met in Muscotti's and traded stories about all the silly improbable things that had happened to them. They'd carefully avoided the other things, the things neither wanted to remember. The only times they'd come close to the other things were when they talked about the trouble they were having getting to sleep some nights or when they woke up in sweats, panting, staring at the night around them and wondering if anybody else was waking up like that. But before they could bring themselves to talk about the nights, they would have had a lot to drink, and despite the alcohol, they never broke the reserve both seemed to need then. They would talk about missing the sleep, or about having it disrupted, or about how hard some days were because the nights didn't seem to be getting any easier, but they didn't talk about the dreams they were dreaming or the memories they were trying not to remember. They went so far and no further and that seemed to be enough. They always wound up talking about baseball.

Balzic spun on his heel and went running back into the building. The switchboard operator looked at him as though she'd never seen him before. She slid open the window and waited.

"C'mon, lady, open the goddamn door. I just went out. I was just here, remember?"

"Whom do you wish to see?"

"Tom Murray. I was just talking to him."

"I'll see if he's at his desk. No one is permitted into the newsroom without an escort." She closed the window before Balzic could respond.

He stood there, waiting with his hand on the knob, for her to do the officious dance, but before she could get Murray to answer his phone, a young girl with a camera bag in her hands pushed open the door and broke into a trot past Balzic.

Balzic ducked through the door and headed back the long corridor with the operator's protest that he was not allowed in trailing after him. By the time he reached Murray's desk—Murray was at the other end of the room talking to a young woman—a private security guard was pushing his way past Murray and had fixed his gaze on Balzic.

Balzic held up his hands when the guard got near. "I know, I know, nobody's permitted in the newsroom without an escort."

"You want to see somebody?" the guard said.

"Yeah, I want to see Tom Murray. And I'm the chief of police here."

"Well, I don't know anything about that, but my orders are not to let anybody in without an escort and the operator told me—"

"I don't care what she said. All you got to do is turn around and ask Murray if it's okay for me to be here—"

"Who's he? Murray who? I don't know any—"

"You're brand new on this job, huh?"

"That makes no difference one way or the other, my job—"

"Hey, Murray!" Balzic hollered. "You wanna come here and tell this guy to lighten up?"

"I'm sorry but you'll have to leave. You can't shout in here. This is a workplace. People are trying to work here, and—"

"Hey, you wanna take a fuckin' walk."

"Oh you can't talk like that in here. You can't use that kind of language in here. There are ladies in here. Oh my no. You'll have to come with me." He tried to take Balzic's arm.

Balzic spun away from him. "Hey, talkin's one thing. Touchin', that's something else. Murray! C'mere and tell this guy to take a walk." Balzic could see that Murray not only wasn't moving, but, worse, was enjoying the encounter so much he was coughing with laughter.

"Now look, I don't want to have to get stern with you but I'm a trained officer. I've been taught how to handle unruly persons in situations like this and I think you better think about that." The guard reached again for Balzic's arm.

Balzic slipped out of reach and thrust his finger in the old guard's reddening face. "You listen to me. You put your hand on me again and I'm gonna show you what bein' trained really means."

"Now don't you threaten me here. Now don't you do that. You just come along before I'm forced to take action here."

"Oh will you shut up. Murray! Get over here! C'mon, quit messin' around."

"Why?" Murray hollered back, sputtering with coughs and laughter.

" 'Cause this is ridiculous and I wanna tell you something."

"Are you going to come along or not? Now I don't want to take action against you but you're bringing this on yourself."

"Murray! You're trained, huh? You oughta sue the assholes that trained you, 'cause if this is what they taught you, you're gonna get hurt. Murray!"

"You need some help, Balzic? Huh?" Murray called out and started to walk toward them, mirth splashed across his face.

"Hey," Murray said to the guard as he drew near, "he's okay. I know him. He's all right. You can take a break now."

"Well exactly who are you to be telling me what to do?" the guard said. "I don't take orders from you. I don't know who you are."

Balzic howled. "Oh listen to this, listen to this. Go 'head, Murray, tell him who you are."

"Well if you'd open your goddamn eyes when you go paradin' through this goddamn room you might have some idea who I am goddammit."

"Oh-oh, you can't use that kind of language in here. There are ladies in—"

"Hey, who the fuck do you think you're talking to? I decide what kind of language gets used in this room. Me! I decide that. I'm the boss in this room. I'm the managing editor."

"You're the boss here? The managing editor?"

"That's right. And he's the chief of police."

The guard shook his head. "Well, I'll tell you, you fellows just talk like you belong in the gutter. Just a sign of a poor vocabulary, that's what I've been taught to believe. And in front of these young ladies in here, why you two ought to be ashamed. I mean, I can understand if he's the chief of police because he has to be around some rough customers, but you, there's just no excuse for you. If you're who you say you are, why my goodness, words are your business and you talk like that? Well there's no excuse for you at all. None, no sir."

Murray looked at Balzic and Balzic looked back and they shook their heads.

The guard continued to shake his head and ramble on that they had no respect for women and that they ought to develop their vocabularies and that there were lots of books on the market to help a fellow do just that and that they ought to consider what bad examples they set, men in their position—if they were really who they claimed to be. "I'm going to check on that, don't you worry," he said as he strode out of the room, shoulders well back and chin high.

"Fucking moralists everywhere," Murray said. "What'd you want to tell me anyway? What'd you come back for?"

Balzic shrugged and shook his head tentatively. "Hell I don't know. Had something to do with baseball."

"Huh?"

"Oh, I was thinking about a long time ago. All that time we spent talking about baseball, I don't know. I just wanted to say something about what we should've been talkin' about."

"Oh Christ," Murray said. "Why don't you get out of here before you say something stupid. Go on. I got work to do. Uh, I'm sorry you got a problem with old lady Hart. I can't help you. That's how it is."

"That's how it is. That's how it is," Balzic said, turning and trudging through the door and down the narrow hallway and past the switchboard operator who was listening to the security guard telling about the "disgraceful language they're using. It was just incredible, men in their position. Who are kids supposed to look up to these days? Why, my God. . . ."

❧❧❧

As usual, when Balzic felt crowded by what he called life's stinking little realities, he headed for Muscotti's. The older he got, the more the stinking realities seemed to crowd him, or maybe it was that he became less able to deal with them the older he got, or maybe it was that the older he got the more the little realities struck him in the nose first. What he'd just learned from Tom Murray had hit him in both nostrils, and the odor was sharp, like an acid he remembered being thrust under his nose in a high school chemistry laboratory. It had stung his nose and made him recoil and brought tears to his eyes and made him retch. Worse, he remembered that the chemistry teacher had taken pleasure in that, had made it a point to single out Balzic's inability to deal with the smell of what was "just part of the chemistry of life." The teacher had been a long, bony, blond-haired man with long teeth with gaps between them where they receded into the gums. He'd joked about Balzic's reaction to that acid smell, and every time he introduced some new chemical, he asked Balzic if he wanted to smell it. He'd smile when he asked that question and more so when he waited for the class to laugh. Balzic found that there was only one way to defend himself against that kind of attack: he refused to learn what the blond, bony man had to teach. He flunked chemistry, flunked it three times out of the six grading periods and eked out barely passing grades the other three grading periods. He defended himself the only way he could, even though he knew that he was hurting himself more than he could ever hurt the teacher. It was a pitiful exercise, and no amount of thought could dilute the impact it had on him.

Now, walking into Muscotti's, deserted in mid-morning, he tried to make some sense of what he'd just learned from Tom Murray. All he could think of was the smell of that acid, the long-toothed smile of that chemistry teacher, and his own refusal to learn what could have been taught because he had no other defense against the way a stink had been presented to him.

Dom Muscotti, wearing a white shirt open at the neck, rumpled trousers, and a sour face, walked out from the little kitchen. "You're getting early, ain't you?"

Balzic shrugged and settled onto the last stool at the bar, near the kitchen Dom had just left. "How come you're here? What's the matter with Vinnie?"

"Ah, he's gettin' some teeth drilled. He won't be worth a pint of cold piss all day. What're you doin' in here? It's not even ten o'clock. Huh? You sick?"

Balzic shook his head no. "I ain't sick but I feel like hell. What kind of wine you got?"

"What kind you want? Whatta you mean, what kind do I got? Here, lemme get some real light stuff. This is only, uh, it's not even ten percent alcohol. It's German."

"You drinkin' German wine? Since when?"

"Hey, I drink it every day for breakfast. I never told

you that? I been drinkin' this stuff for forty years." Muscotti stepped into the kitchen and reappeared shortly with a green bottle and a fine lead crystal glass. He put the glass and bottle on the bar and walked up the bar to get a plain bar glass for Balzic. He came back and filled both glasses. "Try this out. This'll fix you up."

They touched glasses and drank. Balzic held the wine in his mouth for a while and then let it slide down. "Hey, that's not bad. What is it?"

"This is a Moselle. Comes from beside the rivers there, in Germany, where the Moselle and the Rhine rivers get together. No other place in the world makes wine like this. They come close in California, but all that stuff out there got too much alcohol in it. Twelve, twelve and a half percent, Christ, who wants that in the morning? You can drink six, seven ounces of this, puts a nice taste in your mouth, you're ready to go. You drink that other stuff the only place you wanna go is back to bed."

"This is different," Balzic said. "Huh. As long as I been alive I never drank anything like this. Wonder why."

"Ah, you're probably still pissed off at the Nazis. You see German words on a bottle you'd probably think it was a front for a swastika factory."

"Come on."

"Hey, I know you from way back, don't give me that shit," Muscotti said, snorting. "So whatta you doin' in here now? What's wrong?"

Balzic blew out a long sigh. "Lots of things. Too goddamn many."

"So?" Muscotti said, shrugging. "C'mon, I need a laugh, let's hear 'em."

Balzic sighed again and glanced at the front door as it

opened and a rumpled, raw-eyed shell of a human staggered in. His clothes were three or four sizes too big, one of the soles on his shoes was flopping, and he was so filthy he looked like he'd been standing downwind of burning tires.

Muscotti walked away from Balzic and stood behind the center of the bar.

The raw-eyed shell tilted to his right and shuffled up to the bar in front of Muscotti. He fumbled in his pocket and came out with a wadded-up dollar bill that was as grungy as he was.

"Gimme big wine." The effort of saying those words caused him to back up two steps.

"I'm all sold out," Muscotti said.

"Whiskey. Gimme shot." Those words took another backward step out of him.

"Sold the last one right before you came in," Muscotti said.

The raw-eyed shell squinted at Muscotti and then focused on all the bottles behind him, two shelves of whiskies and wines, and not an empty among them.

"Sold last one?"

"The absolute last. I'm outta everything."

The shell rubbed his raw eyes until they watered and he looked at all the bottles again. He turned and shuffled toward the door, his sole flopping. "Sold out . . . sold the last one. . . ." He was repeating those words when the door closed behind him.

Muscotti came back down the bar and scowled at Balzic. "You wanna know the difference between a drunk and an alcoholic?"

"What?"

"The difference between me and that guy that just left. Huh? You know the difference? He's a drunk. I'm an alcoholic. You know the difference between him and me? He ain't got any money."

"What're you telling me?"

"You know the difference between a guy that's dyin' and a guy that ain't, huh?"

"What is this, mob homily time?"

"Just listen to me. Just listen. To the guy that's dyin', what he knows is, all the money in Pittsburgh ain't gonna make any difference. If those pill-rollers can't cure what he got, all the paper on Wall Street don't mean crap."

Balzic scratched his chin and nodded. "I'm goin' down to my office and write all this down. And then I'm gonna study it, and I'm sure if I study it long enough, sooner or later, your message is gonna come to me."

"You dummy," Muscotti said, "you worry too much about stuff you can't do nothin' about. I saw it in your face, the way I handled that lush. You were lookin' at him trying to figure out who you could get to help him out, and—"

"Oh bullshit."

"—and, and you came in here with half the world on your back and I'll lay a yard against a doughnut, it's about something you can't do anything about. Want to bet? Huh?"

"Yeah? Okay, you're so goddamn in tune with reality, okay, so listen to this. Tom Murray's dyin'. He just asked me to lead the parade to the cemetery. How'd you like that?"

"Yeah, I know."

"You know? When'd you find out? Who told you?"

"He did. About a month ago."

"Well why the hell didn't you say something?"

"There you go," Muscotti said, throwing up his hands. "What I just say? What the hell difference would it've made if you knew about it three weeks ago? What were you gonna do? Huh? I'll tell you what you—"

"That's not the point."

"—I'll tell you what you'd've done. You'd've come in here lookin' just like you're lookin' now."

"So what?"

"So you worry too much about fuckin' things you can't do anything about."

"So what're you tryin' to tell me?"

"I'm tryin' to tell you what I been tryin' to tell you for forty years. It's no good to worry about stuff like that. It's bad for your mental health, bad for your health all over."

"Hey, first homilies, now it's medical advice. You gonna pass the basket or send me a bill?"

"Hey, this is no joke, I'm trying to help you out."

"Well what're you hollerin' for?"

"I ain't the only one hollerin' here. You been goin' pretty loud yourself."

"Well what're *we* hollerin' for?"

Muscotti chewed his cheek and thought for some moments, staring off toward the other end of the bar. " 'Cause, uh, 'cause I'm gonna miss that sonofabitch. 'Cause I ain't been able to tell nobody about it and I got to tell my mother and I, uh, I can't do it."

"Your mother? Why can't you tell her?"

Muscotti shook his head. "Hey, my mother loves Murray. She thinks he's the best thing that happened since garlic."

"Your mother? I didn't even know she knew him."

"Yeah, yeah, she knows him. And I'm the one who introduced 'em. Yeah. I took him home, but she took him in. Christ, he was so busted out, so goddamn skinny, so polite, you know, she just wanted to sit on him till he hatched. He still eats dinner with her at least once a month. You didn't know that?"

"I just told you, I didn't even know he knew her."

"Christ, when I tell her it's gonna break her heart."

"Whatta you mean, you took him home, she took him in, what's that mean?"

"It means when he come to Rocksburg here, when he come in here I felt so friggin' sorry for him, I took him home. He didn't have nothin'. He had two pairs of pants, one coat, two shirts, one tie, couple pairs of socks, nothin' matched, he was livin' in the Y in Pittsburgh, he was coming out here on a streetcar, I think he was makin' about twelve bucks a week, he didn't know nobody, all he wanted to do was write about sports, he didn't know shit, and he heard this was a place nobody'd bother him in, so I felt sorry for him. I took him home with me one night. My mother filled him full of pasta, she didn't ask him no questions. He thought she was the Virgin Mary and she thought he was a stray dog if she didn't feed and clean him up a little bit somebody was gonna gas him.

"And you know, I wouldn't eat nothin' but filet mignon, I wasn't gonna eat pasta every day like some wop off a boat, and she thought pasta was what God gave Italians just like He gave manna to the Jews, you know, so here's this skinny Irish kid, he never ate so good in his life. He never ate pasta before I took him home. I didn't know anybody could live that long and never eat pasta. And you know, I'm a big shot, and my mother didn't want me goin' the way I was goin', so here was the kid who was a good boy and he loved her cooking and she loved to watch him eat and she'd talk to me in Italian, you know, right in front of him, he's sittin' there like a dummy, he don't know what's goin' on, she's hollerin' at me in Italian, why can't I be like him? Ha. So that's what I said, I took him home, and she took him in. And I gotta listen to her complain about me, how I was gonna wind up like some goddamn hoodlum with a bullet in my head and he was gonna make his mother proud.

"I never told you any of this, right?"

"Never." Balzic shook his head. "But all the years you two used to argue in here, I thought you two never got along. And all this time he's going to your mother's and eatin' dinner with her?"

"Yeah, once a month. But, see, what happens is when he quit writin' sports and he starts being a regular reporter, you know, writing city hall stuff, then he finds out about me, and then, he can't figure out what to do. He got this Irish conscience, it's big as the goddamn Vatican, and he don't know how to handle it. So every chance he gets he starts an argument with me. 'Cause what he really wants to do is make a name for himself writing a big story, big exposé or whatever you call it, and as far as he's concerned, you know, I'm the biggest story there is in this place. I mean, from his eyes. But what's he gonna do? Is he gonna write something bad about me or what?

"Besides, he didn't understand how taxes work, you know. I mean, he was a real clean kid. He believed all that shit about how us dagos corrupted those Irish pricks in the courthouse. I mean in those days he don't know straight up.

"So anyway—here, have some more," Muscotti said,

filling his own glass and pouring what was left in the bottle into Balzic's. "So anyway—"

"What was I doin' when all this was goin' on?"

"You? What the hell do I know? You were making a big name for yourself, yeah, you were the only dago cop. Half-dago. You know what we used to call you? Huh? We used to call you Earparini. Wyatt Earparini."

"Get outta here."

"It's the truth," Muscotti said, raising his right hand.

"Earparini my ass. You gotta be kiddin'!"

"Hey, that's what we used to call you. You were the first paisan—half-paisan—on the force. Think about it, who was on the force then? All them goddamn Irish, except for that *tuzone* Ruggles. Hey, that was a big deal when they made you a cop. All those dagos up on Norwood went crazy. You didn't even know it, did you? Hell no, you didn't know it. You were too goddaman wound up around your own head then."

"What're you talkin' about?"

"Hey, you don't like to think about stuff like that, you always liked to think that stuff was all below you, but I'm gonna tell you what it was like. It was like, uh, remember when Jackie Robinson got in the major leagues, huh? 'Member how the niggers went crazy? Huh? Well that's what all the old dagos got like when they made you a cop."

"Oh bullshit."

"Ha, listen to him. You don't remember none of that, but I'm tellin' you it's true. Ask your mother. Ask my mother. They'll tell you. Those old dags, they were throwin' parties."

"Not my mother," Balzic said. "She didn't talk to me for about a month. After all the shit those union guys got from cops, my mother thought I was spittin' on my father's memory."

"Yeah yeah yeah, I know all about that. But I'm tellin' ya, most of the old-timers were proud as hell. You were half one of their own. And that meant something to those people whether you believe it or not. 'Course you never believed it, 'cause you were gonna be a cop for everybody, not just the dagos."

"Yeah? Just how long you think I would've lasted if I wasn't?"

"I'm not sayin' anything, am I? Everybody knew real fast how you were gonna be. But nobody was bitchin'. They understood."

"Hey, forget all this. Get back to Murray. You were starting to tell me something about him when I interrupted you."

"Huh? You mean his conscience and that?"

"Yeah."

"Oh, well, he was in a real jackpot. See, he was like you, he wants to do good, you know, be a good reporter, expose corruption and all that crap. But he don't know what to do about me. 'Cause he knows if he writes something bad about me, he's done with my mother—"

"And you weren't thinking about that when you took him home?"

"Hah? Nah nah nah, nothin' like that. For crissake, he was a sportswriter then, what're you talkin' about. Meantime, until I took him home, I had my mother all to myself. How'd I know she was gonna turn him into my brother? You think if I'd've known that, I'd've taken him home, ruined that for myself? Bullshit. Hey, she used to holler at me, but I didn't have any competition. So—"

"So that's why you two are always arguin'."

"Hey, whatta you think? Me, you know, big shot, big time, I feel sorry for the guy and I wind up inventin' a brother for myself. You don't know how many times I kicked myself in the ass for that one." Muscotti shook his head. "Too late now. Now I got a different problem with him. Anyway."

"Yeah, so what did he do about his conscience?"

Muscotti laughed feebly. "He didn't do nothin'. 'Cause that's when his boss hired old pigface to work the courthouse."

"Who?"

"You know who I'm talkin' about. She's giving you trouble right now."

"You mean Mary Hart? You mean she worked for Murray's paper before she did that thing in that magazine?"

"Now you got it, now you got it. You don't remember that, do you?"

"Hell no. I must've been sleepin'."

"You must've been."

"So what was goin' on? He was workin' City Hall and what—she was workin' the courthouse?"

Muscotti nodded emphatically. "That's it, that's the way it was. So you remember who was D.A. then. Huh?"

"Yeah. Leo Roberts."

"Right, right. And Malley was president judge, and the county commissioners? Huh?"

"Oh, Christ—"

"Yeah, yeah, the three snakes Saint Patrick chased outta Ireland. Ryan, Bryan, and Maloney."

"Oh God," Balzic said, shaking his head.

"Yeah. Those guys gave crime a bad name. I learned more about stealin' from those guys than I ever learned from my father. You think I'm jokin'? Hey, they were on their way out when pigface did her number on them. They were gettin' ready to retire. You should've seen them when they came in in 'thirty-two, riding on FDR's tail. That's when they all got started. A week—you hear what I'm sayin'?—a week after the election, they came in here, all of 'em except Malley—Leo Roberts sat on that stool right where you're sittin' and Ryan there and Bryan next to him and Maloney next to him.

"And they call my father over—I'm sittin' up there in the back where the restaurant used to be, and I hear 'em call my father. 'Hey, Paulie,' they say. They don't say Mister Muscotti, or Paolo, uh-uh. No, it's, 'Hey Paulie.' So I come around the corner see who's talkin' like that, real smart mouth, you know.

"So one right after the other, they all say the same thing, 'Whiskey.' One word. Now I don't know these guys from nobody, I never saw 'em before. It's lunchtime. Place is crowded. Nobody drank in here in the daytime. My father wouldn't serve booze until all the women went home. This bar was strictly coffee during the day. So I hurried up, I run down the back stairs, come in through the kitchen and I get a coupla pieces and stick 'em in my pants and I grab the shotgun we used to keep back there and held it down by my leg and I come out right to the edge of the door there.

"My father says, 'No whiskey. I don't sell whiskey.' And Roberts—I didn't know what his name was, but he was real dark, you know, so I couldn't tell what he was from lookin' at him, but the way they're actin' I knew something was up. So Roberts says, 'You sell lots of whiskey.' And he gets this real shitty look on his face and he says, 'You want to keep on sellin' it? You better sell some right now, Paulie.'

"And right then I started debatin' with myself. Should I shoot this sonofabitch or not? If I shoot him, I gotta shoot 'em all—I knew that right away. There's no way I could just hit him, and if I do, how am I gonna get out of it? I'm thinkin' all this stuff. My head's goin' a hundred miles an hour, and I figure the only way I can do anything is if they make a move on my father.

"So my father says, 'You guys wanna talk, I'll talk to you. But not now. You come back later.'

"And that Roberts prick, he says, 'We'll talk now, Paulie.' And the way he said it, I just took the heat and I come around the corner and stick that shotgun right up under his chin, and I said, 'You get the hell outta here.'

"And my father, I hear him groan, and he starts telling me in Italian, 'You donkey, you know who that is? That's the new district attorney, and you know what you just did? You just made him my partner.'

"Me? I'm standin' here thinkin' I'm a big tough guy, and here, they had two cops waitin' outside. Ryan or Bryan, I forget which, he goes and gets the cops and I'm still standin' there the same way, and my old man's saying, 'Put the gun down, put the gun down,' in Italian, and all I can think is, what difference does it make if I put the shotgun down, I got two pistols in my pants. And here come the cops, and there I am. And now you know how all those Irish pricks got in the booze business. And everything else we had."

"That's the way it happened? No shit?" Balzic said.

"Certainly, whatta you think? My father had 'em till he died and then I had 'em. And all because why? C'mon, you tell me."

"You were showin' your old man what a good son you were."

Muscotti threw back his head and laughed. "Yeah. Yeah. And all I showed him was how dumb I was. You know, he let me sit in the joint for a whole goddamn week before he even came to see me. And when he finally showed up, you should've heard the new ass he chewed me.

"I'll never forget what he said. He grabbed me by the ear and he said, 'Pay attention. This is America. This is a place where the people elect their bosses. They elect the guys who make the laws. You gonna make your livin' breakin' those laws, the first thing you got to do is find out who wants to be boss. And if you're too lazy or too stupid to do that, then you're gonna spend your life being a tough guy in public, and tough guys in public, sooner or later, they wind up where you are. Those guys knew all about you, but you, you didn't even know who they were. They knew how to pinch your nose, and you didn't even know their names.' Then he started to cry, the only time in my whole life he ever cried, and he said, 'And if you didn't have me for a father, they wouldn't know your name either.'

"I'm tellin' you, when my father quit talkin', we were both bawlin'. Mario, you'll never know how glad I am I only got daughters."

Balzic shook his head and looked at his lap. After a moment, he said, "So, uh, what was goin' on with Murray and whatsherface, Hart?"

Muscotti thought for a second. "Well, see, this got real confusing. For me, for Murray, it was a mess there for awhile. But the thing that started it was old pigface wouldn't shut up during the commissioners' meetings. She'd interrupt the meetings, always askin' 'em questions. Not like they're good questions, you know how she is, her yap goin' all the time. And those Irish pricks just got tired of listening to her. So what are they doin' anyway, huh? It's a public meeting, strictly routine, taxes, bids on ashes, road stuff, fix the roof, buy a truck, hire this guy, fire that guy, but she wouldn't shut up. She had to stick her nickel in on everything.

"So they close the meetings. They're gonna hold—what the hell they call 'em?—Oh. Executive sessions, right? No reporters, no spectators, no nobody—just so they wouldn't have to listen to her run her mouth all the time. And that was what did it. If they'd've just put up with her big mouth, those bastards would still be running the county. Well they're all dead, but you know what I mean."

"Wait a minute," Balzic said. "Are you sayin' that's what set her off on them? They shut her out of the meetings?"

Muscotti nodded emphatically. "Yeah. Exactly."

"You mean she never wrote anything bad about them before that?"

"You kiddin' me? What bad? What bad did she know about?"

Balzic was incredulous. "Are you tellin' me she never tried to expose those guys until they closed her out of their public meetings."

"That's exactly what I'm tellin' you. You think I'm makin' this up?"

"That thing, that big exposé she did in that magazine—what the hell was the name of it?"

"I forget. It ain't been around for so long I can't remember."

"She did that after?"

"You got it."

"Well what the hell was she writin' about all the while she was going to the meetings?"

"Nothin'. She was their biggest fan. She's Irish just like them. Maiden name was Hanrahan or something. But she never made a peep till they shut her out."

Balzic snorted. "For crissake, she's been bragging for thirty-five years how she's the world's greatest muckraker. Every goddamn year she puts that story in the paper, how she got together with that bunch of ministers to clean up the county and throw the bums out of office."

Muscotti smiled and peered intently at Balzic. "You mean you thought she was on the square? All-American reporter, gangbusters, huh? Christ, you must've been asleep."

"I can't believe I never heard this before," Balzic said.

"Hey, you can check it out. All you gotta do is go down the *Gazette* and read it yourself. They got it all on microfilm. What she wrote before, what she wrote after, it's all there. Or if you don't wanna do that, go ask Valcanas. He'll tell you. That's when he got tied up with Froggy, that's when he was Froggy's campaign manager when Froggy ran for D.A. the first time. Christ, the Greek hates her."

"I'll be goddamn," Balzic said. "I believe you. I'll ask Valcanas. I know he hates her, I know he always did, but, you know, come to think of it, I never asked him why. . . . Wow. Must've made Murray look pretty bad."

"Whatta you think? He's been pissed off at me ever since."

"You kiddin'? He's just been givin' you the hard time because he couldn't bring himself to do what he thinks he was supposed to do. Must've played hell with his mind. No wonder your mother loves him."

They sipped the wine and said nothing for some moments, both thinking of all the complications.

Balzic grunted. "Christmas," he said. "What a fuckin' Christmas this is gonna be. . . ."

⦿⟐⦿

After lunch, Balzic found Sgt. Ruggiero Carlucci waiting for him back at the station. Carlucci was fiddling with a fingernail clipper on his key ring, clicking it open and closed and looking bored.

Balzic paused to check the dispatcher's log and, finding nothing out of the ordinary there, motioned for Rugs to follow him back to his office. Balzic collapsed onto his chair and loosened his tie.

"What's the good word, Rugs? And please make it good. All I been hearing today is bullshit times two."

Rugs canted his head and screwed up his face. "I don't know how good it is. I thought you'd be pretty happy 'cause those vets weren't around."

"They weren't?" Balzic stiffened smartly, jumped up and hustled out to the duty room to look out the window. In a moment he was back, smiling broadly. He fell into his chair again. "I'll be goddamn. I walked right past where they've been standing and I didn't even notice they were gone. Where'd they go, I wonder."

"I don't know. I asked Royer and he said one time he looked out the window and they were there and the next time he looked they were gone. He's not even sure when that was."

"Heyyyyy," Balzic said, chortling. "Best thing happened in a week. Now we can get on to other stuff. So?"

"Well, one thing I know is gonna make you happy for sure. Mrs. Garbin, Mr. Garbin, separately or together, they had no accounts in this town. No savings account, checking account, no Christmas Clubs, no nothing."

"You checked them all?"

"Every bank, ever S and L. Hey, with these computers the banks have, it took about fifteen minutes. And most of that was me looking up the phone number. She might've saved some bucks, but if she did it wasn't in any bank in this town."

"I thought so," Balzic said.

"I told you she was running a game."

"Well, good. That clears that up. Good work, Rugs." Balzic leaned back in his chair and clasped his hands together over his head and stretched.

"So don't you want to know about Murlovsky?"

"Yeah, sure. We might need it."

"Well, turns out he was the center of attention in both places, here and in that Legion in Pittsburgh. Nobody knows how the beefs got started exactly, but everybody's pretty sure he started the action both times. Bartender in the VFW here says there's no doubt in his mind Murlovsky threw the first punch. And before the punch he made some big speeches, a whole bunch of crap about how he put his ass on the line for his country and his country just wants to hang him out to dry and a lot of other similar nonsense. After that, everything gets cloudy. None of the guys who got collared that night seem to remember exactly what his bitch was, but in so many words they all had the idea he was looking for some action and when they all got enough beer in them, you know, one thing turned into another."

"How about the thing in Pittsburgh?"

"Well, all I could get there was what the magistrate remembered and one pretty bad carbon, all smudged up, of a report from the precinct that handled it. I wouldn't bet two bucks on anything except that Murlovsky was the only guy to lose any time and there were approximately the same number of people involved. All the rest just had to give up some money. Biggest fine was fifty plus costs. Only thing the magistrate said he remembered was Murlovsky struck him as a guy carrying around a giant grudge for somebody."

"Hey, Rugs, that's good work."

"There's more."

"Well, don't stop now."

"Okay," Rugs said. He had been standing, but now he put away his nail clipper and took a chair on the other side of Balzic's desk. "I want you to know I worked real hard on this."

Balzic laughed. "So hard you think you have to say so?"

Rugs held up his hands. "This is about Mrs. Garbin. And I already told you I thought she was—never mind. You remember what I said about her."

"Yeah. That she's a pain in the ass."

"Right. So when you don't like somebody, you just have to work extra hard to make sure you're not—hey, you know what I mean."

"Just tell me what you did, okay? I'll figure it out."

"Okay. I went over that intersection where she said she got rolled. I talked to everybody with a window that looked out on that intersection. And nobody saw anything except two people. One guy works in that Boron station, and he's the one who called the ambulance. The other one's a secretary works in the second floor of that real estate office across the street, G and G Realty?"

"So?"

"The guy in the Boron station was working on a car, he was taking off a muffler and he had the bay door down. So there's windows only in the top half of the door, right? You know the kind of door I'm talking about?"

Balzic nodded.

"Okay. So he takes a glance out just out of habit to see if there's somebody pulling in to the pumps. And he doesn't see any woman walking across that intersection. Not that he's looking for one. But he didn't see one. So he gets down on the creeper and slides under the car and he's under there long enough to find out that all the nuts and bolts are rusted so he can't get the muffler off without a power chisel. So he gets back up to hook up the chisel and he looks out the window and there she is, down on her hands and knees. So he runs out to see what's wrong, finds her, comes back in and calls nine-one-one, and goes back out to wait for the ambulance with her. Okay?"

"I'm with you," Balzic said.

"So he says there's no way he's under the car longer than ten seconds. And before he went under the car, he didn't see her. Now he's got a clear view of all three corners. The only way his view's obstructed is, he can't see anybody coming down Third Street beside his station. Okay? In other words, if that woman would've been walking up Pittsburgh Street the way she said she was, he would've seen her. You still with me?"

Balzic nodded again.

"Okay. So when I talk to the lady in the second floor of the real estate office on the other side of the street, she's absolutely sure of two things. First, Mrs. Garbin did not walk up Pittsburgh. She came down Third Street beside the Boron station and turned left up Pittsburgh. She saw her coming from that direction. No doubt. Now, the other thing she's sure of is, the woman is already bleeding when she turns the corner."

"She saw the blood from across the street?"

"Absolutely positively. Now. She sees the woman, sees the blood, tries to make up her mind what to do, decides she got to go help her, goes and gets her coat, and then goes back to the window to make sure she's not seeing things, and that's when she sees Mrs. Garbin down on her hands and knees and the guy from the Boron station running out to help. She says she was away from the window five or six seconds, tops."

"What about a car?"

"I'm coming to that. She said she saw lots of cars. But she says she can't say for sure whether any of 'em stopped for anything but the light. She can't swear to it, but she has the feeling that no cars stopped for the light. They were all moving. But she's not sure about that. She says she was too busy looking at the woman."

"Okay, so what about pedestrians?"

"Neither one of 'em saw anybody but her."

"Okay, okay," Balzic said. "So then what?"

"So then I go back down on Third Street and start knockin'. One block away there's a light at the intersection of Stanton Avenue. It's got a pedestrian button on it. Old pain in the ass Mrs. Garbin backed up about three steps from that pedestrian button, you know how they got a ridge runs all the way around that button?"

"Yeah. Don't tell me. She ran at it headfirst?"

Rugs nodded. "And I got a lady, Mrs. Mary Wolinsky, 101 Third Avenue, lives on the second floor, saw her do it. She was waiting for her granddaughter to come back from the store and she was looking out the window watching for her. The little girl went to get some bread and stuff and Mrs. Wolinsky was worried about her. The girl stayed a couple minutes longer than she should have, so the lady was watching out the window, and here comes Mrs. Garbin, stops at that button, runs her hand all over it, backs up, and runs right into it with her face."

"And Mrs. Witness didn't say anything to anybody 'cause she didn't want anybody to think she was seeing things, right?"

"That's it," Rugs said. "So there's your Christmas Club robbery for you."

Balzic shook his head in admiration. "Rugs, I'll tell you what. You put in one hell of a day. You're gonna get my top-shelf, first-class, All-American letter of commendation for this one. Sergeant, you just saved me a bunch of grief."

"Uh, if it's okay with you, you don't need to make any big deal about this, okay? I mean, usually when a guy gets a letter, they get it at the FOP dinner and their picture gets in the paper and all that warm noise."

"You don't want that?"

"Mario, when I found Mrs. Wolinsky, I got all the warm noise anybody needs. You know what Mrs. Garbin did to me once?"

"I didn't know she did anything to you."

"Yeah. Well let me tell you. Once, when I was nine years old, some kids were chasing me after school up at Mother of Sorrows, and I was really scared, so I was running between the houses and hiding and I ran down beside her house and I guess I must've stepped on some plants or something. So I hear some lady holler, 'Hey you!' And I turned around and she whipped a rock at me. Hit me right in the chest. Tore my shirt, I started to bleed, and when I saw the blood it scared the piss outta me. I mean it, I pissed myself. And then when I got myself all together, the kids that were chasing me found me and when they saw my pants all wet, they didn't even do anything. I didn't know what they were gonna do anyway. They just laughed like crazy and told everybody in Norwood about it. I was never that humiliated before or since. So, uh, that's what I meant before when I said I really had to work hard on this, keep my objectivity about her. But I don't need any commendations, I really don't."

"Hey," Balzic said. "Nobody'll know a thing about it. I'll just put it in your record, and, uh, you can just go on about your business knowing that I feel as good about this as you do. Good enough?"

"I don't know, Mario. I haven't felt this good since I was nine."

<hr>

Balzic didn't know what to do first. He wanted to call Eddie Sitko and tell him to stuff a lid on the Garbin Christmas Club; he wanted to call Tom Murray to tell Mary Hart to start writing retractions, corrections, and apologies; he wanted to buy a bunch of balloons, blow them up, take them to Mrs. Garbin's hospital room, and stick pins in them as they floated around her bed; he wanted to go to a bakery and buy a cream pie and heave it into Mary Hart's face. He wanted to do a whole lot of mean, silly, delicious things, but what he did was fill out a letter-of-commendation form for Rugs Carlucci and take it out along with a blank and put them in the typing basket for one of the city's typists to complete. Then he stood and looked out the window at the spot where the four vets had been standing naked for the past two days, and he felt very good at not seeing anything.

He went back into his office, found the phone number for the newspaper, and called Tom Murray.

"What now, Balzic?" Murray said, when he was connected.

"I just thought you'd like to be the first to know. When I was down there this morning, I said your paper may be party to a fraud."

"And?"

"Well you can change the 'may' to 'is.' "

"Are you changing it?"

"That's what I'm doing. So whatever you gotta do to cover your ass, start coverin'."

"I'd like to hear the details."

"Carlucci checked out the victim's story. None of it holds water. He checked all the banks and S-and-L's in town. Mrs. Garbin didn't have any account anywhere. You gonna sit on the other end and tell me you didn't already know that?"

"No."

"That's what I thought. So your information's the same, right?"

"Yes."

"Is somebody with you—is that why you're giving me these long answers?"

"Yes to both."

"Okay, so you don't have to say anything. Here's the

rest of it. We got two witnesses who put the victim where she claimed to be, but not how she said she arrived there and not in the condition she said she got into after she got there. Also, I got an alibi witness for the guy she said did it. Also, we have a witness who saw her run face-first into a crosswalk button one block away from where she says the assault and robbery took place. The woman is trying to work a scam, and several people, I'm happy as hell to add, have just been nominated and elected to the Dipshit Hall of Fame. How's that grab you?"

"It might be fun to be there at the induction. Thanks for calling. G'bye."

Balzic cradled the phone and stood and whooped until his throat hurt.

He then dropped back into his chair and drummed his fingers on the desk for a moment, plotting, scheming how best to get the most out of Mrs. Garbin and her wonderful little Christmas Club. He reached for the phone, found the list of attorneys in the yellow pages, and scanned it until he got to Alan Cecconi. He picked up the phone again and dialed the number.

"Cecconi and Martin. May I help you?" a girl's voice said.

"Alan Cecconi, please. This is Mario Balzic, chief of Rocksburg P.D."

"Mr. Cecconi's busy at the moment. May I—"

"Tell Mr. Cecconi to get unbusy. Tell him that I can't make him pick up this phone and talk to me if he really doesn't want to, but you also be sure to tell him that I can make him awful goddamn sorry he didn't."

"Just—just a moment, please."

Balzic counted the seconds. He was up to twenty-three when a voice said, "Alan Cecconi. May I help you?"

"You can help yourself a hell of a lot more than you can help me."

"Uh, is this the chief of police?"

"Your secretary told you who I am, Mr. Cecconi. Now pay attention. You—"

"Before you go any further, I don't like your tone. If you wish to speak to me, please do so in a civil manner."

"Okay. How's this? Your name appeared in the *Rocksburg Gazette* as the attorney for the Garbin Christmas Club. Does that tone suit you?" Balzic said, softening his voice only slightly.

"Yes."

"Well I'll try to stay on that same level then. The point is this: you had better make a fast audit of the money that's been collected so far and you better get it into an escrow account just as fast as your little buns can move. Mrs. Garbin is about to be arrested for fraud. The big question as far as you're concerned is, why'd you become a party to this without checking with me first? I think that's the question the bar association's gonna ask, don't you? Why not take the time to make one little phone call to the police? Huh? Fact is, I'd like to hear the answer to that myself. You got one?"

"Chief, uh, can I call you back? I have a client—"

"No you can't call me back. I don't give a rat's ass how many clients you got there. I don't give a rat's whole body if this is a little inconvenient for you at this moment. It was apparently very convenient for you when you were talking to the fire chief and, uh, the voice of the downtrodden—old Mary Hart."

There came a deep sigh on the other end.

"Are you, uh, are you sure about what you just said? I mean, do you have any doubts?"

"When I get through talking to you, I'm gonna call Eddie Sitko and Mary Hart and I'm gonna tell them to meet me at the hospital so they can watch me make the arrest. Let me ask you something. Have you still not checked the banks to find out if that woman had an account—any kind of account?"

"Uh, I really have not had time. I've been swamped with calls from people wanting to know where to send the money."

Balzic shook his head. "Uh, Mr. Cecconi, tell me something. I don't recall seeing or hearing your name before today. You just set up practice here?"

"What you mean is, how green am I, don't you?"

"I suppose that's what I mean, yeah."

"Well. Well. Pretty green. Pretty raw."

"So, uh, you and your partner, uh, Martin is it?"

"No, it isn't. I mean it used to be, but he left four weeks ago. He went back to his dad's firm."

"So you thought this would be a good way to, uh, get a little good P.R., right?   A little free P.R.? Don't answer that. Just tell me, uh, how'd you get wired with Sitko? How'd that happen?"

"Well, if you must know, please try to understand I got so desperate . . . uh, I got very desperate. I started going to the Mutual Aid garage. I know what you're thinking. I know it sounds terrible. It *is* terrible. . . . It's worse than terrible. I can't pay my secretary. I don't have the money. I don't have the nerve to tell her I don't have the money . . . I know, I mean, it's easy enough at the moment to say I should have investigated this more thoroughly, but . . . oh God, I can't, I can't stand to hear myself bitch, that's all I've been doing. Bitch bitch bitch bitching and bitching. . . . Anyway, that's where I met Mr. Sitko. At the Mutual Aid garage. That was about three weeks ago. And the other night when he called I couldn't believe it. I mean, I was really getting to the point where I was shaving in the shower, I mean, my God, chasing ambulances is one thing. But sitting around the garage pretending you're interested in becoming a paramedic? Oh Jesus. . . . What, uh, what happens now?"

"Uh, has anybody—who's been counting that money besides you?"

"Well, Mr. Sitko counted some of it this morning, but, uh—"

"Oh Christ. Have you deposited any of this money yet?"

"No. I haven't had a chance—"

"Good. Then count out what you owe your secretary in wages and stash that someplace."

"What? Wait a minute—"

"Mister, you don't have time to wait, and don't argue with me. Just do what I tell you. After you do that, you call attorney Myron Valcanas and tell him that you need an accountant right away and tell him that I said for you to call him. Then you tell your secretary to stop taking all calls about this fund except from me and Valcanas. You got that so far?"

"Wait just a second, Chief, please, for God sake, wait a minute! I know I'm green, but if what you said is true then what you're doing is conspiracy to commit another fraud. What you're—"

"Hey! Shut up and listen. You can't do no good from jail, Cecconi. And you can't do no good on an empty stomach. And I'm not in jail and my stomach's full. You do what I told you to do. And you talk to no one about this, you hear? Me and Valcanas and that's it. You hear?"

"I hear, but I don't—"

"Never mind what you don't. And if Mary Hart should call you, you don't know anything. Same for Sitko. Tell your secretary you can't talk to them. But if that doesn't work, if they get by her—either in person or on the phone— tell 'em you're in the process of setting up an escrow account and you're busy as hell. And don't talk! Now cut out your secretary's pay and stash it somewhere and call Valcanas. Do it now! G'bye."

Jesus Christ, Balzic thought after he'd hung up, where do they come from?

Ten minutes later, Balzic was still sitting at his desk. Every time he tried to think of what to do next, the thought bombarded him that he had just done the dumbest thing he'd ever done. For crissake, he thought, I just told some goddamn jerk attorney I've never seen to steal money to pay his goddamn secretary out of a fund that should never have been started. And then I tell him to make Valcanas a part of it. Valcanas is gonna shit. Valcanas is gonna look at me and say, oh Christ, I can hear him now, he's gonna say, "Hey, Mario, next time you decide to involve me in conspiracy, at least give me the opportunity to refuse. I would like to be able to look at a judge and tell him with a straight face that I said no." Christ, that's the nicest thing he's gonna say to me. I can give some bullshit answer to that one. But what am I gonna say when he asks me how I figure I was doing something better than they were? 'Cause right now I can't even say how what I'm doing is even different. . . .

"I got to shut that woman up." he said aloud. He lunged for the phone and dialed the hospital.

After his preliminary inquiries he was connected to a clerk in the discharge section.

"Mrs. Garbin was discharged at eleven."

"Well, listen, wait a minute. How did she get out of there?"

"I don't follow you, sir."

"Well you got to pay your bill, right? The whole world knows you don't get out of the hospital without making arrangements to pay the bill, right? So how'd she do that?"

"Oh. I see what you mean. Well, a woman named Mrs. Hart was with her. And she made some arrangements with the billing supervisor. And the director of the hospital came down and he approved it. But I can't give you the details. Maybe you should talk to them. In fact, I think you should talk to them. This is strictly confidential information, sir. In fact, why don't I connect you with—"

"Never mind," Balzic interrupted her. He said thanks and hung up. "Now what?" he said to himself, jumping up and pacing around his desk, pushing hard on his jaw, rubbing the flesh up and down. After a few agonizing moments, when he thought he was probably going to have a bruise on his face from where he'd been pushing, he hurried out into the duty room and asked Royer if he knew where Rugs Carlucci was.

"Probably up at his mother's eatin' lunch."

"Well, find him if you can. And—"

"I can find him, Mario. He's wearin' a beeper."

"Oh, I keep forgettin' about those damn things."

"I know. The mayor asked me last time I saw him why you weren't wearin' yours."

"I keep forgettin' to put the goddamn thing on. I hate those goddamn things. Makes you sound like a doctor. The whole world sounds like doctors. You can't go anywhere anymore without one of those goddamn things goin' *beep beep beep beep*. One of 'em goes off and everybody starts reachin' for their belt. Hey, hey, look at me, look how important I am, people can't get along without me. What a crock."

"Well," Royer said, "they come in handy when you're looking for somebody—like now."

"Aw up yours. Just tell him when you find him to go find Mrs. Garbin and sit on her. Don't let her out of his sight. And tell him be obvious. Don't hide."

Royer nodded and went about it, hiding his face so that Balzic wouldn't see him trying not to laugh.

"And quit laughin' at me," Balzic said. "I can't help it me and this electronic crap don't get along."

Balzic started toward his office and stopped. "And if he wants to know where she is, tell him she's either gonna go home with Mary Hart or else she's gonna go home to her house. Either way, tell him to put out a sign. I want him to piss 'em both off. . . . Where d'you think that fuckin' Sitko is now?"

Balzic again headed for his office and then hesitated, still trying to decide what to do.

"Sitko's on a washdown," Royer said offhandedly. "A truck hit a car down on Pittsburgh and South Main."

Balzic grunted. He kept trying to figure his next move, but nothing came to him with any clarity, except what he'd said to Cecconi about his secretary's wages, and every time he tried to think of something else, there that was, full in his face and demanding justification. There was none. And the more he thought about it, the more he tried to justify what he'd told Cecconi to do about that, the more muddy it became.

"I got to get the hell out of here," he said, and practically ran for the door.

"Where you goin'?" Royer hollered after him.

"I can't think!" Balzic shouted back and bolted for his cruiser. He was out and in it and pulling into traffic and heading toward the Flats and the river for no reason he could explain. He just had to get out of the station, as though getting out would give him better air to breathe and more room to think. He might as well have tried to run out from under his own head. But moving was something, driving was something, even while he knew that it was only for its own sake. "Who you kiddin'?" he said aloud. "You just didn't want Royer to see you about to have a goddamn panic attack . . . Jesus."

He turned the cruiser onto Lafayette Street and went down the slope toward the Flats—beside the Conemaugh River. . . .

The Flats was about a mile long and at most a half-mile wide. When it was booming, as it always was during a war, thousands were employed in its forges and machine shops and fabricating plants and on the docks where the coal and ore and oil barges unloaded and in the railroad repair yards and truck terminals. But everything that had brought casting and machining and fabricating to a round-the-clock frenzy during both World Wars had seemed to diminish during the Korean Conflict. One of the bleak, black jokes that made the rounds then was that if the politicians had quit calling it a "police action" and called it what it was—a war—the work would have lasted a lot longer and more hunkies would have gotten rich. By the time Vietnam got into everybody's ears in the Flats, they all knew it was going to be bad because the politicians couldn't even decide to call it a police action. No Vietnam War, no Vietnam Conflict, no Vietnam Police Action, just Vietnam, and that single word didn't generate much of anything in the Flats, least of all work, because by the time Vietnam put itself in conversations, all the mills and foundries and machine shops had been closed for years. Somebody had taken the names off the factories in the Flats and painted them on buildings in the South, in states where it was okay to run a mill without worrying about whether the workers thought a union was a good idea or a bad idea or any idea at all.

What struck Balzic as he drove through the Flats was a sense of organized desolation, building after building with their doors rusted shut and their windows shattered, no smoke coming out of their pipes or steam out of their vents, and, worst of all, nobody going in or coming out of their gates when the shifts should have been changing. Balzic thought of Jack Garbin working here, 4-F and making artillery shells, and then not working because the artillery shells were no longer needed, 4-F again in a pathetic new way. The organized desolation suited Balzic just right. At that moment, it looked like desolation was something he was very good at organizing.

At the end of Lafayette Street stood the three-story hulk of what had been a can factory that once employed two thousand people. Now only the first floor was used, and that was to warehouse magazines. Fewer than a hundred employees, nearly all of them part-timers, worked for minimum wages and no benefits. Behind that was the shell of a plant where springs for railroad cars had been made for fifty years. Balzic couldn't remember when it shut down—sometime in the early '60s. Four blocks west, downriver, was the shell of what had been the largest boxcar assembly plant in the Northeast until it closed about a year before the springs plant. Two blocks north, with its back to the river, stood the blackened brick-and-steel mass of the railroad wheel and axle division of what had been America's largest steelmaker. A wheel hadn't rolled out of that plant since the early '70s.

Near the river, where the docks had been, where the flatboats and barges had been unloaded since Colonial times, there were two new warehouses, one of yellow corrugated steel with a white roof and the other yellow with a gray roof. They were filled with beer that was brewed someplace else and would mostly be drunk someplace else and filled these warehouses only because large tax advantages had been offered to the owners to put their warehouses in Rocksburg's Flats. The great increase in employment the tax advantages were supposed to create had never happened among the people of the Flats, many of whom had long ago resigned themselves to a life on public assistance. Not many people were needed to move beer out of one truck and into another, and even with the tax breaks not many businesses seemed to believe moving to the Flats was a move for the future.

What was left in the Flats were the churches and the church clubs, the bars and social clubs, the corner groceries and storefront restaurants, the barber shops and funeral homes. St. Gregory's Russian Orthodox Church was next door to St. Matthew's Roman Catholic, which was called St. Matthew's by its members and St. Slovak's by the

Russians who attended St. Gregory's. A block east and a block south, on Mary Street, the Flats' main business street, was St. Mary's Ukrainian Orthodox Church. A half-block away on the other side of Mary Street was St. Stephen's Byzantine Catholic Church, which the locals called the Bell Russian Church because it had the biggest bell of all the churches in the Flats. A half-block farther east was St. Joseph's Polish Catholic Church, called St. Eagle's because of the five-foot-high eagle on the roof of the White Eagle's Hall next door to it. The eagle hadn't been painted in so long it was hard to say what color it was. . . .

The radio crackled, catching Balzic's attention.

". . . request help . . . Club. . . ."

"You're breakin' up," came Royer's voice.

". . . request help. . . . Petrolac . . . Ukrainian. . . ."

"Repeat. You're breakin' up. Switch to operations channel."

"You ain't kiddin' I'm breakin' . . . get some . . . the hell down here . . . Ukrainian Club . . . got trouble goddammit. . . ."

"I'm right here," Balzic said into his mike. "I'm on my way." He made a fast left turn into the alley behind the Rocksburg Hotel and Bar and then shot across Mary Street and spotted Petrolac's black-and-white next door to St. Mary's Ukrainian Orthodox Church in front of the Ukrainian Club. Balzic skidded to a stop behind Petrolac's cruiser and jumped out and ran toward the door of the club.

He found Petrolac sitting just off the walkway into the club, his back against the club's front wall. There was some blood around his nostrils and he was holding his left shoulder and breathing hard.

"What's up?" Balzic knelt beside him. "Where you hurt?"

"I think my collarbone's busted . . . just picked me up and threw me against the bowling machine."

"How many?"

"Just one. He's bigger than a fuckin' horse. Drunk . . . God this hurts . . . Chief, I ain't tellin' you what to do, but if you go in there you better take a shotgun. That bastard's crazy . . . and big. God is he big."

Balzic searched Petrolac's face. It was white with fear and pain. "Listen, young fella, just grit your teeth for a little while. I'm gonna call for an ambulance and you'll be in the hospital and people will be takin' care of you in no time at all. You hear me?"

Petrolac nodded. "I'm okay . . . watch yourself. He picked me up like I . . . like I wasn't even there."

Balzic patted him on the head and hustled back to his cruiser. He called for an ambulance and a backup unit, and he told them to use their lights but no sirens. He didn't want an announcement about who was coming. Then he hurried back to Petrolac's side. Just as he got there, the sound of somebody singing mixed crazily with the crashing of bottles.

"You stay here," Balzic said. "No matter what you hear, you don't come in, you understand me? I know what you want to do, but you're not gonna be able to help me, and I don't want to have to worry about you, understand?"

Petrolac looked up at Balzic but said nothing.

Balzic bent down and put his face close to Petrolac's. "Petrolac, I know you think you fucked up and you're feelin' stupid and you're feelin' useless, but I want your word you're gonna stay here and get in the ambulance when it comes. So speak to me. Tell me what you're gonna do now."

Petrolac closed his eyes and said, "I'm gonna wait for

the wagon . . . and I'm gonna get in it when it gets here."

"One more thing. Anybody comes up here before that—including the guys in the backup—you tell 'em to stay on the sidewalk and stay away from the door. You got that?"

"Yes, sir."

"Good man."

Balzic straightened up just as it started to snow. He took his raincoat off and put it over Petrolac's chest.

Balzic took a deep breath, spit, wiped the corners of his mouth, and pulled open the door of the club.

". . . better watch out, better not cry . . . better not pout, I'm tellin' you why," sang something large off to Balzic's left.

The bar was in the shape of a U. The bottom of the U faced the door and was perhaps fifteen feet across. The two legs of the U were about a dozen feet long and in the middle of the U was a row of shelves, three high, filled with bottles. Blinking Christmas lights were wound around two poles near the corners of the U and over the faded mirror that hung on the wall at the back of the bar, at the top of the U, opposite where Balzic stood trying to get his bearings. To his right, three old men huddled against the wall. Each of them held a bottle of beer, which they sucked on tentatively. Beside them, but nearer the corner, with his arms behind him, was a bald round man in his late fifties. He wore an apron around his middle, and it seemed to Balzic as though he was trying to turn his gaping mouth into something inching up on a smile.

". . . he knows if you been sleep-pin' . . . he knows if you're awake," came the monotonous growling on Balzic's left. The mass surrounding the voice wobbled slightly, then righted itself.

". . . he knows if you been bad or good, so be good for fuckin' sake." What had passed for singing was now snarling into a speech.

". . . he's makin' a list, and checkin' it twice . . . gonna find out who's naughty . . . or nice, San-ta Claus is comming to townnnnnn . . ." He was singing again.

Balzic eased forward slowly and settled onto a stool, loosening his tie.

"Hey, John. Ho, John. Got a customer, John. Better check, see if he's a member . . . he knows if you been— no, that ain't right . . . lost my place . . . HO, JOHN! Wait on a fuckin' customer!"

The bald rotund man with the apron lifted the door in the bar and approached Balzic, walking as though fearful his feet might make noise. He stopped in front of Balzic and bent his head forward. "I think you'd be better if you went someplace else."

"Gimme a beer. Whatta you got on tap?"

"He don't look like no member, John. Better check him," came the voice from off to the left. He was standing in the dark, near a pool table. Balzic could not distinguish anything but his size, plus the fact that he was weaving ever so slightly and belching under his breath.

"If you ain't a member, I can't give you anything anyway. You a member?"

"No, but I know Henry Walsylko. He still president?"

The bartender nodded. "But he don't want me to serve nonmembers. Too much trouble. We lose our license, and, uh . . . why don't you just—"

"He's ma-kin' a list . . . checkin' it twice, gonna find out who's naughty and nice, San-ta Claus is com-ming to townnnnnn . . . hey, buddy, hey. Hey, you!"

"Oh Jeez," the bartender said, and cast his eyes down.

"You talkin' to me?" Balzic said.

"Yeah, I'm talkin' to you. Whoda fuck you think I'm talkin' to?" He took two large steps forward and stopped, swaying and opening and closing his eyes.

Balzic felt his eyes go wide in spite of himself. Standing half in the light, his torso tilting an inch or two first to the left and then to the right, he was bigger than anyone Balzic had ever seen. He was easily six feet six, maybe taller, and he weighed, Balzic guessed, close to three hundred pounds. His belly was large, but it wasn't soft, and his shoulders looked to be two and a half feet across. His little fingers were thicker than Balzic's thumbs, and Balzic had to look carefully to see the neck of the beer bottle in his right hand.

Slowly, methodically, the hulk went into a pitcher's windup, kicked his left leg high, struggled to maintain his balance, and then fired the bottle into the darkness to his left, where it exploded against the wall. Despite his clearly advanced state of drunkenness, his coordination was impressive.

"Steeeee-rike three . . . the crowd goes wild," he shouted, and then, cupping his hands, he made a sound like a crowd's roar of approval.

"Gimme 'nother one, John. Ho, John. 'Nother beer. And don't gimme no fuckin' sermon this time neither, hear?" He turned toward Balzic, and, while eyeing him, put his hands out to reach for the bar, but misjudged the distance and fell against it. Balzic felt the impact.

"Movin' the goddamn bar again, John? Told you 'bout that." He grinned idiotically, sheepishly, at Balzic as he straightened himself. "Gimme BEER!" he bellowed, hammering the bar with the side of his fist. Cardboard coasters bounced on that side of the bar.

Oh shit, Balzic thought, still impressed with the large one's coordination.

John the bartender shrugged and opened another bottle of Iron City. He placed the bottle gingerly on the bar. "I'm not gonna give you a sermon, Andy. I'm just gonna ask you please one more time, don't break nothin' else, please. Don't be mad no more. You been mad all day—"

"All day! ALL DAY! I BEEN MAD MY WHOLE FUCKIN' LIFE! All day, shit . . . I been mad for thirty-two years. No. Thirty-two years and nine months! I was mad the whole time I was in my mother's belly. And ain't nothin' I seen since I been out made me change my mind . . . all day . . . shit, old ladies get mad for one day. Little fruits play in the band get mad for a whole day . . . little girls get mad for a whole day . . . little fruity faggots get mad for a whole day . . . fuckin' PRIESTS, fuckin' priests get mad for a whole day. . . . I been mad for thirty-two years and nine months. Whattayathink now, John? Ho, John, you don't know nobody in your whole life been mad long as I been, tell the truth. Huh?"

"I don't know," John said. "I ain't seen you since your mother passed away, God bless her."

"Ain't shittin' there. 'Cause I ain't been here for a long time. Last time you seen me—ONLY time you see me in this fuckin' town is when I gotta be here for funerals. Last time you seen me before yesterday was when my old lady died. I got the fuck outta this place. . . . And I didn't come back—if my sister didn't die I wouldn't be here yet, whattayathink of that, John? Huh?"

"Your sister was nice," John said.

"She was a—she was an asshole."

"Not to me she wasn't. She was a nice person. You shouldn't talk like that about her. She always spoke nice about you."

"Oh, oh, oh, nice person. Ouuu, big fuckin' deal. 'Cause she stayed around and took care of that cocksucker, that motherfucker? Huh? She was stoooo-pid. Dumb. Like in stump. Dumb and stupid, you put 'em together, and they spell stump. What dogs pee on. That's what she was."

"Can I have that beer?" Balzic said.

John threw up his hands. "What do I care. You want a beer? Here. Here. Take two. They're small. Free. On the house. Here, take three." He lined three bottles up on the bar.

"Gimme a shot, too. And give him one too." Balzic nodded to his left.

John put his hands on his hips. "You want to buy him a shot? Is that what you want?"

"That's what I want."

"Hey, you want it, you can have it. What kind?"

"Vodka. You got Stolichnaya?"

"Sure. Here. Right here. Only you gonna buy for him, you gonna pour it yourself." John plunked the bottle of vodka and two shot glasses on the bar. Then he walked as far away from them as he could get. He went to the wall and sidled up to the three old men who were still huddled against the wall, still sipping fearfully at their beers.

"Here, Andy," Balzic said, pouring two shots of vodka.

"Whatsat for?"

"Santa Clause. For comin' to town."

"I ain't drinkin' to that sonofabitch. Whoda fuck ast him come to town? Huh? Surenshit wasn't me."

"Well. Then here's to his rapid departure."

"Oh ha. Oh hou. Now you got it. Drink to that every day. Oh yeah." He wobbled up to Balzic, banged into him, hoisted the shot glass, and downed its contents.

Balzic dumped his vodka on the floor while Andy had his head back, gulping.

"And here's to all his reindeer goin' with him," Balzic said, filling the glasses again.

"Don't get . . . don't forget the som-mabitch Rudolph, red-nose prick. Don't get him . . . forget him. . . ."

"To Rudolph's rapid departure. May the little red-nose prick lead 'em all out of town." Balzic raised his glass to his lips, then dumped the vodka on the floor when Andy drank his.

"Hey, buddy. Ho buddy. You're awwright. No shit. But lemme ast you. Who ast that fat fart come to town in the first place? D'you ast him? I dint tell him . . . whoda fuck tol' him check my list? D'you tell him? I dint tell him. . . ."

"Not me," Balzic said, filling the glasses again.

"Whoda fuck ast him stick his fat nose in my bed-room . . . find out I'm 'sleep? Huh? D'you ast him?"

"Here's to people mindin' their own business."

"Goddamn right." He gulped down the shot and staggered backward a half-step.

Balzic brought his glass to his lips, then put it back on the bar and immediately filled the other glass as soon as the large one put it down.

"Hey, you drink fast. Huh?"

"Fast? Not when we're drinkin' to the early departure of nosy fat guys in red suits. Can't drink too fast."

"Ol' man used to get me drink . . . used to come my bed . . . tell me quit playin' with myself . . . gimme

drink . . . sam-ma bitch . . . fat fucker . . . all time checkin'
my list . . . make me drink 'at shit . . . laugh, grab me
byda teat . . . I holler . . . fat fuck pour it down my
throat . . . Momma tell him quit, he'd punch her
out . . . bet-ter watch outtttt, bet-ter not cryyyyyy. . . ."

The door opened, and patrolmen Fischetti and Johnson
started in. Balzic threw up his hand to stop them and
pointed twice for them to get back outside. They looked
at him, puzzled, then Fischetti asked if he was all right in
a whisper. Balzic nodded and motioned again for them to
leave. After a second, they did.

Andy turned ponderously around. "Zat cops?"

"Nah. Just a couple guys. Uh, so, uh, who was that
used to check your list? Your old man? What was his
name?"

"Prick. Name was prick . . . used to get me drunk
. . . whoa, place spinnin' . . . hate that, fuckin' spin . . .
yeah was my ole man . . . knows when you been sleep-
pin, knows if you're a-wake, knows if you been bad or
good, so be . . . so be, uh, howda fuck's it go?"

"He knows if you've been bad or good," Balzic sang
out, "so be good for goodness' sake.

"You better watch out,

"You better not cry,

"You better not pout,

"I'm telling you why

"San-ta Clause is com-ming to townnnn."

Andy roared approval. He hung his arm around Balzic's
neck and peered woozily into Balzic's eyes. He blinked
heavily and his head dipped and then jerked upward.

"One more for old Saint Nebshit, whatta you say,"
Balzic said heartily, refilling the glass again.

"One more I go . . . one more I go fuck-king bed-dy bye."

"To Saint Nebshit," Balzic said, hoisting his glass. "To Saint Nosy."

"Rahhh. To Saint Nose-shit. Saint No-shit." Andy was staggering, and he wobbled against Balzic, straightened himself, and with mighty deliberation poured down the vodka.

"Ain't . . . goin' . . . make . . . it," he said between sluggish breaths while he tried to set the glass on the bar. It slipped out of his fingers and rolled away. His eyes closed, opened for a second, then closed again, and, mumbling softly, he sank to his knees and fell face first into the bar. Within seconds he was snoring.

Balzic blew out a long sigh, closed his eyes, shook his head, and then tossed down the vodka in his own glass. "Okay, gentlemen," he called out to the four men backed against the wall. "War's over. You can start cleaning up now."

He put a five-dollar bill on the bar. "Get those fellas a beer, will you? John? You hear me?"

"Yeah, I hear," John didn't move.

"Well, what's the matter? Isn't five enough?"

"Oh yeah, sure. That's too much."

"Let 'em drink it up. What's this guy's name?"

"Huh? Oh, Starenchko. Andy. His sister just died. Her funeral was yesterday. He been drinkin' for three days."

"He got any other relatives?"

"Uh, no. I don't think. She was the last one." John came forward and started to wipe up the bar and set out three beers for the men who had left the wall and sidled onto stools.

"Well, if anybody should want to know where he is, tell them he's in the Drug and Alcohol Unit up the hospital, okay?"

"Yeah, sure. I don't think nobody's gonna ask, but I'll remember," John said. "Uh, what can I say? Thanks. It just came to me when them two cops came in who you was, you know? I didn't mean to get smart with you little while ago, okay?"

"Forget about it. Just tell me what happened to the officer who came."

"Huh? Oh. I didn't see that. I was in the back there sweepin' up the bottles he busted and I didn't even see the cop come in. Next thing, bang! I turn around and there he is, fallin' off the bowling machine. And then Andy just picked him up and put him outside and came back in like nothin' to it. And then he went over and took a stool and smacked the phone, and I thought here we go, here we go, you know. But he didn't do nothin' but throw those empties back there and then you showed up and, hah, listen to him now. Jesus, he'll be shakin' the bottles he snores any louder."

"Okay, John. Anybody else get hurt?"

"No, no. Everybody come in, they see him, they'd leave. Is that cop okay?"

Balzic shrugged. "I'm going to check now."

He went outside in time to see Petrolac being helped into the back of a Mutual Aid ambulance. Balzic trotted over and told the driver to get another ambulance and at least four paramedics back there, and to bring a straitjacket. Then he told Fischetti and Johnson to go inside and put handcuffs on Starenchko until the paramedics got back with the jacket.

"Oh, and call D and A and tell them what they got to look forward to. Tell them when this guy starts to come out of it, make sure they get something polite in his veins before they take the straps off. Tell them this guy is very depressed and very angry. You got that?"

Fischetti and Johnson nodded that they did and hurried toward the door.

"Hey, wait a second," Balzic called after them. "How come that wagon's just leavin' now? When'd it get here?"

"It was here when we got here," Fischetti said.

"Well then why didn't it leave?"

" 'Cause Petrolac wouldn't go until he figured you were okay."

"So when'd he figure that out?"

"He said it was gonna be all right when you started singin'," Johnson said. "But I gotta tell you, he said he never heard two guys sing that bad. He said you were terrible."

"Is that a fact?"

"Yeah," Fischetti said. "He said the big dude had the worst voice he ever heard, but you were second for sure."

"Oh yeah? When you two clowns get inside—which is where you should've been already—you'll find out why I was singin'." Balzic turned on his heel and set out toward his cruiser, growling and muttering all the way.

In his cruiser, Balzic felt himself trembling as he turned the key in the ignition. Every time he braked for a stop sign or a traffic light, he put his hands out and stared at them. The tremors in his fingertips were unmistakable. He could hear his pulses thumping in his neck and temples and he could taste perspiration on his upper lip. His shirt was damp with sweat and he was having a hard time slowing his breathing. "Jesus," he said aloud several times, "I'm getting too old for this shit. . . ."

Minutes later, after calling the station to have someone sent up to the hospital to check on Petrolac and notify his wife, Balzic parked by Muscotti's back door. He got out of the cruiser and stood for a minute or so on the sidewalk breathing deeply, expanding and contracting his diaphragm fully until his breathing was close to normal.

He was inside, on the steps going down to the bar before he saw Mo Valcanas at the bar. Before Balzic could turn and run, Valcanas spotted him and sang out, "Mario. Old friend. Decades-long companion. Seeker after truth, justice, fair play, not to mention the American way. Come, have some refreshment, and then, then, let us reason together."

Oh shit, Balzic thought.

"Innkeeper! Wine for my friend. Wine for my—shall I say it? Of course I shall. Wine for my fellow officer of the court."

Balzic tried to be as casual as he could muster, given the state of his nerves. He parked on the stool beside Valcanas as Vinnie, lips still numb from his visit to the dentist, set a glass in front of Balzic and asked what it would be.

"Your finest jug wine," Valcanas sang out.

"Listen, Mo, I can explain—"

"Mo? Mario, have I ever told you how much I detest that name?"

"Uh, you drunk?"

"Certainly not. This drink you see here is the first I've had today—it's the first I've had a chance to have. I've been busy. Consulting. A consulting lawyer, if you'll allow me to explain, is one who is referred to other lawyers to advise and counsel them when they have problems with nuances of the law that they may not understand, and—"

"Mo, I really can explain."

"Uh, I don't wanna break up this fuckin' romance," Vinnie said lop-sidedly, "but who's payin'?"

Valcanas gestured grandly toward Balzic. "The good chief is paying, of course."

"You wanna quit talkin' like that, Mo, huh? No shit."

"You wanna gimme some bread?" Vinnie said.

"Put it on my bill," Balzic said, snapping out each word.

"I can't put it on your bill," Vinnie whispered loudly. "The Liquor Control Board's down there by the door. Last time they found out we were running bills they shut us down fifteen days. Just gimme some money, huh? I got a headache, okay?"

"Mo, I don't have anything on me, just a bunch of dimes."

"No money? My word. You've given it all to charity perhaps? To worthy causes perhaps? Helping your fellow man perhaps?"

Balzic sighed and looked away.

"Oh, allow me," Valcanas said. "I insist. I hope I can find some small pleasure in this gesture of congeniality."

"Lighten up, Mo, Jesus Christ."

Vinnie took the money and left to wait on other customers.

"Now. Where were we? Oh, yes. My name. Mo. Did I ever tell you how stupid that name sounds? Did I ever tell you how just the sound of it irritates me? Did I ever convey to you how deep I have to dip into my well of tolerance to let people call me that day after day?"

Balzic shook his head glumly.

"Well perhaps you'll understand if I tell you that my name has no equivalent in English. People think my name is Myron and they think it comes from Myros or some such."

Balzic put his elbow on the bar and rested his cheek on his hand. "You're really gonna make me pay for this one, aren't you?"

Valcanas stared off haughtily. "My name is not Myron, because it was never Myros or anything remotely like Myros. I don't have any goddamned idea where or when people began to confuse my name for something else. I suppose it was when they began to confuse me for somebody—or some*thing*—else, when they began to look at me and see not *me* but something or somebody they thought was me, when they began to see a person who would do things they thought I would be or do—I suppose that was when they started to call me Myros, and thus Myron, and thus Mo."

Valcanas paused to sip at his double gin. Then he turned and hunched forward and got his face about a foot away from Balzic's.

"But I am not Mo. I am not Myros. I am not Myron. I am Panagios. The nearest I can render it in the Roman alphabet is P–A–N–A–G–I–O–S. And how in the fuck anybody *in* anything approaching normal human intelligence could take that that perfectly adequate Greek word and turn it by degrees of stupidity into *Mo* is something that rankles me every day of my life. And what rankles me most is that they did it . . . and that they do it . . . without . . . my . . . con-sent . . . and with-out . . . the courtesy . . . of even . . . inquiring . . . whether I mind."

Balzic studied his wine and then drank half the glass.

He chewed the inside of his lower lip and shrugged. "I have, uh, I have fucked up."

"My friend," Valcanas said, "what you did, is take the bonds of friendship and lay them out in a muddy path and set loose a herd of diarrhetic goats on them. My friend, my arthritis is the only thing keeping me from socking you in the nose. My friend, I have just come from counting what you told that certain other person to call me to call a C.P.A. to count. And I counted it because I was goddamned if I was gonna get a C.P.A. involved. Because If I had gotten a C.P.A. involved then my name would be My-ron and I would deserve to be called MO! Because that's the sound some assholes make when wind passes through them."

Balzic nodded throughout Valcanas's last speech. "You're right. Everything you say is right. I was not right. For that I apologize—"

"Don't you dare," Valcanas said. "Don't you dare apologize. I don't want to hear a goddamned apology. I want to hear what you're going to do next. And it better be good. Because if it isn't, I am not going to allow myself to hear another goddamned word you say."

"Aw, hey, listen. What'd you want me to do? Maybe you need to be reminded of something," Balzic said, fortifying himself with the rest of that glass of wine. He held up the empty for Vinnie, who came and refilled it.

"You still buyin', Greek?" Vinnie said.

"My name is not 'Greek.' It is Panagios. Literally translated, it means 'all saints.' Figuratively translated, it is the masculine equivalent of the Virgin Mary."

"No shit. Does 'at mean you're still buyin' or not?"

Valcanas grimaced and waved his hand majestically.

"Hey, Greek, what's that fuckin' wavin' mean—you buyin'? Yes or no?"

"Yes, I'm buying. Without gestures. Unadorned. Yes."

Vinnie scowled, took the money from in front of Valcanas, and left, complaining of his headache.

"I started to say," Balzic said, "you need to be reminded of something—"

"I doubt that, but I'm listening—for the moment."

"You remember what it was like when you started out?"

"Oh wait just a moment. Are you going to tell me that there is some similarity between when I was getting started in this business and this little, uh, what do I call it? Misadventure? This little misadventure you shoved me into?"

"Now wait a minute, for crissake. I'm just trying to remind you of how tough it was when you were getting started, and—"

"My friend, all lawyers dance the dance of the desperate when they're starting out. Not all lawyers, however, are invited by a cop to dance with a strange partner while the band plays 'the felony frolic.' You gotta do better than remind me of how tough I had it trying to get on the dance-floor."

"I'm trying. If you'll just let me. Huh?"

"I've been trying to let you try. And I am still listening."

Balzic groaned. "Okay. I'm gonna try again. When I called that kid, I was all set to stick it to him. If anybody had it comin' he did, if for no other reason, he could've saved everybody a ton of trouble if he'd just made some phone calls. But that's how goddamn desperate he was. He wouldn't let himself make the calls, he—"

"Is this gonna get any better or is this pretty much the

way it's going to go, because if this is where you're going, Mario, you can stop now. Your appeal to my compassion is a waste of time. I don't care how desperate he is or was. I don't care that I was once just as desperate. What you set me up for leads to the two worst 'ments' I know, i.e., indictment and disbarment. And piss on his despair. What do you think my hopes would be at my age, with my liver, and my tastes, if I were to wake up one morning knowing that all those state cops I've pissed off over the years were out gathering evidence to guarantee my conviction? Let's not even think about the D.A.s and their assistants. And then, while we're not thinking of them, let's not think of the judges who've been reversed on my appeals. What do you think my prospects would be, what do you think my despair would be if that's what I had to wake up to one morning? Hmmm?"

Balzic sighed heavily and started to speak, but Valcanas wouldn't let him.

"Well, I thought about that and I thought about that and I thought about that, and I knew there was only one way out, because there are too many people in this county who wouldn't miss the chance if there was even the appearance that I might have stepped into something, so—so I swallowed real hard and I took the kid and his money down to my man in the bank and I had them set up the account. Their signatures are on it. And then, in front of my banker's eyes, I wrote our desperate friend a check so he could pay his bills—including his secretary's wages."

"What? What did you say?"

"You heard me."

"Oh you sonofabitch," Balzic said, grinning maniacally. "You goddamn beauty you."

"Your compliments, charming as they are, change nothing. I am still seriously pissed off."

"Hey, be pissed off. Good! Stay pissed off long as you want. That's great, Mo, no shit."

Valcanas winced. "Don't call me that, for crissake."

"Well what am I supposed to call you?"

"How about 'sir'?"

"Hey, Vinnie. Ho, Vinnie. Give us a drink here. And, uh, Sir's still buying."

"I got your 'sir,' " Vinnie said.

"Uh, Vincent, my boy," Valcanas said, "try to remember who it was that settled your last, uh, romance with that lady's front porch?"

"Okay, okay, I stand corrected."

"Restrained, not corrected. God, what's the use." Valcanas turned back to Balzic. "Listen, I didn't solve anything. All I did was postpone the inevitable. Which is neither here nor there. What I want from you is your oath that you will never involve me in anything even remotely like this again."

Balzic shrugged. "Okay, you got it."

"Oh no, oh no. I want to hear better words than those."

"Okay. I promise not to put you—hey, how often's something like this gonna come up for crissake?"

"I'm hoping that it never comes up again, but if it does and you happen onto the scene, I want your oath that you will not call me."

"Okay, okay. I give you my word, if something like this ever happens again I will not call you. Better?"

"Much. Now. I'm curious. You mind telling me how you plan to clean up this little mess?"

"Why should I mind? I don't have the first idea what to do."

Valcanas snorted. "Then you ought to seek some guidance because there's over four grand in escrow right now, and I'm sure there's more on the way."

"God! Four grand already. What the hell's wrong with people?"

"What's *wrong* with people? That's an interesting way to look at it. I would not have looked at it that way. Not at this time of year."

"Yeah. Christmas." Balzic raised his glass. "To Christmas. To Mrs. Garbin, to Eddie Sitko, to Billy Lum, to Mary Hart, to the whole goddamn bunch. They oughta take each other to the goddamn prom."

"Prom?"

"Yeah, to the prom. That's what I said and that's what I meant—even if it doesn't make sense. Makes sense to me. Fuckers oughta spend the rest of their life dancing with one another."

"Mario, the reason you're pissed off at them is they exhibit your most sentimental qualities. One of them doesn't; she's just trying to make good on those sentiments. But the rest?"

"Billy Lum?"

"No, I mean Sitko and Hart."

"Mary Hart exhibits my most sentimental qualities, is that what you said?"

"What do you call them? Never mind. The point is, you're pissed off because that otherwise insufferable pile of protoplasm has some compassion in her, and because it's the same thing that causes you to turn me on to Cecconi, you have doubts about yourself, and those turn very quickly into rage at her. A wise man once said, 'I'll never forgive anybody for being as morally good as I want to be.' "

"What wise man said that?" Balzic said.

"Me. I said it." Valcanas slapped the bar. "Vinnie! Another here. And for my worried friend who thinks he's been found out."

"What the hell are you talking about?"

"Come on, come on. You know it just eats you up to know that Mary Hart is capable of feeling the same thing you're feeling for the same reason. You're no different from anybody else. You can't stand it when somebody you despise has the same noble emotions you have."

"Oh yeah? Where does that leave you?"

"Where else? It leaves me a partner in your crime. As I said before, what do you plan to do about it?"

"Hey, you're the goddamn genius here."

"Are you asking for suggestions?" Valcanas said, finishing his gin.

Balzic thrust up his hands and looked at the ceiling.

"Well, then," Valcanas said. "In no particular order—I mean just as the ideas come to me—you have to negotiate a deal with the alleged victim—"

"Her promise to shut up in return for my promise not to bust her."

"Bravo. Now. Something must be done with Saint Edward, the fire chief."

"Uh, not that this has anything to do with the subject, but I take it you don't have much use for him."

"Oh he's a fucking martinet. He's got a couple of hundred little boys who wanted to be firemen when they grew up, and they think he's some kind of hero, so he can bully them any way he wants. He's got this great reputation for putting out fires and saving cats in trees and all these charity drives, but nobody talks about all the marriages that have gone to court because his volunteers love him more than they love their wives or kids.

"From the look on your face, Mario, it's clear you think I'm exaggerating."

"I didn't say anything. I'm just listening."

"I just arranged the support payments for a woman whose husband climed off before he reached his orgasm—not hers. His. Just because the siren blew. Off he went, and that was the last straw for her."

"Okay, so there's two sides to good works. More like fifty. But let's get back to us. You know? Our own good works?"

"Well, Sitko is a problem. All I can suggest is you tell him what an asshole he's going to look like if the truth be known. If you can think of anything else to deal him off with, do it. You know how he loves to be modest in public when people tell him how wonderful he is."

Balzic frowned. "He's gonna have to have a story to tell all his people where that money went."

"That can wait. I'm sure somebody will be able to think of someplace four grand would be welcome. For now, he just has to have a reason to shut up."

"Okay. I don't know what that is right now, but don't let me hold you up. You're movin' right along. What about the paper?"

"The paper? Or Miss Goodie Two Teats?" Valcanas's mouth curled as he spoke the last. "Innkeeper! Vincent!"

"I'm comin', Jesus Christ, I'm comin'. You ain't the only people in here." Vinnie poured their glasses full.

"Courtesy, Vincent, is always a virtue. Especially when dealing with a lawyer to whom you have not made the first payment for your romance with—"

"The lady's front porch," Vinnie said with exaggerated disgust.

"Exactly. The choice is clear I think: either courtesy from you or the collection agency from me."

"Yes, sir. This one's on the bartender, sir. Is that polite enough, sir?"

"Vincent, you learn so fast one wonders why you set your goals so low."

"Oh fuck you, sir, huh?" Vinnie hustled away.

"Where were we?"

"The paper," Balzic said.

"Yeah. Well. You talked to Murray?"

Balzic nodded. "I told him what was happening and he had somebody check it out himself."

"So the paper's no problem. I mean, it's not *the* problem. The problem's, uh, Hart. Does she still call that puke she calls writing—is she still turning out that column, what the hell does she call it? Hartbeats? Is that it?"

Balzic laughed. "You mean you don't read it?"

"God. Last time I looked at one of those Carter was president, and she'd managed to call him a communist twice in one paragraph. There wasn't any insinuation. 'That communist in the White House,' is what she said." Valcanas sighed. "You know what's scary about her? There's a judge who actually begins to stammer when he hears her name, that's how frightened he is of her. I've seen that myself. And he's clean. He's just scared that someday one of his decisions might not meet with her approval.

"And you know what the commissioners do? Huh? They keep appointing her to all those goddamn boards and committees and authorities just to pacify her, just to get her out of their hair. That's how scared *they* are of her."

Balzic shrugged. "They probably have good reason."

"That's not the point. The point is, she gets on these boards, she's involved in decisions that affect a lot of people, and she doesn't have the first goddamned idea what she's doing. Do you know she's a member of the county water authority board, the community college board, the board of the juvenile home, and the redevelopment authority?"

"I knew she was scattered around, but, no, I didn't realize it was that bad."

"That's not the half of it. She got these appointments years ago, and all the succeeding county commissioners just keep renewing her appointment because they're afraid to kick her off, so for all practical purposes she's got the same job security as a goddamn federal judge."

"I don't want to say anything, Mo, but you're practically frothin' at the mouth."

"Hey, Mario. You have any idea how much money passes through the redevelopment authority in one year's time? You have any idea what the competition is like to get those loans? For crissake, those loans—give or take a point, a point and a half—are two-thirds of the prime rate."

"You sayin' old Mary's dirty? Is that what you're sayin'?"

"Oh come on. That woman isn't for sale for something as trivial as money. She doesn't collect anything but expenses for being on those boards."

"Then what're you tellin' me?"

"What I'm tellin' you is she extracts a price in a different way. She throws her vote for the loans to the people who think the right way, you follow me? The people who have their hearts and minds on the right side of the voting machines."

"So? If she doesn't take money, so what?" Balzic shrugged. "Far as I know, that's the way the system is supposed to work."

"Of course, of course. But the point is, each new county administration—or state or federal or city, makes no difference—new pols, new appointees. That's the way it goes. That's how you get new blood, new ideas. This woman's been tromping around in this county for decades—and nobody elected her. She's forever yapping in her column about throw the bureaucrats out, throw the rascals out, throw the bums out, they're the people who raise our taxes, yap yap yap, welfare cheats, welfare bums, but who gets a chance to throw *her* out? Who gets a chance to vote against *her?* Nobody. Because all the new county commissioners are terrified of her for what she did to a bunch of thieves thirty years ago—or whenever it was. Now do you get my point?"

"I don't like her either," Balzic said, grinning widely.

"I see you think this is all a big joke."

"Hey. A little while ago you were makin' suggestions about what I should do to straighten this mess out, and the next thing I know you're makin' a speech about the evils of appointed officials. Get back to the point: what do I do about her?"

"What are your objections to assassination?"

"Jesus, I need more wine. Vinnie!"

"You know anybody with syphilis? Maybe he could be persuaded to rape her. Nah. He'd probably want too much money."

"Vinnie! Yo, Vinnie! Two more here."

"Vinnie, yo, Vinnie, two more here," Vinnie mimicked him. "You ever think maybe you should go, 'Yo, Vinnie, two more here and get yourself one'—you ever think of that?"

Valcanas scowled at Balzic and said, "I truly love people who owe me money who try to make me feel bad because I haven't done something charitable for them."

"Well?" Vinnie said, bottles poised over the glasses. "Is it gonna work?"

"Why not?" Valcanas said. "It won't be the first act of idiotic charity I've performed today."

The phone under the bar started ringing, and Vinnie, after pouring, scurried to answer it. He listened for a few seconds and then returned, grabbing a small bottle of beer out of a cooler along the way. "We all got our problems. I got you guys, and you, Mario, old paisan, you got the mayor. He wants to talk to you right now. Five minutes ago, if not sooner. He's in his office."

"I knew something else had to go wrong," Balzic said, sighing.

"You mean there's something else left to go wrong?" Valcanas said.

"Who knows. He was in Florida all last week. Probably dreamed up twenty new ways to put an end to crime. I hope that's all it is."

"Uh, why don't you get him to fall in love with Hart, get both of them out of your hair," Valcanas said.

"Hey. Speaking of which, how 'bout comin' up with something about her, huh? I mean it, Mo."

"I'll give it my totally divided attention. And don't call me that."

"Yeah. Sure. See ya, Panag—Panagus—"

"Pan-ag-i-os. PANAGIOS!"

Mayor Kenny Strohn, deeply tanned and looking fitter than when last Balzic had seen him—which was fitter than anybody ever looked to Balzic because nobody Balzic knew took as much care to keep himself as fit as the mayor did—was pacing in his office when Balzic opened the door. Strohn practically leaped at Balzic.

"Mario, what in hell have you done to Mary Hart?"

"Hi, Mr. Mayor. Nice vacation?"

"Mario, that woman has been blistering my ear for the last half-hour! She's demanding that I fire you. And bring charges of harassment against you. She's—"

"All right if I sit down, Mr. Mayor?"

"Sit, stand, I don't care. Mario, that woman is—is . . . She's very powerful, she's—"

"I know who she is," Balzic said, taking a seat in front of the mayor's desk.

"I know you know who she is. What I want to know is, what have you done to alienate her?"

"Alienate?"

"Aggravate, irritate, make her furious. Forget the words. She says that instead of helping some woman who's been robbed and beat up, you've done everything you can to harass the woman. She says that thousands of dollars have been collected for this woman and that you have somehow turned the attorney, uh, oh what's his name—"

"Cecconi."

"Yes! That's it. She says that he won't talk to her now on instructions from you and they don't know what's happened to the money. The money's missing! And she says—"

"She's full of crap."

"She may be that, Mario, but she is full of powerful crap. And she has made serious charges against you—and, by inference, against me! I am—"

"Mr. Mayor, do I get a chance to—"

"Mario, she says that at this very minute you have a detective, uh, Car—Carliucci—"

"Carlucci."

"Yes. That's it. She says you have ordered him to follow her—"

"Oh that's bullshit. I told him to park himself in plain view in front of the alleged victim's residence. Old Mary Hart just happened to take the woman to her house. He's not following anybody. And he's sure as hell not harassin' anybody."

"Mrs. Hart says his mere presence there constitutes harassment."

"According to her idea of how the law's supposed to work, I guess it is. But the law doesn't operate the way she thinks it ought to. If it did, all cops would be wearin' white sheets and pointy hats and takin' orders from her."

"Mario, this is serious. That crack was beneath you."

Balzic cleared his throat and waited.

"Look, the story she told me is going to put your department and my administration in a very ugly light. She has demanded that I fire you—"

"You said that before. Are you ever gonna ask me what's goin' on here? Or you gonna keep tellin' me what kind of trouble I'm in?"

"All right. All right. Then tell me. By all means. Please tell me!"

Balzic nodded gratefully and told the mayor everything

he knew about the incident, leaving out only the details of the conversation he'd just had with Valcanas in Muscotti's.

". . . so the important point is this, Mr. Mayor, the money is not missing. Furthermore, all the money that Cecconi had has been counted by three people at least: Cecconi himself, attorney Valcanas, and an officer in Valcanas's bank. Furthermore, any money that has not been counted has not been counted because it's still in the hands of people who've been collecting it. In other words, if we don't know about it, it's because it hasn't been turned in to Cecconi. You follow me?"

The mayor nodded. He had been standing and pacing all the while Balzic was talking, but now he relaxed somewhat and sat at his desk.

"Mario, you have conclusive, absolutely conclusive proof of what you're saying?"

"No doubt about any of it."

"You don't doubt the work of your detective, uh, Car—"

"Carlucci. No, sir."

"Well would you mind telling me why you have him up there by that woman's house? I don't understand that."

"Simple. I want the woman to know we're wise to the scam. I also want her to know we're not gonna go hide because old Mary Hart is runnin' her mouth. And I also needed some time to figure out what to do."

"Well? What are you going to do?"

"Well, in no particular order, we gotta put a stop on the money. Then we got to give Eddie Sitko a story to tell all his people who've been workin' their buns off to collect the money. Then, I got to give the woman a choice of shuttin' up or gettin' busted, and then I got to think of something special for old Mary. She's been a pain in the world's ass for a long time. World owes her one."

The mayor stood and began to pace again. "Mario, I know that you and I have a lot of differences of opinion. I know that you think I'm naïve to the point of, uh, well, to put it bluntly, I know you think I'm a fool. But I'm not naïve about this woman. She has a reputation. She's fearless. She's tenacious. She's—"

"She's a goddamn liar."

"Mario! Her reputation—my God, are we talking about the same person?"

"There's only one Mary Hart. Thank somebody for that."

"Oh come on now. I mean really, Mario. The Mary Hart I have heard about for years is as honest as the day is long. She brought down public officials who were totally corrupt, commissioners, a district attorney, the sheriff, judges—that story is famous. Are you telling me that—"

"I'm tellin' you that she's a goddamn liar. You ever talk to the people she interviews, huh? Afterwards, they all say the same thing, which is that they never said the things she says they said."

"Yes, but, Mario, come on now. If that's true, why don't these people sue her? If that's true, why has no one sued her?"

"People *do* sue her. It just never goes to court and it never gets in the paper. Don't take my word for that. Call the guy who runs the paper. You know Tom Murray?"

"Of course I know him."

"Then call him."

"But how is this possible? If what you say is true, then

how is it possible that she is held in such high regard? It doesn't make sense."

"Look, Mr. Mayor. People get a rep. They do something. People talk about it. Everybody who talks about it adds a little something to it. It grows. I don't know why people do it, but they do. In this woman's case, maybe five percent of what people say about her is true. The rest is bullshit—and don't think she doesn't contribute to it. The dedicated muckraker lookin' out for the little people, lookin' out for the taxpayers' dollars. Bullshit. Look, in the first story she wrote about this woman, she said she called my house repeatedly. I was home all day. My wife and mother were home all day—except when they went to church. She never called. I don't care how many times she writes that. I don't care if she believes it. I don't care how many other people believe it. It didn't happen. And she's been doin' that kind of crap for years and years."

"Well, all I can say, Mario, is that whether or not Mary Hart deserves the reputation she has, the fact is she has the reputation. And many, many, many people believe it is justified."

Balzic shrugged. "I can't argue with that."

"Then how are you going to stop her? Mario, she's committed to this. She wants your resignation. She—"

"Hey, no time like the present to do it. You want to come along and watch?"

"What are you going to do?"

"I'm goin' to put it to the victim. In front of Mary Hart's face. Uh, a word of caution."

"What's that?"

"The old bag carries a piece. It grieves the shit out of me every year I gotta sign her permit, but there's nothing

I can do to stop her. If I didn't sign it, she'd find ten state cops who would. Course, I have been known to keep her sittin' around for hours before I get around to signin' it. It's my contribution to gun control."

"My God, has she ever shot anybody?"

"Oh hell no. But it wouldn't hurt to keep one eye on her purse. I mean, she's not gonna want to kiss me when I stop talkin'."

"Oh God," Strohn said. "Oh God."

They started for the door with the mayor on Balzic's heels, but Balzic stopped abruptly and said, "Mr. Mayor, see how a rep gets built?"

"What? What are you talking about?"

"I said, do you see how a rep gets built? The fact is, I just made up all that stuff about Mary Hart havin' a gun. If she has a gun she sure doesn't ask me to authorize her permit. I'm the last cop she'd ask. But see how easily you believed it? I mean, it's the sort of thing that would fit with her reputation, wouldn't it?"

Strohn looked exasperated. "Why are you always doing this to me?"

"I'm not doing anything to you."

"God, Balzic, you are always instructing me. I feel like a—never mind."

"Mr. Mayor, if I was tryin' to make you look like a jagoff, I'd do it in public. I'm just giving you information here, that's all."

"I wish you would find another way to do it."

Balzic shrugged apologetically. "Sorry. Uh, you ready to go?"

"Of course I'm ready."

They rode in Balzic's cruiser up to the Garbins' house

on Norwood Hill. Neither of them said much, just passing remarks about what was going on in traffic, but right after Balzic shut off the engine Strohn touched him on the arm.

"Mario, tell me the truth this time. No games. Okay? No games. Does Mary Hart have a gun or not?"

"Uh, no games, right?"

"Right. Exactly."

"Well, tell you the truth, I don't know. It is something to think about though, isn't it?" Balzic lurched out of the car before the mayor could answer, but he did hear the mayor groan.

∽✠∾

Detective "Rugs" Carlucci scrambled out of his car and hurried to join Balzic and Strohn on the sidewalk in front of the Garbins' house.

"They still in there?" Balzic said.

Carlucci nodded emphatically. "Unless they went out the back. Old lady Hart's Buick is right in front of my car. They're in there."

Balzic led the way up the steps, but before he could knock, Mary Hart jerked open the door. "It's about time," she said in her deep voice, ragged from decades of smoking. She planted her short, blocky body in the doorway, her pale eyes bristling with contempt that seemed even more menacing because of the distortion created by her trifocals. Her face always reminded Balzic of a peeled potato that had sat out in the air too long, lumpy and white and reddish-brown on the outermost surfaces.

"You've got a lot of explaining to do, buster," Mary Hart said.

"Am I gonna have to do it out here while you let all the cold air in, or are you gonna let me come inside?"

"You got any warrants?"

Balzic looked at Carlucci, and they both laughed. Strohn didn't think it was the least funny.

"Now what would I need one of those for?" Balzic said. "You doin' something bad in here?"

"You're not funny, buster. You're not funny at all." She turned toward the room behind her and said, "Okay if I let them in? It's up to you, you know. He says he doesn't have any warrant, and this is your house. Just say the word and I'll throw the bunch of them right the hell off the porch."

"Mrs. Hart," Strohn said, "I believe we're here to talk, is that right, Chief?"

Mary Hart turned back with a snarl. "I'd watch what I'd say if I were you, Mis-ter Mayor. You're in this just as deep as he is. You're his boss and don't you for-get it."

"Mrs. Hart, uh, would you let us come in, please? Really, we just want to talk—the chief has some things to say I think you really ought to hear."

"Aw let 'em in for cryin' out loud," Jack Garbin said. "And shut the door. Lettin' all the hot air out and all the cold air in."

"Well it's up to you. Your home is your castle. You've got rights here—"

"You heard the man, Mary. You wanna step aside?"

"Go ahead. Go ahead. Just keep talking like that, buster. You'll be singing a different tune in front of a judge." She glared as hard as she could at Balzic, but she stepped back into the house.

"You're all heart, Mary," Balzic said, leading Carlucci and Strohn inside. Carlucci coughed, trying to suppress laughter, but Strohn didn't think that was funny either.

Balzic stepped just far enough into the room to let the others in, and then he waited until Mary Hart had closed the door and walked around them to take up a place beside Mrs. Garbin, who was seated on a creaky rocker in the far corner of the room. The air was blue-brown with cigarette smoke.

"You want to talk?" Mary Hart growled, taking out another cigarette and lighting it. "Then go ahead and talk. My tape recorder's already turned on."

Balzic and Carlucci exchanged looks, but had to turn away to keep from breaking up.

"I don't think that's, uh, that's really not necessary, is it?" Strohn piped up. "This is all going to be pretty much off the record, isn't that what you had in mind, Chief?"

Balzic looked directly at Mary Hart. "Even if Mrs. Hart has a tape recorder, Mr. Mayor, which I doubt, it won't make any difference."

"What? Why not? I don't think—"

"Because she never listens to anybody anyway, doesn't matter whether they're on tape or not. And if she is gonna write about what's happenin' here, she'll do what she always does, which is say what she thinks we said."

"Aw get off your high horse, Balzic," Mrs. Garbin said. "You think you're so goddamn smart. You got something to say, spit it out."

"You tell him, honey," Mary Hart said.

"All right, Mrs. Garbin. To the point. You got no savings accounts in any bank or savings-and-loan in this town. You—"

"I never told you where I was savin' the money. I never said it was in no bank."

"I didn't say you did. I'm just tellin' you what we know

you don't have. Next thing is, we got one witness that saw you get to the place where you say you were robbed from a different direction than you told me. You said you came up Pittsburgh Street from the Sons of Italy Club. The witness says you came up Third Street. More important—"

"That's a lie."

"—more important, the witness says you had blood on your face before you got to Pittsburgh Street."

"That's a lie," Mrs. Garbin said, her voice growing louder.

"Furthermore, the man you accused of robbing you has at least one witness who puts him someplace else—"

"Probably another lyin' nigger just like him."

"Why that degenerate wasn't locked up forever years ago is beyond me," Mary Hart said. "You'll have to answer for that when you meet your maker."

"He may be a degenerate, thief, bum, rat, whatever you wanna call him, but a reliable witness has placed him somewhere else."

"Didn't I tell you this was gonna happen, Jack, huh?" Mrs. Garbin screeched at her husband, who was smoking hard and walking in and out of the room, not looking at his wife. "Didn't I tell you the bastards were gonna do this?"

"A couple more things, Mrs. Garbin," Balzic said. "First, you got nobody to corroborate your story. You got no friendly witnesses. In other words, you're the only person who saw this thing happen the way you said it happened."

"Well, that's not her fault, buster. If you'd do your job, she'd have some witnesses, instead of looking for witnesses for the other side."

"The other side? That's an interesting way to put it. Well. Never mind that. Mrs. Garbin, if you push this thing, I'm gonna have the coroner take those bandages off and measure your wounds. He's an expert in this kind of thing. He'll take pictures, he'll take measurements, and he'll examine your face very carefully, and then he'll be able to say how you got those injuries."

"I already told you how I got 'em." Mrs. Garbin's voice was brittle.

"Yes, you did. But we both know that's not true. And Detective Carlucci here knows it's not true because he knows how you got those injuries."

"He's fulla crap too," Mrs. Garbin said, smoking now as fast and hard as her husband was.

"We have a witness, Mrs. Garbin, who saw how you got those injuries—"

"That's crap. You're makin' this all up. I told you they was gonna do it, Jack. Didn't I tell ya? Huh?"

"—and when we put the information from that witness together with the information we get from the coroner, there won't be any doubt about how you got those injuries."

"Well just how the hell *did* she get those injuries, buster? You say you know this and you know that and the other, but so far I haven't heard a goddamn thing to convince me."

"I don't have to convince you, lady. I just have to convince Mrs. Garbin. She's the one who has to make the choice."

"What choice? What're you talking about? Sounds like a bunch of crappola to me. I've been covering the police and the courthouse since before you were born. You haven't convinced me of anything. You haven't got anything that even looks like a case."

"Mrs. Garbin," Balzic said. "Mrs. Garbin, listen to me."

Mrs. Garbin scrambled out of her rocking chair. "Oh shuddup. Shuddup and get the hell outta my house! Jack! Tell 'em get out. Tell him!"

"Oh I ain't tellin' 'em nothin'. You tell 'em. Tell 'em yourself."

"Mrs. Garbin, pay attention here. I'm giving you about a minute to decide. You and I both know you're trying to work a fraud."

"Shuddup shuddup shuddup! I don't wanna hear it!"

"One minute, Mrs. Garbin. Either you forget this or you're in a lot of trouble. Nobody's gonna put you away, but you will be convicted, I guarantee it. And before you're convicted, your face, your name will be all over the place, newspapers, radio, TV, everybody'll be talkin' about you. It'll be embarrassing as hell."

Mrs. Garbin was standing in the center of the room, trying hard not to look at anyone. She folded her bony arms in front of her and began to scratch them slowly and methodically.

"Just get out of my house. Just go away. Just giddout!"

"Can't do that, Mrs. Garbin. I'm giving you a hell of an opportunity here. You get nothin', or you get a real humiliation."

"My picture already been in the papers. So what else is new?"

"Mrs. Garbin, this is the last time I'm gonna ask. I want you to think about this. You can walk away from this reasonably clean. Or you can open up a real mess for yourself."

"Open up a real mess for myself," she said, mocking Balzic. "What the hell you think I got here? Huh? Whatta you think I got here all my life? Guess you think this is paradise!"

"I didn't say that, Mrs. Garbin."

"You didn't say this, you didn't say that. Whatta you know? WHATTA YOU KNOW! . . . Take a look around, you high and mighty bastard you. You see any Christmas tree? Huh? SEE ANY PRESENTS? Come up here Christmas Eve you won't see none either. Christmas mornin' neither."

"That's enough, okay?" Jack Garbin said, his voice breaking.

"Aw you shuddup too. You wanna talk so much, go 'head. Talk. I ain't stoppin' you. Tell old high-and-mighty here when's the last time we had a Christmas tree, go 'head!"

"That's enough, I'm tellin' ya. Just 'cause you made a jerk out of yourself doesn't mean you gotta try and make one out of me."

Mrs. Garbin turned to confront her husband. "Oh yeah? Well just tell me one thing. Why would I have to try?"

Jack Garbin started to speak but couldn't. His face grew very red and his throat filled with phlegm. "Well . . . thanks. Thanks a lot, missus." He turned unsteadily and hobbled out of the room.

"Sure, that's it. Leave. Go down the cellar and pour yourself a big wine. Then sit there and stare at it and pout! Go 'head." Mrs. Garbin wheeled around and glared at all of them. "Whatta youse lookin' at? Whatta youse want from me? Why don't youns go home and wrap up some presents? . . . You know what I'm gonna do? Huh? I'm gonna sit around and wait and see if somebody brings me a turkey. . . ."

"But, uh, my God, Mrs. Garbin," Mayor Strohn said, "surely you're getting food stamps. Surely you qualify—"

"FOOD STAMPS! Who are you? Who are you, I don't even know who you are and you're in my house tellin' me about food stamps!"

"He's the mayor, honey," Mary Hart said. "Mayor Strohn."

Mrs. Garbin took a couple of steps toward the mayor. "Izzat who you are, huh? Well lemme tell you something, Mayor. I get food stamps. Know what I do with them? I sell 'em. Why don't you ask me what for?"

"Uh, uh, what for?"

"Gee. You're real quick on the uptake, ain't you? I sell 'em to get money to pay my gas bill. So I won't freeze when I go to the bathroom. Four years ago we could heat the whole house. This year we're down to three rooms. This one, the kitchen, and the bathroom. I notice youse ain't took your coats off yet and youse ain't complainin'. Don't that add up to nothin' in your head?"

"God," Strohn said. "I don't—I don't know what to say."

"I'm goin' outside," Carlucci said. "You want anything, Mario, just holler."

"Yeah, okay, Rugs, go ahead." Balzic licked his lips and wiped the corners of his mouth, which was starting to feel all cottony.

"Mrs. Garbin, lots of other people are in the same fix you're in—"

"You go blow it out your ass, Balzic. Don't you preach

at me. Don't you tell me you know what it feels like to sit around waitin' to see if the Salvation Army got a turkey with your name on it. Don't you try to give me that crap."

"Lady, the only thing I'm givin' you is the choice I gave you a little while ago. You can forget this or you can get yourself arrested. And if I arrest you, I'm gonna see that you get convicted."

"Mario, Mario," the mayor said, "maybe we can talk about this. Maybe we can work something out here."

"Nothin' doin'. Not a chance."

"But, uh, why are you being so hard about this? I don't see that there might not be another way. Obviously, this woman was under great duress."

"Bullshit. This woman could've made up any story she wanted. She could've said, 'Some black guy did it,' or 'Somebody I never saw did it,' or anything. But that isn't what she said. What she said was, 'Billy Lum did it.' And that takes it out of the duress category as far as I'm concerned."

"But if he didn't do it and we know he didn't do it, I don't see what the problem is."

"First off, the problem is, what she did is a misdemeanor, two counts. She made up the whole thing; that's giving false information to a law officer. Then, she gave false information when she accused a specific person. Second, this is theft by deception, and considering the money that's involved, it's a felony."

"But she doesn't have the money yet."

"That's not the point. If I hadn't got my nose open, she would've taken the money. That's still not the point. The point I've been trying to make for a long time now is I'm giving her a choice: forget this thing, or I'm gonna make a lot of trouble. From where I stand, that sounds like the best offer she's gonna get."

"Mario, I don't think really, I mean, couldn't we work out something here?"

"Mr. Mayor, what do you think I've been doin'? I've already worked something out."

"Yes, but it seems to me all you're doing here is giving the woman a choice—what I mean is, no choice at all."

"Okay, Mr. Mayor. Since obviously I haven't got through to you, what do you think ought to happen here?"

"Well . . . I'm not sure." Strohn screwed up his face and took a deep breath. "Maybe, maybe some of the money could, uh, you know what I mean."

"You sayin' the woman should get some of the money, is that what you're sayin'?"

"Well there *is* a lot of money, Mario. And these people— well, look around."

"Mr. Mayor, I don't have to look around. I know what's here. What's here isn't the point."

"You keep talking about the point, buster," Mary Hart said, "but if you made one I don't know what it is yet."

"You wouldn't. But I'll make it again. Mrs. Garbin here just didn't make a general accusation, and she didn't make it to a general audience. She accused one person and she made that accusation to the fire chief."

"So what?" Mary Hart said. "From what I hear you weren't available—and that's putting it mildly. The word is, you were loaded when you finally got to the hospital— about six or seven hours after the fact."

"I'll let that one pass," Balzic said. "But are you startin' to get an idea how this stuff gets rollin', Mr. Mayor? Huh? No, I can see from your face that you aren't. Well. The fact is, Mrs. Garbin didn't report this assault and robbery to the police. She said something to the paramedics and they didn't tell the police either. And when they got Mrs. Garbin to the emergency room, the people there didn't report it to the police either. The first time I heard about it was when the fire chief called me at home at one o'clock in the morning. By my addition, Mrs. Hart, that's seven hours after the fact. And now we come to the point."

"Hallelujah," Mary Hart said.

"Yeah, sure. By the time I got to the hospital, the admissions clerk was already convinced that, number one, it happened, and, number two, a nigger on welfare did it. Is it startin' to add up, Mr. Mayor?"

"I follow you. Go ahead, I'm with you."

Balzic wondered how much of his breath he was wasting. "Uh, oh boy. Okay. I've gone this far, what the hell. Mrs. Garbin here, like most of the people in this town, knows Eddie Sitko's reputation for charity things. Hey, why am I doin' the talkin'? Mrs. Garbin, you wanna tell the mayor why, from the time you say you got rolled until around one-thirty the next morning, you still hadn't called a cop? Why the only person you told was Eddie Sitko? You wanna do that?"

"I can answer that," Mary Hart said. "Nobody down at your station would answer the goddamn phones."

"There's more journalistic objectivity for you, Mr. Mayor," Balzic said. "That's lame, Mrs. Hart. Even for you, that's lame. Whatta you say, Mrs. Garbin? Wanna tell the mayor why you didn't holler cop?"

"Nobody answered the goddamn phones!" Mary Hart said again.

"Okay, we'll do one thing at a time. You wanna do the

phone thing first? Fine. Did you have the phone in your room hooked up, Mrs. Garbin? Of course not. And you know yourself, Mrs. Garbin, how simple it would be to check that. Forget that. The fact is, there is no call from you in the dispatcher's log, and I don't care what you think, Mrs. Hart, dispatchers who work in my department answer the phones. Besides which, she didn't have to call my station. All she had to do was call nine-one-one. You gonna tell me *they* don't answer the phones? The point is, Mrs. Garbin did not tell a cop because she wanted to tell Eddie Sitko.

"Mrs. Garbin, you wanna tell the mayor where Eddie Sitko is every Friday, Saturday, and Sunday from eleven at night till seven in the morning?"

"How the hell should I know?"

"No idea, huh? Bullshit, lady. You must've been on Mars for the last twenty years. Everybody in this town knows where he is. Same place he's been ever since he started the Mutual Aid ambulance thing. He's somewhere in the Mutual Aid garage. Every weekend. Hasn't missed one." Balzic squinted hard at Mrs. Garbin. "What's the other thing you're gonna say you don't know about Sitko?"

"What is she? A mind reader? What kind of double-talk is that, buster?"

"Oh she knows exactly what I'm talkin' about, don't you? You want to tell the mayor why you pulled Billy Lum's name out of the hat, Mrs. Garbin? No? Okay, I'll tell him. Because there's not one black fireman in this town. Hundreds of volunteer firemen, scuba divers, guys with the bloodhounds, and not one of 'em black. And there's no mystery there either, right, Mrs. Garbin? It's Sitko's blind spot. He hates black people."

Balzic turned to the mayor. "Mrs. Garbin knows the fire chief, Mr. Mayor. She knew what buttons to push. And that's why I'm not doin' anything else for her. 'Cause all those firemen, hundreds of 'em, by last Saturday mornin', were already convinced of two things: one, something good ought to happen for Mrs. Garbin; two, something bad ought to happen to Lum. You startin' to see the problem, Mr. Mayor?"

"That is the damnedest cock-and-bull story I ever heard, Balzic," Mary Hart said. "And if Eddie Sitko was standing here, you wouldn't have the guts to say any of it."

"I've known Sitko for a lot longer than you have, Mrs. Hart."

Mary Hart advanced on Balzic, her chin thrust out, her face ruddy with anger. "You wouldn't say any of it if he was here 'cause he's twice the man you are and always has been and you know it!"

"Mrs. Hart, Eddie Sitko is a man among men. I've seen that guy go into places after people when everybody else wouldn't even think of it. I saw Eddie bring a guy back in an accident. A doctor said the guy was dead. Eddie jumped in that mess, I don't even know how he got inside the car, started beatin' on the guy's chest and giving him mouth-to-mouth. Next thing everybody knew, the guy's breathing. The doctor comes back—he was already in his car, gettin' ready to leave—and Eddie spits on him. I saw that. But you know what? If the guy in that car had been black, he would've stayed as dead as the doctor said he was, 'cause Eddie would've never touched him. And if Eddie was standin' here right now, he'd tell you that what I'm sayin' is the truth."

"Well you can bet your badge I'm going to ask him, buster. I never heard such bull-oney in my life."

"Whatta 'bout you, Mrs. Garbin? What's it gonna be? Last chance."

"Don't let him bluff you, honey."

"He ain't . . . he ain't bluffin'." Mrs. Garbin studied the floor, scratching her arms under the sleeves of her sweater. "You win, Balzic . . . bastard."

"I want to be specific, Mrs. Garbin. I want you to say exactly what you mean to do."

"Okay okay okay okay. I won't do nothin'. Does that suit ya?"

"That suits me fine. You heard it, Mr. Mayor, right?"

"Yes, I did. But I—"

"Just as long as you heard it, Mr. Mayor, that's all that counts."

"Wait a minute! Wait just a damn minute here," shouted Mary Hart. "What in the sam hill is going on here? Do you mean to say he's right?"

"Aw listen to you," Mrs. Garbin said.

Mary Hart put her hands on Mrs. Garbin's shoulders and tried to turn her around, but Mrs. Garbin squirmed away.

"Wait! Oh wait! You mean to tell me you made up this whole goddamn story?" Mary Hart was crimson.

"Aw listen to you. Mrs. Wonderful. Go'wan. Get outta here and leave me alone."

"Well, I don't believe—why, my God, woman, you've made a complete fool out of me."

"Okay, Mrs. Hart, that's enough," Balzic said.

"Oh sure. Easy for you to say. My God! . . ."

"Listen to me. Both of you. I want to see you in the *Rocksburg Gazette* building tomorrow. In front of Tom Murray's desk. Ten o'clock."

"What? What is this, buster?"

"Just be there, Mrs. Hart. You too, Mrs. Garbin. I'll have a car pick you up at nine-thirty. Wear something nice. And, Mrs. Garbin, don't think about not coming, 'cause the man I send for you will have orders to bring you one way or another. In other words, don't give him a hard time, you understand me?"

"Blaaaaah," she said, and stuck out her tongue.

Balzic spent the rest of the day setting things up. It took all day. The easiest part was convincing Cecconi, who would have done anything to get out from under the weight of his part of the scam. Next easiest was Tom Murray, and he was "next easiest" only because he was second on Balzic's list. Murray promised, with a vengeful mirth, to arrange things at the *Gazette*.

Eddie Sitko was third on Balzic's list, and Sitko took some doing, first because Balzic had to spend hours just locating him, and second because Sitko refused to believe he'd been had. All of Balzic's persuasion went for nothing; it was only after he'd taken Sitko to talk to the woman on Third Street who'd seen Mrs. Garbin run face-first into the crosswalk button that Sitko was convinced. He was convinced, but there was nothing resembling satisfaction in it. He felt used and foolish and gullible; and, as used to having his way as often as he did, Sitko was having a hellish time smothering his rage.

"Goddammit," he said finally, "you better be right about this, Mario. And another thing. You better never ever tell me that if I'd've listened to you in the first place none of this would've happened. 'Cause you do, you sonofabitch, I'll knock you right on your ass."

"I give you my word," Balzic said.

"Aw stick your word up your ass. Five years from now, you're gonna be drunk someplace and you're gonna start lippin' off at me and I'm gonna pop ya, you hear me? 'Give you my word'—shit. I know you, you sonofabitch. You'll never forget this one. But I'm warnin' you right now—"

"Aw cut it out. Christ, you're startin' to sound like I set it up instead of what I'm doing, which is, my friend, coverin' your ass, you know?"

"Yeah? Well just don't gloat, that's all. Can't stand you most of the time. When you're gloatin' I can't stand you at all."

Balzic saved the worst for last, and he collected reinforcements first.

"What's this all about?" Valcanas said as they hurried past the security guard and switchboard operators in the *Gazette* building.

"You'll find out," Balzic said, leading the way through the maze of desks and cubicles to a corner of the building occupied by Mary Hart.

Valcanas stopped when he saw where they were going. "What in the hell possessed you to bring me here?"

"I brought you because you're the, uh, lemme see, the best talker I know."

"Oh horseshit," Valcanas said, starting to turn away.

Balzic grabbed him by the sleeve. "I need a backup here, Pa—Panag—Panagus."

"Not *gus*, for crissake. *Gios*. Pana*gios*. What the hell's so hard about that?"

While Valcanas was distracted, trying to correct Balzic's pronunciation, Balzic tugged and steered him into Mary Hart's cubicle.

Her cubicle didn't look like a part of any office Balzic had ever seen. Beside her desk, which was piled high with old newspapers and magazines, she had a bookcase, four shelves high and six feet wide, stuffed with paperback books, mostly mysteries and spy novels. A framed sampler above her desk said, "GOD ISN'T A COMMITTEE," and another said, "DUTY ISN'T FREE IN THIS PORT," and another said, "GOD SO LOVED US ALL HE MADE AMERICA," and they were all sewn with red thread on white backgrounds, and the frames were all blue metal. Spread among the samplers were framed photographs of Richard Nixon, J. Edgar Hoover, Ronald Reagan, and John Wayne.

Valcanas was making noises like he was going to be sick.

Mary Hart had her back to them. She was engrossed in copying something in longhand from a book. Balzic had to speak to her twice before she heard him; the second time he had to lean so close he could see over her shoulder, and he saw that she was copying words from a spelling book. She had made three columns of words on an unlined tablet and was working on the fourth.

She whirled around, startled, the second time Balzic called her name. Then her eyes hardened into slits. "Whatta you want? You caused me enough trouble today, buster. My God, I've had a headache all day."

"Well, that wouldn't make us anywhere near even, lady. You've been givin' me headaches for a long time."

"Oh yeah. Sure. Well, cut the baloney. Whatta you want?"

"I have a proposition for you, Mrs. Hart," Balzic said. "I think it's a way to make us all, uh, well, if it doesn't make us look real good, at least it won't make us look like a bunch of jerks."

"Well if it's something to do with that woman you can just count me out. She already made a complete fool out of me. I won't be able to show my face in this town."

"If only that were true," Valcanas said.

"What? What did you say?" She squinted meanly at Valcanas. "Oh for God's sake. It's you. I thought you died."

Valcanas snorted. "I know you pray to the death-fairy every night for my departure, madam, but as you can see, your prayers are not heard."

"Okay, okay," Balzic said, holding up his hands, suddenly doubting his decision to bring Valcanas. "Listen, Mrs. Hart. Just listen to me for a moment." He went on to explain with as few pauses as he could manage what he had in mind.

When he finished, Mary Hart's mouth was forming a horrified and indignant oval. After a long moment, she said, "Well you can just kiss my rosy red ass, buster."

In spite of himself, Balzic shot a supplicating glance at Valcanas.

"Madam," Valcanas said, "while I must say that I despise everything about you, I have to concede that I have a warm spot in my checkbook for you. The cases that have been settled in chambers because of you have given me great pleasure—and a lot of money."

"Get to the point for cryin' out loud."

"All I want to say, madam, is that if it weren't for you, I'd have a lot less money. In other words, while I wish you much pain and suffering, I don't wish you so much that you'd do something so dumb you'd lose your credibility with the idiots who read you."

"Is there a point to all this bull-oney?"

"What I'm trying to tell you, madam," Valcanas went on, "is that if you screwed up so bad you lost your readers, the publisher would quit printing your crap, and if he did that, then that would mean nobody would sue you, ergo, I'd make a lot less money. So, in spite of myself, I have a stake in seeing to it that you don't make a complete ass of yourself."

Balzic jumped in before she could reply. "Uh, I think you better give this some thought. I mean, we do it my way, you come out lookin' pretty good. And then, don't forget, or maybe I didn't tell you, Cecconi and Murray and Sitko already said they'd go along."

"I don't give a tinker's damn what they said they'd do. They're not me. I have a—my God, how do you think I'm going to live this down?"

"Well just how do you think you're gonna live it—no, never mind. Just what do you wanna do, huh?"

"Nothing! Which is exactly what I'm going to do. Nothing!"

"Madam," Valcanas said, "you have already done something. You have excited a lot of people to give their money away. And they didn't give it to some goddamn telephone operator for a bunch of nameless children with unpronounceable diseases. You stirred up a crowd for one woman with one name and one address. And that crowd is going to want to know how this operetta turns out. They want a happy ending. And goddammit you're gonna give it to 'em."

"Says who?"

Valcanas smiled his slyest, most cunning smile. "Says me, lady. 'Cause we're not gonna settle this one in chambers. This one doesn't lend itself to being settled in chambers. This one calls for public pronouncements. And you have my word that you try to fade into the night on this one, I will make pronouncements in every public place I know."

"What the hell're you talking about? You can't threaten me. You don't have anything to threaten me with!"

"I don't, huh? Woman, if you believe that," Valcanas said, "then you're stupider than I think you are, and Christ knows I think you're stupid."

"Okay, Mo, okay," Balzic said. "Look, Mrs. Hart. Those firemen, those people who collected the money, the people who gave the money, they're gonna talk."

"Of course they're gonna talk. You think I don't know that? But if I go along with what you want—hell no! I won't do it. I'll be a bigger fool."

"That's impossible," Valcanas said. "I just want to leave you with one thought, woman. As a matter of professional ethics, I have never once publicly discussed any award I've ever gained, or any suit that led to that award, in any matter involving you or this newspaper. But you play the stubborn witch on this one, and I'll tell the world about your record for truth and veracity."

Mary Hart swung slowly around in her chair. She folded her hands and rubbed her fingers and thumbs. She swung back, and snapped, "You two can go to hell. I'm not doing it."

Balzic sighed. "Mrs. Hart, be here tomorrow. Ten o'clock."

"I'm here every day at ten o'clock. I'll be here tomorrow.

But I'll be damned if I do what you say. You two think you're so goddamn smart. . . ."

Valcanas raised his eyebrows and canted his head slightly. Balzic sighed and nodded toward the door.

They were out in the parking lot before either spoke.

"How do you think we did?"

"Who knows?" Valcanas said. "Let her sleep on it."

"I don't know. She's a tough old bird."

"Tough? Nah. Stubborn. Stubborn people always want you to think they're tough. That's their game. That's how she scares dumb politicians. She just won't leave. They think they got to talk to her, otherwise she won't leave. And so they talk, and they always wind up sayin' something stupid. And that's how she gets 'em."

"Uh, listen," Balzic said. "Were you tellin' it straight in there about makin' money on her?"

"Did you think I was makin' it up?"

Balzic shrugged. "I don't know. I just never heard you talk about it before."

"Isn't that what I said—that I'd never talked about it?"

"Well yeah, but—"

"Mario, threats are just like cake. You can't have 'em if you use 'em up in barroom conversations."

"I'll try to remember that," Balzic said. "Well. What's it gonna be, where you wanna go?"

"Las Vegas. Tahiti."

"Oh, sure. Look, it's either your office or Muscotti's. Take your pick. I'm goin' home."

"Muscotti's. Muscotti's . . . is just another word for jail."

Balzic got in the car and started the engine, looking at Valcanas as he did.

"You okay?"

"Oh drive for crissake."

On the morning of the day before Christmas, Balzic was as excited to get out of bed as any child would be on Christmas. He woke at least three hours earlier than usual, and he hurried in his underwear and bare feet to the front door. He twisted open the handle lock before he remembered to open the chain lock, and barely avoided slamming his face into the edge of the door. The noise of the door being stopped by the chain lock made him wince.

He finally got the locks undone and snatched up the newspaper. He closed and locked the door quietly—though he was sure he'd already made enough noise to waken his mother—and padded out to the dining room to find his spare set of reading glasses. Then he spread the paper out on the dining room table and opened it, quickly searching for what he wanted to see.

He'd gone through three sections and was starting to get anxious when he got to the fourth and final section, the one with the obituaries and classified ads.

And there it was. "Hot damn," he said. "Look at 'em."

And there they were. To the left under the picture a small two-line headline said:

In The Nick
Of Time.

To the right of that was this:

Mary Hart (front-r.), Rocksburg Gazette columnist, presents a check to Mrs. Jack Garbin, of Norwood, who was beaten and robbed of her savings last week. Standing (l. to r.) are attorney Alan Cecconi, Rocksburg Fire Chief Edward J. Sitko, and Rocksburg Police Chief Mario Balzic. Sitko, with Cecconi's assistance, led the collection drive, dubbed The Garbin Christmas Club, to replace the money Mrs. Garbin lost. Chief Balzic said the investigation was continuing.

Oh sweet Jesus, Balzic thought, look at 'em . . . look at 'em. Damn, that's beautiful. Just beautiful . . . best present I ever gave myself. Look at Hart, look at her. Goddamn phony smile . . . be a while before you live this one down, lady. Yeah. Anytime anybody wants to know what was on that check, you're gonna have to explain it. Anytime anybody wants to know . . . and you're gonna be squirmin' just like you are right here. Like you're on the Turnpike and you got the runs and you're ten miles from the next rest stop . . . love it. God, I love it!

He folded the paper into quarters so he could look at their faces while he went into the kitchen and dialed the *Gazette*. When the operator answered he identified himself and asked to speak to Tom Murray.

"Murray."

"Balzic. Hey, Tom, ho, Tom, God, I love it. You have made me a happy man."

"I'm feeling pretty good myself."

"You ought to. Damn, you ought to! Listen, you didn't tell me yesterday how you got old Mary baby to go for it. And that's something I have to know. You said before you had nothing to do with her. And then there she was, and not a peep. What d'you do?"

"Well, it was a pretty routine threat. Either she sat for the picture or I wrote a piece myself for page one, spillin' the whole thing, her lousy reporting, you know, that sort of, uh, nice, decent little threat—in keeping with the season."

"What'd she say?"

"She pitched a royal bitch. Headed into the publisher's office. Fortunately, he wasn't there. So I just closed the door and I told her what I've been wanting to tell her for thirty years."

"Oh God, tell me, what'd you tell her?"

"Aw it's too goddamn long. Can't remember it all anyway."

"C'mon, Murray, I wanna hear it."

"Look, the only part worth repeating is this: I said to her that if she didn't sit down for the picture, my last ethical act as a newspaperman would be to expose her for the two-bit fascist she is and the lousy reporter she's always been. It wasn't a great speech. But it gave me a lot of satisfaction to say it. Is that good enough for you?"

Balzic started to say that Murray was leaving something out, but he caught himself and said instead, "Well, I think it was a great speech. I'll never forget it, you can—"

"Hey, Balzic, I don't know about you, but I got work to do. See ya around."

Murray hung up before Balzic could say goodbye. Balzic put the phone on its cradle and looked out the window. It was starting to snow heavy, large, wet flakes. Balzic's deck was already covered.

Balzic was so elated by the sense of triumph he felt from seeing the picture in the *Gazette* and from having engineered its production and from hearing how Mary Hart's participation had been gained that he gave himself the day off to go Christmas shopping. As usual, he was unprepared, both emotionally and practically. He had no list, and the card he had carried in his wallet listing all the sizes he thought he should know was badly out of date. Every year he vowed that next year would be different, that next year he would give himself plenty of time to survey every member of his family about their wants or needs and about their sizes, from hats to gloves to shoes, but every year something came up and every year he found himself muddling among the shoppers fortified with nothing but a sense of urgent good will.

From nine until noon, he plodded from one shop to another in what was left of Rocksburg's business district. Pickings were meager; most of Rocksburg's retail merchants had long ago abandoned the town for the malls that had blossomed east and west of it, sprawling across what had been strip mines and, before that, farms.

Even in those seemingly rare times when the retailers weren't celebrating a holiday with a sale, the malls made Balzic uneasy. Maybe it was the vast parking lots with roadways defined only by arrows painted on the macadam which drivers seemed not to notice or to ignore; or maybe it was the air-conditioning and the fountains and the unfamiliar trees and plants that together combined to create their own odd weather; or maybe it was the private police forces that were connected only to the businesses; or maybe it was the music that never stopped or caused anybody to stop; or maybe it was that nobody lived there, that when the stores shut everybody got in their cars and went home; or maybe it was that Rocksburg seemed to lose something more than just commerce when the malls were built. It was probably all of those things, and it made Balzic uncomfortable. Walking among the throngs of day-before-Christmas shoppers, he felt edgy and found himself thinking about the days after World War II, when the streets of Rocksburg used to be as crowded as this mall.

Now, when the retailers were celebrating their biggest day of the year, when poinsettias and wreaths and silver and gold balls and tinsel jangled his eyes, and when every recorded carol jingled his ears, Balzic felt doubly uneasy.

By three o'clock, he found himself empty-handed and leaning glumly over the balustrade of the second floor watching a miniature train going round and round on a set of tracks below him. The train made two circuits of the track with its load of tots and toddlers, stopped and unloaded them, and then took on another collection of kiddies and made two more circuits around a fantastic village cluttered with animated reindeer and elves and dominated by an artificial silver tree that rose to the roof of the mall.

Balzic felt someone lean on the railing and turned and saw Harry Lynch.

"You too, huh?" Lynch said.

"Me too what?"

"Ah, you know, Christmas. I'll be glad when all this crap's over."

"Is that what I look like?"

Lynch nodded and shrugged.

"Well, if I could figure out what to buy for presents I probably wouldn't look like—like whatever I look like."

"Give 'em money. Everybody loves to get money. You buy what you want."

"Is that what you do, Harry?"

"Certainly. And then I get myself a fifth of good Irish whiskey and, if I'm lucky, when I sober up it's time for New Year's."

"That's a good trick if you don't have to go to work."

"Not me. I had five sick days left, and I took 'em. I don't have to go back to work till New Year's Day. That's what you ought to do."

"Take five days off between now and New Year's?"

"Sure. When's the last time you took a vacation?"

"Jesus," Balzic said, snorting. "I can't remember."

"Hey, Mario," Lynch said, staring off, "nobody ever asks me for advice. I'm the big stupe. Big, dumb Irish. But you ask me—and you didn't—take off someplace. Be the best present you'd give your family, I'm not shittin'."

Balzic leaned over and rested his cheek on his fist and watched the train going around.

"Hey, Harry. D'you ever find your notebook?"

Lynch worked his lips sheepishly and shook his head no. "I guess it really didn't matter, but for a little while there, I really thought I had something that would stick on that bastard Lum."

"Ah, forget about it. We didn't have anything as soon as the shootee took off. Anybody ever make that guy?"

"Nope. Sloppy work all the way around. Me, the hospital. Sloppy. Real sloppy." Lynch straightened up. "Hey, I'll see you, Mario. I gotta go. Merry Christmas."

"Same to you, Harry. And thanks for the advice."

"Huh? Oh. Yeah. I'll see ya."

Balzic turned around and leaned his elbows on the balustrade and watched Lynch amble off through the crowd.

Balzic watched the people for a moment and then brought his gaze down the row of shops, looking for nothing in particular, and there, directly in front of him, his eyes fell upon a sign: *Horizon Travel Inc.*

He looked inside and saw a lone woman talking with great animation on the phone. He watched her for a moment, trying to decide, and then he lurched off the balustrade toward her.

"Hi," she said brightly. "May I help you?"

"Uh, I don't know. You got, uh, you got someplace close by I could take, say, an old lady, and a lady my age, and two girls, uh, college age—and me? You got anything like that?"

"Well, what would you like to do?"

"I don't know. Go someplace nice. Not too far. Just, uh, go someplace."

"Well. Let me think," she said, studying him. "Do you like winter sports?"

"You mean like skiing and ice skatin' and stuff like that?"

"More or less, yes."

"Uh, I don't know. Never did anything like that."

"You mean you just want to get away, is that it?"

"Yeah. Yeah, that's it."

"Well, there's a wonderful place less than an hour's drive from here. Seven Springs. Did you ever hear of it?"

"Oh yeah. I've heard of it. But I just heard the name. You think that'd be a good place to take my family for a couple days?"

"Oh my, yes. It's a wonderful place. Let me get you some brochures, okay?"

"Okay. Sure. Lemme see what they got."

Balzic led his mother down the steps of St. Malachy's after midnight Mass was over. His wife, held by his daughters on each arm, followed them out onto the sidewalk, and they stood together as a mild wind pelted them gently with large, wet flakes of snow.

"Listen," Balzic said, "I want to make an announcement. You listening?"

"Oh oh," Ruth said.

"No, nah, it's not what you think. Don't be jumpin' to conclusions."

His daughters glanced at each other, and then all four women looked at each other.

"So?" Ruth said. "You're going to make an announcement, so make it."

"Okay, okay. I'm gonna tell you what your gift is right now."

The women peered with a combination of suspicion and wonder and mirth at each other and at Balzic.

"Uh, we're takin' a vacation."

"What?" his mother said.

"We're takin' a vacation. From tomorrow until New Year's day."

They all looked at him. They said nothing. They just looked.

"Hey, it's not like you're goin' to jail, you know? It's a vacation. You know? We're goin' to Seven Springs. It's only about an hour from here. You go to a hotel and you eat in a bunch of different restaurants, all different kinds of food, and you can ski if you want to, or swim, or just sit around and watch other people ski—or swim. Or get a suntan. Or get a massage or sit in a sauna bath."

They pondered this and then looked at each other and then at him.

"Somebody wanna say something? Like 'Yea' or 'Boo' or something?"

Before anybody could respond, Balzic felt a tap on his arm. It was Patrolman Larry Fischetti.

"Whatta you say, Larry. Merry Christmas."

"Yeah. Same to you. Uh, you better come over here."

"What's up?"

"Uh, you better come on, I'll tell you in the car."

"Uh, go 'head. I'll catch up." Balzic turned back to his family with a heavy shrug. He shook his head several times and shrugged again. "Look, I'll be home as soon as I can. Promise. Okay?" He kissed them all hurriedly, Ruth last. "Sorry, Ruthie."

"Don't apologize," she said.

"Yeah, I know, but . . ."

"Oh get goin'. We'll be okay. It's no big deal."

Balzic shrugged again, and then turned and hustled to get in the car with Fischetti.

"Okay, what's up?"

"Hey, I didn't mean to take you away from your family on—"

"Just tell me, okay?"

"Okay. First, Lum's in the hospital. He's really fucked up. Beat up bad. They tried—they were tryin' to cut his, uh, they were tryin' to cut—"

"You tryin' to say they were trying to castrate him?"

"Yeah," Fischetti said, and laughed. "I don't know what the hell I'm laughin' for. It ain't funny."

"Never mind. What happened?"

"Uh, Frank Lomicka just stumbled on it. He was cruisin' down by the Flats and they were in a playground where that old school is, the one that's all boarded up? He said there were four of 'em. But three of 'em got away, and he just collared the one. He said if that guy split, he probably wouldn't have grabbed him either. But the guy just stood there laughin' like an idiot. Never tried to run."

"So, uh, what about Lum?"

"He's in the hospital and they went to work on him right away. That's what Lomicka said. Said he was bleedin' real bad down there, you know? Said his face was a mess. Said the doctors were more worried about his head than they were about the, uh, you know, the other thing."

"So did Lomicka take 'em both to the hospital?"

"Yeah. He said he was too scared to wait for an ambulance. Cause Lum was bleedin' so bad. And then—Cheesus—then he said this asshole was standin' there—God this makes me sick. He said he was standin' there and when Lomicka collared him and told him to drop the knife, the guy looks at him and says—he opens up his other hand and he says something like, 'You want me to drop this too?' or somethin'—and, oh shit, he's got, uh, he's got it in his hand." Fischetti gagged.

Balzic put his hand on Fischetti's shoulder and waited.

"I'm okay," Fischetti said after a moment. "Uh, so anyway—Cheesus, I'd've never thought of this—so Lomicka goes and gets a baggie and tells him to drop it in there. He said he thought maybe they could sew it back on, or in, or something. Turns out they can't, but it's something to think of that. . . ."

"Uh, what you're sayin' is the guy went easy? Made no effort to run?"

"Yeah, weird, right? That's what Lomicka thought. He didn't know what was goin' on. He didn't know whether the guy's flipped out on somethin' or what the hell—but the guy just got in the cruiser and when they got up to the hospital he walked in with Lomicka and sat down in the waiting room. I mean, he didn't help Lomicka get Lum in the car or into the emergency room or anything like that, but he could've split any time. But Lomicka said he just kept grinnin'. Really gave him the creeps."

"Where's he now?"

"In our lockup. Uh, I don't like tellin' you this, but I guess I got to. He gave me a message for you. Told me to be sure you got it."

"Gave a message for you to give to me?"

Fischetti nodded. "Yeah. He said he did your investigation for you. He said you can close the case now."

"What case? What the hell's this about?"

"Mrs. Garbin. He said he saw the picture in the paper. Said you said the investigation was continuing. Said to tell you he took care of it."

"Oh Christ," Balzic said, covering his face with his hands. "Oh Christ. God. Come on, let's go up the hospital."

"Okay." Fischetti put the cruiser in gear and pulled out into traffic, turning on his lights and passing everybody before Balzic told him to slow down.

"Uh, what's this asshole's name?"

"Jeez, I'm not sure. It's Polish. Starts with an *M*."

Balzic felt his mouth drop open. "Oh no. It's not Murlovsky?"

"Yeah, that's it. How'd you know?"

" 'Cause he didn't run. 'Cause he gave you that message."

"Huh?"

" 'Cause he didn't run. 'Cause I put him in with Lum and then I turned him loose. God-dammit! Tried to prove a god-damn point, and look what the sonofabitch does."

Fischetti pulled into the emergency room parking lot and turned off the lights. "Uh, you want me to come inside?"

"Huh? Oh. No. I just want to see how Lum is. You don't have to hang around."

"Hey, Chief, is that the guy that, uh. . . ."

Balzic leaned inside the open door after he'd gotten out. "The guy that knocked me on my ass last Friday night?" Balzic snorted. "Naturally. Who else would do this and not run? He showed me, didn't he? I'll see ya later."

Balzic was directed by the emergency room receptionist to a small cubicle containing just a desk, chair, and some file cabinets. Balzic had ten minutes alone before the doctor who'd worked on Lum came in, and they were ten very long minutes because Balzic used every second to berate himself for handling Murlovsky the way he had.

The doctor, except for his heavy beard, looked hardly old enough to be going to medical school, never mind running an emergency room. He was board-thin, and his skin looked whiter than it was because of the blackness of his hair and the bluish cast of his beard. His name tag said "Beans."

He dropped into the seat on the other side of the desk and said, "So you're the chief fuzz, huh?"

"You're Doctor Beans? Is that what that says?"

"Nah. Rules say I gotta wear a name tag. They didn't say it gotta be my name. So I put my nickname on it. Whatta they care, right?"

"Okay. Doctor Beans, what—"

"Just 'Beans.' Well, whatta you wanna know? Is he gonna die? No, he definitely will not die. What else?"

"Well, I heard he was worked over pretty bad. Lot of blood, lot of head wounds."

The doctor thought for a second, screwing up his nose, and said, "Nah, nah."

"Uh, you seem pretty casual about this. Don't get me wrong, but—"

"Casual? Hey, I spent twelve months in 'Nam. There isn't anybody who's gonna come through these doors either up or flat that's gonna shake my bootie, if that's what you mean."

"You a medic?"

"In 'Nam? Yeah. The stuff I did waitin' for the choppers to get down, man, I should've got the Nobel Prize for medicine. And I didn't even know what I was doin'. Uh, so, uh, casual's not exactly the right word. Never mind. Only problem I had with your boy is, uh, even though the pictures showed no fracture, I was a little tense about noddin' him off. So, it got pretty loud in there while I cleaned him up and closed him up."

"So, there's no permanent damage?"

"You mean about the, uh—"

"Yeah, I guess that's what I mean."

"Nah. He's got a backup. Two's one more than you need. I mean, he's gonna have to get some sweats. He ain't gonna be wearin' jeans for a while, that's for sure."

"So you're not concerned about this?"

"Well, hey, we keep him two, three days, make sure there's no fever, no infection, then, as soon as he can motor, he can move. Nah, there shouldn't be any problem. Long as he stays away from whoever did it and they stay away from him, all he got to do is heal up and cool out." The doctor paused and eyed Balzic. "Uh, you look like you want me to tell you something else. I mean I know he ain't a member of your family, so, uh, what's with the look you're givin' me?"

"Uh, probably I'm looking at you 'cause I never heard a doctor talk like you before."

Beans threw back his head and laughed. "Hey, I'm just a skinny little dago boy from East Liberty tryin' to make good in the world, you know? So far all I learned how to do is the medicine part. Next year maybe I'll start workin' on the talkin' part, who knows."

Balzic stood up and held out his hand. "You're okay, kid. You got any problems with the cops, let me know. I'll probably get you locked up, but then, on the other hand . . . so can I go talk to Lum?"

"Who? Oh, the black guy. One Ball."

"What? What'd you say?"

"One Ball. That's the name I gave him. He didn't think it was funny. Course I didn't think the names he was givin' me were what you call hilarious. Uh, he's up in, lemme think, I think they put him on the third floor. Yeah. Hey, listen, before you go, I only been here a month, and I probably shouldn't be askin' you, but, uh, lemme put it this way. When you wanna crack down on the bookies, you know? I mean, where do you go to crack down on 'em?"

It was Balzic's turn to throw his head back and laugh. "Where you from? East Liberty? And you been here a month? Some dago you are."

"Come on, man, this is serious. Playoffs are on, three weeks it's Super Bowl time. I gotta find an honest broker."

"Okay, okay. You go to Muscotti's Bar and Grille. Tell the bartender I sent you—quietly, okay?"

"Hey, man. You're awright. Listen, somebody hits you in the head with a brick, you know where to find me, 'cept Mondays and Tuesdays. Don't get hurt Mondays and Tuesdays. I'm off and I ain't too sure about the dude works those nights, if you know what I mean."

Balzic snorted. "I'll try to make it a Wednesday. See ya around."

Balzic set off toward the elevators, but he couldn't resist a look back as he heard Beans singing. There he was, dancing down the corridor toward a hefty nurse thirty years his senior, and he was croaking, "Come on, come on, come on, devil woman, you know I'm a dancin' fool. . . ."

Balzic made his way to the third floor, found the duty nurse, showed her his ID, and followed her to Lum's room.

"You think he's awake?"

"Oh I'm sure," the nurse said. "The doctor said absolutely nothing for pain because he's still worried about concussion, and Mr. Lum has been ringing his bell just about nonstop. He's awake. I have to go."

Balzic thanked her and stepped inside quickly and closed the door. Lum was propped up, his feet spread to both edges of the bed, holding an ice bag against the left side of his head. His left eye was swollen shut and there were stitches across the width of the lid. There were more stitches from nostril to nostril just below the bridge of his nose, which was also badly swollen. The left side of his forehead had a walnut-size lump that was covered by a butterfly bandage. He was lifting the sheet and looking with his bloodshot right eye at his groin.

"Motherfucker, whatta you want? What the fuck you doin' here? You come to see how they did me? Is that what you want? Then come look, motherfucker! Come and see how they did me!"

Balzic put his hands up and shook his head. "I already talked to the doctor. I don't have to see."

"And fuck him too! Jive motherfucker did me wrong too. Hurt me worse'n they did. Still hurtin' me too. Won't give me nothin', man. Didn't—you hear what I'm sayin'?—DID NOT give me nothin'. Hurt me so bad I pass out, man, you dig that? I wake up, man, they're wipin' my ass, man. I shit myself from the pain. Motherfucker. . . ."

"Look, Lum, I'm sorry this happened—"

"Sorry! Motherfucker, Balzic, don't be lyin' on me, man. You tell lies so bad, your nose oughta be long as Finocchio's. Know why that dummy was name Finocchio? 'Cause he a lyin' dago like you. Motherfuckers say I shoot that peckerwood in the Legion, run a fifty-thousand bond on me, throw that honkie in the slam with me, and now you gettin' ready to say you didn't set me up."

"Set you up? Are you crazy?"

"Oh, listen at him. Shee-it. Go 'head and say it, man. I wanna hear the words, man. Go 'head and tell me you didn't know what you was doin' when you put that honkie in with me."

"That was a mistake."

"Mi-STAKE! Is that what you call it! Lil' ol' mistake! I done lost half my man-ness and you call it a mistake? Four mothafuckin' honkies cut my ball off and you think it's a mistake! I guess you think that dago doctor done a mistake too. Took every mothafuckin' nurse in the mothafuckin' room to strap me down so he could be sewin' and stitchin' while I'm stone cold awake. Guess that be a mistake, too, huh, mothafucker?"

"He was worried about your head. Still is. You got a hell of a lump there."

"Whatchu see ain't shit. Put your eyes on this, mothafucker." Lum took the ice bag away from his head. A swelling about the size of a third of a grapefruit protruded outward from above Lum's left ear; it caused the top of his ear to nearly fold over on itself.

Balzic winced and exhaled audibly.

"S'matter, Balzic? Ain't it pretty? Ain't it what you wanted? Why can't you look at it?"

"Don't say that. I didn't want this."

"You got a short memory, mothafucker. Wasn't too long ago you was sayin' how you was goin' turn one of your go-rillas loose on me. Goin' tell him get a big towel and wet it and go to work on my legs, or you goin' lie and say you never done that neither?"

Balzic sighed and looked at the floor.

"Yeah, right on. Better lamp your shoes, man.

"Uh, Billy," Balzic said, looking up. "I'm not gonna tell you again I'm sorry this happened because I know you aren't gonna believe me—"

"You got that right."

"—but I have to know some things."

"Oh whatchu goin' tell me now—you gettin' ready to make a case? Huh? Goin' bust some honkies for this? Shee-it."

"Look, bad as I feel about this, I gotta remind you that you squeaked clean again. The guy you shot in the Legion took off and—"

"Whoa. Whoa. Jus' come to a complete whoa. The dude

you say I shot. Ain't nobody else said it. Don't be talkin' no squeakin' shit."

"—the victim took a walk. And there went our case. And you squeaked. That's history. In spite of that, I'm gonna prosecute somebody for this, and I need information. Where were you when you first saw 'em?"

Lum took a long time answering. "Okay. Okay. I was standin' in front of the Legion rappin' with Jimmy Payne's old lady. These dudes went past three times. Third time they backed up and started woofin' about weed. And like a dumb ass I walked out to the ride. Two of them motherfuckers got out and started wavin' paper at me and the next thing I know I'm in the back seat and I can't hardly breathe and some skinny little honkie is spittin' on me from the front seat talkin' all kindsa shit about do I remember this and do I remember that. 'Nother one got me around the throat and 'nother one is jabbing somethin' in my guts."

"Do you remember what? What was he talkin' about?"

"All kinds of jive. Do I remember fuckin' this one and that one."

"What did he mean?"

"I didn't know then. Couple minutes later on, he was talkin' 'bout that bitch got rolled and lost her Christmas Club or some shit, and he said do I remember her and this was for her and all the rest, and that's when I knew it was that honkie you put in the slam with me."

"Why was he sayin' all this?"

"Now how the fuck I'm s'posed to know that? All I know was he be jivin' me to quit all my hollerin', and told him shut up his honkie face."

"You didn't tell him anything else?"

"Hell, man, we was there all night. I told him a whole lotta shit. Told him when I got out I was gonna fuck his momma if he knew who she was, fuck his sisters if he had any."

"What'd you say about the woman who got rolled, lost her Christmas money? You remember that?"

"Shee-it. Probably told him I done that too. Yeah. I did. But so what? So what what I told him?"

"So what is, you brought a lot of this on yourself, that's so what."

"Oh no, oh no, OH NO! You ain't goin' dance this with my shoes, mothafucker. You ain't goin' fry this on my stove. You put that honkie on me, Balzeek, and I'm goin' sue you and all your cops and the mothafuckin' city of Rocksburg for pain and suff'rin'—and for the loss of half my man-ness. I already talked on my lawyer, man. We're goin' to the motherfuckin' federales, man, and get your ass busted for violatin' my civil rights, lettin' a bunch of peckerwoods cut me off half my man-ness. And then, and then, when we get done there, my lawyer say we goin' sue all your honkie asses for pain and suff'rin'. Little P and S time in front the judge. I'm goin' own the mothⁱerfuckin' city, Balzeek, now whatchu think about that?"

Balzic blew out a long disgusted sigh. "Then what I think is you ought to have yourself arrested. If you didn't think it was so goddamn much fun braggin' about all the white women you had, that jerk would've never come near you. You be sure and tell that to the federales."

"I'm goin' tell them everything, man. Everything. Lynch and you and that honkie. Lynch threatenin' me and you threatenin' me and that honkie doin' me. Federales goin' make love to that story, man, goin' come all over it."

Balzic shook his head wearily. "You want to tell me anything I can use, anything that could be used against the—"

"Aw man, why don't you stop! You wanna *use* somethin'? You got my permission to go get my ball and paint it red and hang it on your tree, man. Mothafucker, I already got my present. I got a stockin' with one ball in it—or you want that one too? Shee-it, Bal-zeek! You got the right name for this job."

Balzic turned toward the door. "We'll make the case with your cooperation or without it. Doesn't matter to me. And as far as you ownin' the city goes, well, I wouldn't bet on it. Most you're gonna get out of it is the city'll probably cover your expenses here, but you wouldn't have to sue 'em to get that."

"Aw, man, get to gettin'. I don't wanna hear that mess."

"I'm goin', I'm goin'." Balzic started again to say he was sorry, thought better of it, and left.

⟨✠⟩

Balzic was outside the hospital before he realized he had no car. Rather than go back inside to call the station to have someone pick him up, he decided to walk. Most of it was downhill, and the snow had stopped. The winds were gentle and swirly and the temperature was well above freezing. Balzic set off slowly, lost in thought. He covered the six blocks between the hospital and Muscotti's in no time at all, vaguely aware of the few passing cars, absorbed by pieces of ideas and bits of thoughts that were all connected to the events of the last week or so but which made very little sense. He had passed Muscotti's and was crossing the intersection away from it before it occurred to him that the lights were on inside the bar and that music was coming from it. He went back to Muscotti's front door and peered through the diamond-shaped window in the badly worn door. Dom Muscotti was seated at the bar near the jukebox, staring at the glass he was holding.

Balzic knocked.

"Go home," Muscotti hollered. "I'm closed."

Balzic knocked again, louder. "C'mon, open up. It's me."

"I don't give a fuck who it is. It's Christmas. Merry fuck yourself."

"C'mon, hard head. It's me. Balzic. Lemme in. I'll buy ya a drink."

Muscotti lurched off the stool and weaved toward the door. He twisted the lock and then turned unsteadily and headed back to the stool he'd been sitting on, saying, without turning around, "What the hell you want?"

Balzic followed him and dropped onto the stool next to him. "I said I wanna buy you a drink."

"It's happy hour. Every drink in the joint's six bucks. For you, two for ten bucks. C'mon, you wanna buy me a drink, get some friggin' money up."

Balzic fished some change out of his pockets and put it on the bar.

"You can owe me," Muscotti said. He was breathing heavily. "You wanna drink, you gotta get it yourself."

Balzic looked at the bottle in front of Muscotti. It was Mondavi Pinot Noir. "Is that for sale or do I gotta drink beer?"

Muscotti nodded ponderously, and Balzic went behind the bar and got a glass and filled it. He stayed behind the bar and raised the glass. "Salud. Merry Christmas."

"Yeah, yeah. . . . Hey, what the hell you doin' here? Never mind. I don't wanna know. . . . You know the first rule, Mario? Huh? The first?"

Balzic shook his head no. He sipped the wine and closed his eyes to taste it. "First rule about what?"

"Never, ever, take money from a Catholic doctor. Lawyers? They're different. They know you gotta lie to survive. Catholic doctors, huh? The worst, the worst."

"What the hell're you talkin' about?"

"You know what's wrong with Catholic doctors? Huh? They got these consciouses . . . conscien-nes . . . conscience. Two of 'em."

"Consciences?"

"Yeah. The nuns pound it into 'em. And then they grow up and all of a sudden they get to be a doctor and then, next thing you know, they think they're workin' for God. You know what that means? Huh? Hey, especially surgeons. A surgeon, Catholic surgeon, he fucks up, you know what he says? Huh?"

"No. What?"

"A mickey surgeon, he screws up and he gets caught? You know what he says? Huh? He says, 'Certainly, I did it that way.' He don't say, 'I did it.' Oh no. What he says is, 'Certainly I did it that way. That was the best way to do it. If there was a better way to do it, I'd've done it that way. And you can't prosecute me. I'm a—I'm a surgeon.' "

Balzic was trying hard to follow Muscotti's drunken logic.

"A mickey doctor, he says, 'I'm a surgeon. I do God's work. I heal people. You think God would let me fuck up?' Shit. . . . You know how many mickey surgeons come to me in the last thirty years, come to my house? Yeah. They walk in in their suits from London and their shoes from Italy and they say, 'Here. Here's ten gees. Put it on the street.' Oh, they don't say it like 'at. Fuck no. They use these big pretty words. Oh yeah. But what it come down to was, how many points was I gettin'?''

Muscotti drank the rest of the wine in his glass and motioned for Balzic to refill it.

"Oh yeah. . . . They sit there and look at me and I nod and I shrug and they knew before they ever got outta their car how many points. I don't say a word. They tell me how many points. They tell me! And then, you know what they said? Huh?''

"Uh-uh. What did they say?''

"Ha. Fuckers. They say, 'All I want is a couple points.' Two, three. That's all. Couple little points. Yeah. Couple little points. Just like that. Like here I am, greasy little shylock, I should be honored to take their squeaky clean paper and turn it into a couple points a week. . . . Yeah. Couple points my ass. Couple points short of a hundred points is what they want. Double their friggin' money and they're gonna let me keep three points, that's what they want. . . . People wanna know why I go to a Jew doctor. Ha. Double ha!''

"You ever do it?''

Muscotti stiffened indignantly. "What? I look like some kinda asshole? Huh?''

"Just wonderin'.''

"Don't wonder. Don't ever wonder. . . . That friggin' Murray. Soon as he told me who his doctor was, I said to myself, forget it. It's history. . . .''

So, Balzic thought, that's what this is about. Muscotti must have told his mother about Tom Murray.

"Friggin' mickey doctors. Sooner or later they say, 'Hey, it's outta my hands. Call the priest.'" Muscotti snorted. "And people wanna know how come I don't go to nothin' but Jew doctors. You wanna know how come I don't go to nothin' but Jew doctors? Huh?"

"Why?"

"I'll tell you why. You wanna know? I'll tell you. 'Cause they don't ever say, 'Hey, call the rabbi. It's outta my hands.' They don't believe in the afterlife, that's why. A Jew surgeon got you on the table, he knows. He knows he fucks up it's all over. So he busts his ass to make sure it ain't all over. So 'at's why I don't let no mickey surgeon near me. Fuckers wanna put their money on the street, but when it's jackpot time, they say, 'Call the priest!' And then they go get in their fuckin' German cars and go to the club, play a little gin, play a little golf. . . . And then they wanna take their girlfriend to Mexico, they want twenty gees real fast, they come to me." Muscotti hoisted his glass and touched Balzic's. "Hey, Mario, what the fuck you lookin' so gloomy about. It's Christmas. Merry Christmas."

"Merry Christmas," Balzic said.

"Why the fuck don't you go home? What're you doin' here?"

"Listenin' to you make a speech about Catholic doctors."

"Fuckers oughta all be shot. . . . Soon as Murray told me who his doctor was, I said to myself, forget it. It's history. I told him go to this Jew in Pittsburgh. You think he'd listen? Huh? Fuck no. Fuckin' stonehead Irish. . . ."

Balzic refilled their glasses.

"Hey, Dom, listen to this," Balzic said after a moment. "You'll like this. You know what I'm givin' my family for Christmas?"

"What? Wha'd you say?"

"I said, you know what I'm givin' my family for Christmas?"

"No. What?"

"A vacation. We're gonna go to Seven Springs until New Year's. Gonna leave tomorrow afternoon. Whatta you think of that?"

"Hey, you know what I think? Huh? I think if I was you, I'd go home and put 'em all in the car and take 'em tonight."

"Nah. C'mon. You kiddin'? I don't even know if they want to go. When I told 'em tonight after Mass, they all looked at me like I had two heads or somethin'."

"You don't even know if they wanna go? Is that what you said?"

"Yeah."

"Then what the fuck you doin' here? Get outta here. Go home and find out."

"I am. Soon as I finish this wine."

Muscotti raised the glass to his lips and held it there and rubbed the tip of his nose with his index finger. He peered up at Balzic. "What the hell you doin' here? I'm closed. Go home."

"I'm goin', I'm goin', don't worry. How you gettin' home?"

"Whyn't you quit worryin' about other people? Worryin' about other people don't get you shit. You're always worryin' about other people. What's it get you? Huh? Go home. And don't take nobody with ya. You hear me? Huh?"

Balzic nodded. "I hear you." He emptied his glass and put it on the bar. He came out from behind the bar and patted Muscotti lightly on the shoulder. "Merry Christmas, Dom."

"Yeah, yeah," Muscotti growled. He staggered along behind Balzic to lock the door after Balzic left. At the door, after Balzic stepped outside, Muscotti said, "Ya know, if it wasn't for Jesus, there wouldn't be no mickey doctors. They'd all be Jews—which is the way it was s'posed to be."

Balzic snorted and shook his head. He set off toward Main Street and toward his house, wondering about his family, about how they were going to react to his gift, and he couldn't shake the feeling that he had made a mistake by making all the arrangements for a vacation without talking it over with them first. He went over all the possible reactions they could have, each one less promising than the previous, until by the time he reached his house he was sure he had made another mistake. He thought that he'd had a run of mistakes and that this one was going to be the worst of the run and he really hated making the worst one with his family.

He need not have fretted. When he got inside, they were packing.